SPICE

"…Completely laugh-out-loud funny and the underlying romantic plot is the perfect backdrop for its sparkling characters, Simon and Benji, who are bound to induce a book hangover… Fresh, fun fiction at its best!"

—RT Book Reviews

"Suzanne keeps the humor warm and the sex real."

—Publishers Weekly

"Five Stars… The story is funny and sweet and almost painfully well observed. I loved it."

—Inked Rainbow Reads

"*Spice* is a cute and fun story all the way around."

—Joyfully Jay

PIVOT AND SLIP

"4.5 stars… Balancing laughter with touching emotions, this novella is a great first effort"

—Carly's Book Reviews Blog

BROKEN RECORDS

BROKEN
RECORDS

lilah suzanne

BOOK ONE IN THE *SPOTLIGHT* SERIES

interlude press • new york

ISBN (trade): 978-1-941530-57-3
ISBN (ebook): 978-1-941530-58-0
Published by Interlude Press
http://interludepress.com
Book design by Lex Huffman
Cover Illustration by Victoria S. with CB Messer
Cover Design by CB Messer

10 9 8 7 6 5 4 3 2 1

interlude 🧩 press • new york

"Find out who you are, and do it on purpose."
—*Dolly Parton*

This is rock bottom. It has to be. Nico clings to the last tiny thread of his hopes and dreams that this *is* rock bottom, because if he sinks any lower than being elbow deep in the plunging neckline of the red bandage dress—carefully considered and procured and the fourth outfit of the night for one Hailey Banks, former child star and current trashy tabloid star—then he's packing it in and leaving Los Angeles for an off-grid eco-shack in Montana or Wyoming or South Dakota. One of those square-shaped states. He's not picky.

Nico grunts and struggles with the silicone pads and tape, lifting and mashing Hailey's perky A-cup breasts together to give the illusion that they've magically become a bounteous C-cup. All this, hunched and contorted in the back seat of a black BMW X4 that's parked in an alleyway behind a club in West Hollywood at 4:00 a.m.

"Lean over," Nico hisses, struggling with the left breast that stubbornly refuses to rise up over the line of the bodice evenly with the right breast to become a precarious attempt at cleavage.

He had once imagined helping Hollywood's elite look and feel their best, stepping out onto the red carpet at The Oscars or Golden Globes with the sort of joy that comes from knowing, deep in their souls, that this who they are, this is what they want the world to see.

Apparently, what Hailey Banks wants the world to see are her nipples.

Once the adorable chubby-cheeked tot who starred in movies and her own TV show, Hailey was the angel-faced, squeaky-voiced It Girl of Hollywood and every talk show's go-to guest for a sure dose of adorable and sweet and sky-high ratings. She is now the spindly, hollow-cheeked, train-wreck star of tabloids and gossip sites.

"More," she says, bending lower to strap on her black-and-red suede platform six-inch stilettos, making Nico bend with her and nearly topple from the seat onto the floorboards. She narrowly avoids his crotch as she kicks one foot out. "Ugh, I hate these shoes."

"The shoes you made me fly to New York to find and all but get down on my knees and beg for? The shoes by an elusive designer who seems to think his creations should only be worn by Brazilian supermodels and the ghost of Jackie Kennedy Onassis? Those shoes?" Nico hauls himself back up onto the seat and finally hikes her stubborn left boob up evenly. The dress is tiny, and her pale skin is garish in the flickering light of the alleyway.

"Yeah, I dunno. They're pointy and shit," she rasps, lighting another cigarette and making no effort to direct the smoke toward the open window and not Nico's face.

He coughs and waves the smoke away. "There, that's as good as you're going to get."

Hailey takes a drag and says with smoke drifting from her mouth, "It's beyond time for me to get a boob job."

Styling Hailey may be a nonstop nightmare for Nico, but it's his job to look past the bratty, out-of-control behavior and figure out how to make the person beneath shine. And if she ignores him, well, it's not as though Hailey Banks has been listening to any sort of sound advice since she was twelve and throwing diva fits over being given the wrong brand of bottled water.

"Look, they're *your* uncooperative breasts, so do whatever the hell you want, but I've told you before we have so many options with the shape you have now. Look at Kate Moss. Look at Twiggy. Audrey Hepburn!" Nico fixes some stray hairs that have come loose from her top knot; a red carpet premiere and an after party and an after-after party have taken it from *carefully disheveled* to *just woke up on the floor of a public bathroom after a bender.*

He would know, because he's seen Hailey rock that exact look on the front cover of *CelebWow* magazine and every gossip site on the World Wide Web.

She waves him off, takes one long drag from her cigarette and flicks it carelessly into a cup holder. Nico sighs and drops it into a half-empty (Italian-imported-sparkling-natural-mineral) water bottle instead. As Hailey sends a text on her phone, the sunken contours of her face are illuminated. She looks forty-five instead of nineteen; her once cherubic features are hardened, sharp and world-weary.

"Wish me luck." She winks, and when she cracks the door open just a scant inch, there's a blinding barrage of flashing lights and voices shouting her name. She turns away from Nico, making her mini dress even more mini and—

"Hailey, we talked about the underwear."

Hailey pushes the door open the rest of the way—shouts and flashes and bodies shoving against the car so hard it rocks from side to side. "If I'm gonna give them a show, may as well go all in."

She steps out and closes the door, and the cacophony of light and sound goes with her, leaving Nico in a dark alleyway to clean up the aftermath of the last-second quick change. He struggles out of the car with his arms full of garment bags and his sleek aluminum travel case banging down onto its wheels behind him, gives a wince of battle-weary solidarity to Hailey's driver, closes the door with his hip and then has to figure out how to get back to his own car parked at Hailey's first event. As he rides back across town in a city bus that smells like stale perfume and wet dog, that shack in Montana starts to sound better and better.

When he finally gets home, Nico collapses onto his bed, doesn't even bother to brush his teeth or take his shoes off, still smells like cigarettes and booze and that god-awful perfume Hailey uses to cover up the stench of cigarettes and booze. He's so exhausted and drained he doesn't care, just drops off to sleep at 5:00 a.m., knowing he has to be back at it in just a few hours.

He wakes to a bird happily chirping in the tree outside his bedroom window. "Shh," he tells it, covers his head with his pillow and tries to go back to sleep. The bird seems to chirp even louder.

"Shut up, bird," he grumbles into the pillow.

Chirp. Chirp. Chirp, chirp, chirp, chirp. Twee, twee, twee, chirp, chirp, twee. CHIRP.

"Oh my god, shut the fuck up!" Nico yells, pushing up on his elbows to throw his pillow at the window. The bird is unfazed, keeps on chirping and tweeting away.

He glares at the bird, then at the clock on the nightstand next to his bed. It's nine thirty. He has a meeting with some record producer's daughter for one of those events for the sake of having an event and calling it "networking" that Hollywood is so fond of.

"Fuck, fuck, fucking fuck." He sends his business partner Gwen a message saying he's on his way, which is sort of true, then scours his cabinets for something edible, as he hasn't had time to grocery shop in weeks. He manages to find an old protein bar at the top of his pantry and eats it while he waits for the water to warm up in the shower.

He dresses simply: a striped crewneck shirt, distressed jeans, a dog tag necklace, white leather belt, white leather shoes and aviator sunglasses to hide the hideous bags under his eyes.

Hooking the sunglasses in his shirt for now, he ignores the dark circles and fixes his hair: black and straight as a pin, cut in medium length asymmetrical layers to de-emphasize the way his ears stick out and highlight the sharp sweep of his cheek bones and his naturally dark, thick eyelashes. He shaves, slides his index finger over the arch of his eyebrows, dabs on a touch of cologne and—

He may feel as if he was repeatedly run over by a luxury super-stretch Hummer limousine, but his look says: Nico Takahashi, calm, collected and put-together stylist to the stars. For now that will have to be enough.

Sitting in barely moving construction traffic at—he glances at the clock—ten-sixteen, Nico lays on the horn again. It doesn't do anything, but he *feels* better. Looking put together and feeling vindicated when a sliver of the left lane opens up and he speeds past those suckers in the center lane are the only things going for him today.

After he gets off the highway and leaves the traffic behind, he gets excited and takes a turn too fast while he sips his coffee. It dribbles down his chin and spills on his sleeve, and he now has to pretend that breezy rolled-up shirt cuffs is the look he was going for all along. He cuffs his jeans high at the ankle too while waiting for yet another light to change. Gotta be able to adapt on the fly.

He continues to catch every single goddamn red light, cursing at them and willing them to change with the sheer force of his irritation.

By the time he makes it down Sunset Boulevard and onto a side street, past the Spanish-style office building with the pale stucco walls and a clay tiled roof, wide arched entryway lined with sloping, purple-flowered wisteria trees and towering King palms that houses his office, he can't find street parking. He has to slowly, slowly, *so fucking slowly* follow a woman in an unfortunate baggy beige pants suit around a parking lot until she finally remembers where she parked her car.

He bolts from the car, slams the door, mutters a few curses under his breath for good measure and then, just outside the street exit, he steps in a puddle of something that is definitely not water. After his trudge up the stairs to the fourth floor, Nico has decided to tell Gwen to cancel their appointments so they can focus all of their energy on researching the wilds of Montana for suitable land.

2

The meeting with the record producer's daughter goes fine, particularly since Gwen had already taken her measurements and written down what she was looking for so Nico wasn't the one trying get at the specifics of what "something nice, but not nice" could mean.

Nico scours style magazines, the usual fashion sites and blogs, puts some auctions on watch, saves images, rips out pages to stick in a look-book binder, takes notes and calls a couple of contacts. He shovels down the spinach and quinoa salad Gwen shoves at him late in the afternoon, two more coffees and, after that, a bottle of (regular, boring, probably from the tap) water and two aspirin.

The day is winding down, and Nico is finishing up, very much looking forward to crawling into bed and sleeping for at least ten hours, when Gwen comes in with a stack of magazines. Gwen's look is always a variation of goth-punk-pixie, not one many can pull off, but with her dramatic bone structure and round kewpie-doll eyes, with her hair dyed blonde and cropped in a short undercut style, she somehow turns tartan prints, corsets, black leather and carefully placed chains, hooks and zippers into something totally fresh and interesting. Today, it's leather pants with fishnet side panels, a frilled white blouse with a draping bow, heeled leather boots and a thin silver chain hooked tight around her neck.

"Two things: One. Cosima, our spoiled Daddy's girl from this morning, called and requested that she only work with you because…" Gwen hikes the magazines into the crook of her arm and reads something she scrawled in ink on her palm, holding it in front of her face. "I wrote this down so I'd get it right. She 'likes to surround herself with exotic people.'"

"For God's sake…" Nico looks up with fingertips pressed to both temples. "Did you tell her I grew up in Sacramento? And so did my parents? And their parents?" Gwen bobbles her head and gives him a look that says it wouldn't matter if she did. "Can we at least charge her extra?"

"Already did." She moves across his office space; the interior of the building is done in the same neutral tones as the exterior: tan and beige and off-white, the same natural wood and clay tiles. They've brightened their suite with bold yellow accent walls and polished chrome desks, throw rugs in variegating black-yellow-gray geometric patterns, yellow and black framed graphic art, desk chairs in shining black leather. A glass wall, cushy suede chaise and rows of metal garment racks in the waiting area separate his office from Gwen's. The overall feeling of the space is meant to be down-to-earth but modern, welcoming yet cutting edge.

"This is why I keep you," Nico says, going back to his notes.

"I think it's the other way around, but whatever makes you happy." She drops the stack on his desk and sits in the chair on the opposite side of his desk. Nico drags the top one closer with the end of his pen.

"Second order of business," Gwen announces. "We have a problem." She flips to a dog-eared page.

Hailey Banks punches photographer in ripped Herve Leger dress and peekaboo sheer thong!

"I'll call her manager. I'm not paying for that." It's awful, it was a stunning dress, really, but he dresses her, instructs her team on hair and makeup and sends her off. After that she's someone else's problem.

"Oh, it gets worse." Gwen pulls a different magazine.

Who wore it better?

"Oh no," Nico groans, his head pounding in his skull like the thump of a bass drum.

Troubled child star Hailey Banks steps onto the red carpet in stunning Gucci jumpsuit... after model Claudette Babineaux already strutted her stuff to the delight of the crowd.

"Fuck, fuck." Nico drops his head in his hands and scrubs his hands through his hair. "She's gonna lose it."

"On the bright side, they identified both designers and called the jumpsuit stunning. I wasn't sure about the open-back style of the jumpsuit, but you were right. It looked fantastic on Hailey." She pats his head gently.

Nico looks up with his cheek on his fist, slumped in his chair. "Maybe she'll fire us."

Gwen smiles placatingly. "We can always hope."

Nico sighs and spins his chair to face the little window behind him and watches the path of dozens of purple flowers as they flutter sadly to the ground.

"Uh-oh, he's staring wistfully out the window," Gwen mutters.

"Don't you ever get tired of it, Gwen? It's all so fake and pointless. Put on a show, build people up, tear them down. Rinse, repeat."

"It's entertainment. It's art. It's fun, Nico."

Nico swivels back. "Yeah, it's fun until you're in the back alley of some skeevy club waiting for vultures to eat you alive."

Gwen tips her head and looks at him with her huge, round eyes soft and affectionate. "It's sweet that you care about Hailey."

Nico runs both hands through his hair and sighs. "I really wish I didn't. It's exhausting." He leans forward and reaches for her. "Run away with me Gwen. Let's move to Montana and learn how to ice fish and hunt buffalo and grow radishes and beets."

"I think my wife would probably object to that."

Nico waves a hand at her. "Flora can come." He twists his lips and considers. "Does she know how to ice fish?"

"Okay, I think you need to take a break now." Gwen closes his laptop despite Nico's objections and pushes his notebook aside. "I brought you a little pick-me-up."

This magazine is a more respectable publication: high fashion photo spreads and sit-down interviews instead of close-ups of celebrity beach bodies and the latest infidelity scandals.

"Not bad," he allows.

"Not bad? That is a fine specimen of man and you know it."

"And how does your wife feel about you ogling fine specimens of men?"

Nico straightens the magazine. The splashy headline reads: *Grady Dawson: Country Music's Sexy Bad Boy Strips Down and Opens Up.* The words appear just to the left of a photo of what Nico has to admit is a very attractive man: a naked, save for a strategically placed acoustic guitar, very attractive man.

"Ogling is completely allowed within the confines of our relationship; besides, just because I don't want him doesn't mean I can't appreciate the aesthetics. It's part of my job to appreciate aesthetics. In fact…" She flips the pages and grins wickedly. "On page eighty-six he's wet and wearing nothing but white briefs." Gwen flips to said page. "You're welcome."

Normally he'd roll his eyes and call it a desperate bid for attention and say he prefers his men in a nicely tailored suit, which is true, but it's been a shitty two days, he's running on very little sleep, and Nico may very well be down to nothing but base instincts. So what the hell.

He lets himself enjoy the images: damp sandy blond hair in a mass of thick, tight curls; plump lips and chiseled features, just the right amount of rugged scruff on his strong jaw. Gorgeously sculpted torso and thick thighs and, from what he can tell in the wet underwear shot, pretty impressive assets as well.

"Okay fine, you win. I would lick him if I had the chance," Nico says, closing the magazine and looking up at Gwen.

Her smile turns sly. "Well maybe if you ask him nicely—"

"Gwen, please tell me he's not here."

"He's not here," Gwen says. Nico sighs in relief. "Yet."

"Not today. Even if I wasn't beyond tired and in a shitty mood, I can't deal with one more entitled, self-absorbed train-wreck right now. I've got nothing left to give." Nico stands and steers her out of his office by her shoulders. More than anything, he just wants the sanctuary of his own quiet, simple home and his own cozy, simple bed.

"I know, but his assistant called and said he really wanted to meet with you and that *Mr. Dawson's* time is limited, and I had to make a quick decision," she says, rapid fire and breathless. He steers her to the left, into the open door of her office.

"As opposed to my time?" Nico has to continue this never-ending day because some pretty-boy music star thinks everyone should just bow to his demands? "No. I need this day to be over. Go home to your wife, Gwen."

She resists, bony little shoulders twisting from Nico's grasp. "Just meet with him. This could be the sort of fresh opportunity you need. Try something different, see what happens."

Nico grabs her bag from under her desk, plops it against her stomach and holds her shoulders again, shuffling her toward the exit and—

Outside the door to their suite, one hand raised to knock, there he is. Grady Dawson himself. Even more gorgeous and ruggedly sexy in person.

Gwen greets him, claims to be a fan, which is news to Nico and helps to explain a lot, and then skips away, back to her office.

"Thank you so much for meeting with me," Grady says with a noticeable Southern twang, after getting settled at Nico's desk.

"Well, I was informed your time is very valuable." Nico's bite makes Grady wince a little.

"Yeah, I'm really sorry about that. My assistant can be a little... pushy. But, I have been working on my next album here and in Nashville and after that is the CMAs and then I leave for a short promotional tour." His eyes are a lovely light shade of blue; his hair, lush golden curls that spill down his forehead and spiral over his ears and softly brush his neck.

"And you're here because..."

"Oh." Grady smiles. Perfect teeth, beautiful smile. Nico sighs heavily. "I saw you working an event recently and—let's just say you caught my eye." His accent is thick and viscous like honey; his voice is deep and rough-hewn and stupidly sexy. "I can see you have the article where I talk about wanting to change my image?"

Nico raises his eyebrows and glances at the magazine spread he'd been ogling earlier. "Yes. I... certainly read that article." And did not just drool at the pictures.

Grady smiles again. "Great. So you get it. I want something new. Something different. And when I looked into your work, I knew you were the person who could help me."

Nico falters, releases a breath and tries to think through the fog that is his brain right now, but the last thing he wants is another needy client too full of themselves to listen to anything he has to say. He's *just so done.* "I don't think I can help you. Sorry."

"So you won't do it?" Grady frowns and leans over the desk. His eyes are low and imploring, his mouth is lush and pouting and Nico really, really wishes he didn't find that so damned appealing.

"I don't think—"

"How about just for this photo shoot I have tomorrow? No commitment." Grady flutters his eyelashes and smiles hopefully. Nico can only imagine how often that look gets him exactly what he wants and more.

What Nico really wants is to go home. And the easiest way to do that is to tell Grady, "I'll think about it, okay?"

Grady stands, showing tight jeans and a tight black T-shirt on that incredible body, grins and holds out a hand for Nico to shake. "It's at noon. My assistant will send the details." His hand is soft and warm and strong.

"I didn't say yes," Nico tells him.

Grady's answering grin is sly, cocky. "You didn't say no, either."

3

He should say no.

Nico is propped up in bed with squashy pillows behind his back and head and under both arms, his tablet on his bent knees and the TV on in the background: a nightly entertainment show droning away about a reality star's recent attempt to launch a movie career. Nico has only caught bits of the movie's premise and clips, and it still sounds completely horrific.

On his tablet are the results of a Google search: *Grady Dawson.*

Nico is well aware of the sensationalist nature of Hollywood "journalism." He's stood on the sidelines and observed enough to see it for what it is: a constant cycle of manufactured drama and intrigue and hyperbole designed to keep people watching and reading and clicking and consuming. Some of it is true. Some of it is sort of true. Some of it is so ridiculously fake that it should be on display as a tacky wax figure at Madame Tussauds.

The problem is that Nico is just far enough removed from the crazy at the center that he can't be sure which is which. From where he stands it all looks like angry, churning chaos.

And that's a lot like what Grady Dawson's Google search results are: a storm of rumors and romantic links to almost every person he's been seen in public with since his first single, "Broken Records," went double platinum.

A playboy. Party animal. Romantically involved with dozens of men *and* women in Hollywood and New York and Nashville. He shows up with a wealthy music producer twenty years his senior one night, and then a young Hollywood actor barely out of high school the next. He's dating a pro football player. An actor only rumored to be gay. Three different members of the same rock band.

Article after article about who Grady Dawson is probably sleeping with this week, and none about his music or career, until Nico does a specific search for it.

The entertainment show switches to a behind-the-scenes look at the set of a popular sitcom as Nico wriggles up to a sitting position in his pillow fortress to read reviews and analysis articles about Grady's music. He doesn't know much about country music, but *breath of fresh air* and *visionary* and *soul baring* seem to be universially a pretty damn good take. But there is controversy there too: spats with his record label; a reputation for being impulsive and difficult to manage; speculation that "Broken Records" was an anomaly, a one-hit wonder, that the rest of his music is too odd, too niche, too label-defying to ever be a real success.

Nico closes down the browser, more confused now than when he started. Is it really a simple matter of changing his image, or is Grady just exhausted by all the clashing expectations being shouted at him from all directions? Who *is* Grady Dawson? Could Nico get to the real person hiding behind the bravado and bluster?

He should say no to Grady just on principle. No appointment, waltzes in there with that cocky smile and just *assumes* Nico will drop everything and do whatever Grady asks, just because he's charming and gorgeous and chiseled like Michelangelo's wet dream and *maybe* the image of Grady wet and in briefs *does* keep buzzing at the edges of Nico's brain and maybe Nico's tongue *would* fit perfectly into the groove of muscle along the jutting bone of Grady's pelvis—

It's the principle of the thing. How dare he?

Nico furrows his brows, nods his head at himself for confidence, and sends Grady's assistant a text: *I can't make it until 12:30.*

There. He can at least make him wait a little bit. That'll show him.

The TV switches again, to the local news, so Nico turns it off, grabs one more pillow and shoves his face into it. South Dakota is probably nice. What do they have there, he wonders, his own warm breath puffing against his face. Prairies? Do people still do the frontier thing out there? Probably not. He hopes there's a few buffalo left, at least. He drifts off to sleep on a mountain of pillows and dreams about spending his days threshing wheat and shearing sheep.

The next morning he dresses in skinny-fit light gray chinos, white low-top slip-on sneakers, a green and blue geometric print button-down and a simple silver collar chain for a touch of elegance. He shaves and styles his hair and dabs on a little cologne.

He does a search for Grady once more as he eats sprouted grain toast and SunButter and sips coffee at his kitchen counter. It's a perfect warm sunny morning, except for that damn bird chirping away in the tree next to his bedroom window again. He types a new search for the CMA and ACM and CMT awards red carpet photos from last year.

He is dismayed but unsurprised at the offerings for men's styles in country music. Jeans with T-shirts and blazers. Ill-fitting monochrome suits and ties with black dress shirts. Even some full-on cowboy looks: the hats and snakeskin boots and pearl-snap plaid shirts, Wrangler jeans with oversized gold or silver belt buckles. Nico swallows a mouthful of black coffee and shudders.

He makes the long drive out of town to the address Grady's assistant sent him and parks in a gravel lot, heaves his travel case and garment bag from the car, then stands squinting through the afternoon sun at an old warehouse. Inside it's cool and cavernous, dusty and dirty and littered with construction waste: splintered boards piled in a corner, old pipes and crumbled plaster and rusted machine parts, the walls graffitied and windows broken. The photographer is probably going for gritty and raw, though given its location in Studio City, the warehouse has likely never been used for manufacturing of any kind. It only looks that way.

A backdrop is set up in the back, where lighting is being arranged around it and the photographer is fiddling with a camera. To the right is a makeshift hair and makeup station, a rack of clothes next to that, and Grady Dawson sitting in a tall stool getting concealer applied under his eyes.

"Hey! You made it!" Grady hops up, to the makeup artist's clear annoyance, and pulls Nico into a quick, tight hug.

"Oh," Nico squeaks, "Okay."

"Sorry, I'm a hugger. I should have warned you." Grady grins that megawatt smile. "It's a Southern thing."

"Is it?" Nico straightens his clothes and waves a dismissive hand at Grady's cheerfully confused smile. "Never mind." He hangs his garment bag on the rack, then rifles through the other pieces that someone else pulled for the shoot: faded jeans, flannel shirts, frayed T-shirts, boots, a cowboy hat. Nico clicks his tongue in dismay. "There's even less to work with here than I thought."

"Grady's look says that he's approachable," a voice says behind him, each word crisp with irritation. Nico turns to a young man with neatly parted brown hair and thick-framed glasses who crosses his arms and lifts his chin. He's short and thin, dressed in green chinos, a light pink polo shirt with the collar popped, a cream cricket sweater and brown penny loafers, almost as if he read a how-to manual on how to pull off the perfect preppy style. "People are drawn to Grady because he is approachable. They could have him, if they wanted. Which they do," the kid says with a purse of his lips, now looking at his phone. "But not really, because *obviously.*"

"Mhhmm." Nico had hoped to hear from Grady, not some kid who seems to think he can speak for him. "Well, if you want my *professional* opinion, Grady's look says that he's a tired cliché. You may as well dress him in camouflage overalls and accessorize with an American flag and hunting rifles."

The kid looks up with narrowed eyes. Nico straightens his spine and stands his ground.

"That's Spencer," Grady says, eyes closed as he gets an application of powder all over his face. "My assistant. He's been pulling double duty as an emergency stylist."

Oh. Nico's stomach twists guiltily. He relaxes out of his battle stance. "I'm Nico. Nice to meet you. And hey, I'm sure you were just sticking with whatever the last stylist was doing." Even if whatever the last stylist was doing was terrible. Nico holds out his hand, but Spencer is back to looking at his phone, typing rapidly with both thumbs.

"Pleasure."

Nico looks around. What the hell is he doing here? Why did Grady go to all that trouble to track him down and beg for a meeting with him when everyone seems to have decided everything? Maybe that's the problem. If Grady *doesn't* want to be the guy everyone wants, the guy who beds whoever he wants whenever he wants, the guy who parties and graces the cover of every trashy tabloid in existence. And if that's the case, well. That changes things.

Nico stretches his arms behind him, twists his back right then left, works his shoulders loose and studies the rack of outfits again. "Okay, I was hoping I'd have more to pull from here, but I think we can adapt what I brought in a few different ways." He glances to Grady, still waiting on the stool, watching Nico intently from beneath lowered eyes. Nico crooks a finger. "You. Up."

Grady scrambles off the stool; the metal legs screech harshly on the concrete from the force of it. "Do with me what you will. I trust you."

Next to them, Spencer makes a throaty scoffing sound.

Nico turns his critical eye to Grady, to the shape of his body: wide shoulders, defined pectorals, broad chest and tapered waist. His hips are narrow, his legs thick. Nico moves behind him. Average-sized neck; that makes things easier. Well-muscled back. His ass is rounder than Nico expected, more—he tilts his head—perky. Yet lush. Ample, even. Nico realizes he's been staring longer than is really required to get an idea of how well the suit he brought will fit. He clears his throat and strides to the garment bag.

"Since this was so last minute," he says, curt but not unkind, "I had to go with what the designer happened to have available." He unzips the bag, smooths out the fabric. "I'll have to make some minor adjustments." To the photographer he calls, "Can I get fifteen minutes?"

The photographer, lighting director, Spencer and the makeup artists all stare at him as if he's setting fire to stacks of money and cackling instead of requesting a little more time.

"It'll be worth it," he tries. They all stare. "I'll buy lunch."

The photographer goes back to adjusting settings on the camera, and everyone else waits. "Fifteen. No more."

Spencer hands Grady a can of Mello Yello with a straw before taking lunch orders and disappearing without a word.

"Health tonic," Grady says with the can raised.

Nico lifts his eyes to the ceiling, then holds out the button down shirt and slacks. "Go change."

When Grady comes out from behind the partition, the shirt is untucked, his tie is draped around the back of his neck and his pants are undone. Nico's belly feels as though he swallowed a hot stone. Grady holds his pants up with one hand, shrugs and smirks in a winsome sort of way. "I didn't know how you wanted me."

Nico's thumbs fumble and slip on the clasps of his travel case. Finally he manages to open it with a frustrated grunt and scoop out clamps. He works quickly, smoothing the thin cotton across Grady's shoulders and chest with his warm skin and shifting muscles beneath the fabric, almost against his palms. He twists the extra folds in the shirt along Grady's spine, clamps it into place.

Tucking the shirt in with uncharacteristically trembling hands, Nico tries to find a spot on Grady's body to focus on instead of the hard V of his hips and the flat ridges of his abdominals. His eyes dart from the hollow of Grady's throat to his square chin to his sharp jaw, up the roguishly stubbled line of it to a spot behind his ear. That seems safe. Nico reaches behind Grady, making sure the waistband is clamped taut against his body.

The spot behind his ear looks soft and warm and as if Nico's mouth would fit right there in the crook of it. Nico shakes his head roughly, pulls his hands off of Grady's waist as if he's been shocked and steps back to find himself staring into Grady's blue eyes.

"Hey." Grady wets his lips with the tip of his tongue. Nico swallows, clenching his hands at his sides to keep them steady. He has to crouch down to clamp the material of the slacks around Grady's legs and now there's nowhere safe that he can look, no escape from the fact that Grady's groin is *right there* and his thighs are so delectably strong and Grady's fingers keep twitching toward Nico as if he wants to cup the back of his head and Nico is dizzy from all the blood rushing chaotically through his body.

"Lunch!" Spencer calls. Nico bolts up from the floor and rushes to open his lunch as if there has never been anything more important than his veggie wrap with hummus and bottle of kombucha.

The crew mills around and chats; Grady sits in the makeup chair while Nico props himself on the edge of a stack of pallettes nearby, eats and tries to not notice Grady noticing him. He looks up at the steel beams on the ceiling, out the milky-clouded windows. At the lighting equipment. The desk with a laptop open. The makeup table with bottles and brushes and combs, an electric razor and neat, sharp little scissors.

He looks over at Grady, who holds his gaze until Nico looks away with his cheeks warm and heart thudding.

"Your shirt is amazing," Grady says as Nico takes several long pulls of tea from the bottle. "Paul Smith?"

"Yeah, actually." Nico looks down at the shirt, hooks a finger gently on the chain placed across the collar and tugs at it. "So, you recognize high-end designers and yet you're still being styled like a backwoods Fabio."

Grady snorts so hard he chokes on his ham sandwich.

"Sorry, that was harsh," Nico says, once Grady catches his breath.

"No. Don't be sorry, it's true." He sets his sandwich down and brushes crumbs off his hands. "Let's just say that the country music scene can be a little stuck in its ways." He shrugs and looks at Nico. "People like knowing what to expect. No surprises, nothing too out there. They like doing things the way they've always been done."

"So why hire me then? Why take the career risk?"

Grady takes a bite of sandwich and smirks around the mouthful. "I like taking risks, for one. And I know who I am, what I'm about." His eyes are dark, lingering on Nico's face when he adds, "I know what I want."

This time the photographer breaks the moment, yelling that Nico's fifteen minutes are up, so he stands and brushes crumbs from his lap, balls up his trash and then helps Grady into the jacket. He can't clamp it without destroying the lines and making Grady look bulgy in the wrong places, but if they keep it open, and he adds some of the accessories already here—

"It's wink-wink-nudge-nudge ironic," Nico says. "A fine suit." And a fine man. "With touches that say, 'Hey I'm just a dude in a cowboy hat who happens to be wearing a jacket that costs more than the average monthly salary of my fans, but that's okay because we're all in on it.'"

Grady's mouth curls at one corner. "That's a lot to ask of a suit."

Nico shakes his head, takes a few steps back to survey the outfit. "It's not just the suit, it's the guy in it," he says, distracted by how incredible Grady looks. Still. Something's not quite right. He stares at Grady, and Grady stares at him. Spencer sighs loudly. The photographer has impatience radiating from her in waves.

Finally Nico realizes what's off, snaps his fingers and says triumphantly, "You should cut your hair."

At this, everyone gathered around gasps. "What?"

"You can't," the makeup artist says.

"My editor will have my head," the photographer says. "And there's no time!"

Spencer stares at Nico. "Grady Dawson is known for his hair. It's his trademark." He waves a hand around dramatically. "You're suggesting career suicide!"

"I'm not demanding we shave him bald," Nico protests. How he longs to work in an industry that isn't so infused with theatrics. "Everyone knows Grady for his flowing mane of hair? Well guess what everyone will be talking about, then?"

"This photo shoot," the lighting director fills in.

Nico gives her a nod of thanks for getting it. "And Grady Dawson's bold new image."

The truth is, it could backfire. Good style has a lot to do with straddling that line between classic and surprising, original and personal. Grady could lose something that defines him. But from what Nico saw in his Internet search, and from Grady's own words, that might not be such a bad thing.

"Let's do it," Grady says. He bounces on his toes a little. "Yeah. Let's do it."

Spencer clenches his jaw, but says, "I'll call a hairdresser."

The photographer shakes her head and tosses her hands up. "Fine. Great. Change the world with a hair trim. But we're gonna run out of decent sunlight by the time we get a hairdresser here and get this done. I've already given you extra time as it is."

"No problem. I can do it." Nico rolls his sleeves up to his elbows, waits for Grady to agree, then steers him by his deliciously broad shoulders back onto the stool.

The makeup artist has scissors and a razor meant for trimming sideburns and facial hair, so it's not ideal, but will have to do. The top of Grady's head is level with Nico's shoulders, and from here he can appreciate the splay and scatter of ringlets, the tendrils that corkscrew over his forehead and down his neck, the rebellious locks sticking out from his temples and behind his ears. Nico combs his fingers through, an instinct taking over from so many years of cutting hair. He tugs this way and that, and the curls wind around his fingers.

Grady makes a low rumbling noise deep in his chest, then says in a tone that's even huskier than usual, "So, you cut hair. You're impeccably dressed, smart and shrewd and gorgeous," Grady says as Nico snips a short trim around one ear. "I don't see a wedding ring so I'm guessing you have a long line of suitors just begging for a scrap of your attention, right?"

Nico cuts the other side, the back, moves around to the front. He ducks down to make sure everything is even, so close that he can see that the scruff on Grady's jaw is dark blond, that his eyebrows are carefully groomed. His bottom lip has a tiny white scar in the center. He can sense the warmth from Grady's body and the earthy clean smell of his skin.

"You are shameless." Nico drags his fingers through the newly shortened curls a little more thoroughly than necessary.

Grady grins up at him. Shamelessly.

Nico snips and cuts and tugs; golden curls fall around his feet like fractured sunbeams. Grady's eyes are closed, his mouth pressed tight, and his hands grip and release, grip and release on the armrests. When he tips Grady's chin up and crouches to closely survey his work, Grady drags his eyes open. The intimacy is so intense that Nico's scissors clatter to the ground.

"Okay," Nico says, his voice pitching weirdly high. He arranges the clipped curls in a messy-yet-groomed style; then stands behind Grady and catches his eyes in the reflection. "What do you think?"

Grady tilts and turns his head, touches his hair, pivots the chair to see it from different angles. "You are seriously amazing."

"Well…" Nico lifts a shoulder coyly. "I try." He takes the cape from Grady's shoulders, and then Grady is standing there in front of him looking like one of *Nico's* wet dreams: a gorgeous man in a gorgeous suit, freshly trimmed with his tie hanging undone around his neck. With his pulse pounding against his throat, Nico helps him tie it.

Grady looks down at Nico's mouth, says, "Thanks," and swallows thickly. Nico's eyes track the shift of his Adam's apple, the smooth glide down his throat when he swallows. They both jump when the photographer impatiently calls for Grady.

The photoshoot takes off quickly; the photographer snaps picture after picture rapid-fire, calls out instructions and encouragement.

When she comes to look at some of the shots on his computer, she shakes her head again, but this time she chuckles. "Incredible."

"I figured out what you can tell your editor," Nico says. The photographer arches her eyebrows. "Let them know that they're going to want to move this to the cover."

4

It's not as if he's *waiting around* to hear something from Grady. He's busy. Plenty busy. He has other clients to meet with, boutique owners and designers to lunch with, trends to research and showrooms to visit. Fittings and emails and shopping and borrowing and, every once in a while, eating and sleeping.

He had a full and fulfilling life before Grady Dawson cowboy-sauntered his way into it, before Nico felt the spark of attraction between them that's flared to life under his skin, pulling at his mind and body, before he couldn't quite convince himself that even a brief, no doubt amazing, hookup with Grady would be a terrible idea.

Nico stares at the gray wall of the building outside his office window, thinking about how much he's not thinking about Grady for so long that he loses an online bid for an Hermès scarf that would have been perfect for the look he's putting together for an up-and-coming actress.

Nico sighs and swivels his chair back to the desolate grayness outside.

"You're doing it again," Gwen calls, crossing in front of his office with newly arrived deliveries of clothes and accessories for all the clients they have that *aren't* Grady. Gwen adds over her shoulder, "You're pining."

"I am not," Nico scoffs.

"Whatever you need to tell yourself." She disappears behind a rack of clothes in the center of the office.

Nico's mouth works silently with a protest he can't quite seem to verbalize. "Shut up," he finally says. From behind the rack, Gwen laughs.

Two more days pass and still nothing. *It's probably time to move on.*

Fridays often mean preparing for weekend events, but he has nothing on his agenda, so he's actually looking forward to grocery shopping and vacuuming his little bungalow. Maybe he'll even go for a hike. In the mall. While he's window shopping. And *shopping* shopping.

"Hey, this came for you earlier." Gwen drops a small square package on his desk.

Nico picks it up. The label is from a drink company that he recognizes and occasionally buys from, but he isn't sure why he would be getting a package from them. He pulls scissors from a desk drawer.

"Hey, how's Flora lately?" Nico asks as he slices open the tape on top.

"Okay, I guess." Gwen looks down and away, shifts uncomfortably, then looks curiously into the box at whatever is hidden beneath the packing peanuts. "Things have been… tense, I guess. So what the hell is that?"

Nico tips his head. "Kombucha." He pulls it out, little tan biodegradable packing peanuts scattering everywhere. "Hibiscus and ginger flavored."

There's a card stuck between two of the bottles.

> *Nico,*
>
> *My apologies for not thanking you sooner. I asked Spencer to send a card I wrote but I guess it slipped his mind. Thank you for working with me on such short notice. You're really very remarkable, and I know you're busy. So consider the drinks as a peace offering. I ordered some for myself to see what the fuss is about, but I think it might have been a bad batch. Tasted sour. Hope yours is better.*
>
> *Thanks again,*
>
> *Grady*

Nico hands the card to Gwen and bites down on the stupid grin that's trying to break free. Grady is… sweet. Nico is a little disarmed by sweet. He's not sure what to do with sweet. And he's also not sure how much of the sweetness is Grady, and how much is Grady Dawson, Country Music Star.

Either way, Nico is into it. Really into it. Which is ridiculous, of course. He's mooning over some music star like a middle-schooler with his first crush: Butterflies flit about his stomach and his pulse races when he thinks about him. An infatuation with a guy that can have anyone he wants. A guy that *does* have anyone he wants.

Nico pulls notes from other clients, gets on his computer and starts putting together looks for other people, but no matter what he does Grady keeps intruding on his thoughts. This shirt would look great on him, Nico muses, and puts it on his online wish list before he realizes what he's doing. On an auction site, he wonders what other designers would best suit Grady. At an online vintage store he has a sudden idea for incorporating classic western wear into Grady's new look.

Nico ends most work days banging his forehead on his desk while Gwen looks at him with obvious concern from her side of the office.

Then the magazine spread comes out. Grady has been keeping a low profile, hanging out in the studio putting final touches on his next album. So when the pictures hit the Internet, everyone goes crazy.

Grady Dawson is everywhere, not just in the tabloids or on country music sites. Every celebrity and music and fashion site has Grady Dawson front and center; Grady Dawson as a headline; Grady Dawson as the hot, trending, most shared, most popular, top story.

Grady Dawson, sheared and sexy!

Grady Dawson shocker, click for photos!

Grady Dawson stuns with class and a sleek new look.

You won't believe what Grady Dawson has done now!

Nico follows link after link to articles and discussions about the photo shoot with Grady in the stunning Armani suit that Nico picked for him, Grady with his head tipped up and to the side, his hands wrapped around the tie Nico himself knotted around his throat.

There's a photo with Grady lit by the afternoon sun streaming in from the huge warehouse windows, turned to the right with one hand in the pocket of his dress slacks. One where he's tipping a cowboy hat down over his forehead with his suit disheveled and that gorgeous strong profile perfectly displayed.

And the photo that's a long shot with every detail of the outfit displayed—from his leather boots, to each piece of the suit, to the pocket square and knotted tie, coat open to the perfect fit of the shirt, his short tousled curls and a sexy smirk on his lips—is stunning. Moving. Art.

That one is Nico's favorite.

"Well done," Gwen says over coffee at her desk. "Maybe he'll woo you with more fermented yeast tea now."

Nico laughs and picks up his latte. "A boy can dream."

"Seriously though, really great. And," she says as she sips her mocha and gives him a knowing look, "it's nice to see you so inspired again."

"Thanks, Gwen. You're the best."

"Don't I know it," she jokes. "So I hate to derail the happy train but..." Nico sips his coffee and raises his eyebrows at her. "Flora's been talking about moving."

"Oh yeah?" Nico's gaze flicks back to his computer, where that last photo of Grady has been minimized. He'd like to take a longer look at his work again. No particular reason. "I hear Boyle Heights is the place to buy these days. I mean, it's like up and coming, up and coming. Or something?" He gives in and clicks the picture.

Just stunning work, really. Stunning.

"No, Nico." Gwen shifts so much in the chair that it squeaks and scrapes. "Not in LA. She has family on the East Coast and I guess she's fed up with sunshine and warmth and optimism. I don't know." Gwen frowns and shakes her head. "She thinks it would be good for us."

Nico finally drags his eyes away from the perfect sexy curl of Grady's mouth in the picture. Wait. Gwen is leaving? Gwen can't leave. He's the one who wanted to leave. "But what will I do without you? And you love it here."

"I do." Gwen offers him a sad smile. "But I love her more."

Nico reaches both arms across his desk and she takes his hands. They started Style by Nico together, despite his name being on the door and letterhead. He would be nowhere without her hard work and sacrifice. And despite his frequent soothing fantasies of living the quiet life of a radish farmer in Nebraska, he never really would have left Gwen behind. They're a team.

"Okay." He gives her hands a squeeze. "Just make sure you tell Flora that if left to my own devices I'll become a hermit who only occasionally emerges to yell on the street corner about the indignity of drop-crotch pants, and that I'll die alone and disgruntled and it will be on her head." He lifts his eyebrows and dips his chin. "But I want you both to be happy. So I support whatever you want."

"Thanks, Nico. You're the best."

Nico smiles, and then the buzzer for the door goes off. It's the end of the day, and they aren't expecting any more clients or any shipments. When Nico goes to the door, the delivery person hands him a slim overnighted envelope. Nico signs for it and walks back to the office, sliding his index fingers through the seal to open it.

He reads the little card quickly, and his face must give something away, because Gwen hops up and takes the card from his hands.

"Gwen!"

"Once again, you are amazing. Thank you. Please come to Nashville so I can *thank you* in person," Gwen reads, then says, "Ooooh," in a really obnoxious sing-song voice.

"Shut up."

"I will not. Gee, I wonder what kind of *thanking* he wants to do, hmm?"

Nico snatches the card away from her—she's small and quick like a jackrabbit—and stuffs it in the inside pocket of his blazer. "Very mature."

Gwen sits back down and flicks her fingers at him. "Oh, whatever. You're into him. It's okay, really." Her phone pings with a text from Flora asking if she's working late again. She answers something that Nico doesn't see. "Let loose and have some fun. He's hot, why not?"

Nico sits, too, elbows on the table and chin set on one fist. He makes a face at her. "Because he'll screw anything with a pulse?"

"There is that." Gwen picks up the empty envelope and taps it on her chin, thinking. "Oh wait. *In Person.* That explains the weird cryptic email I got from his assistant that just said 'CMA' and a date." She quickly looks up something on her phone. "Grady must want you to style him for the CMAs. I'll call to confirm."

"I don't know… Tennessee?"

Gwen chugs the rest of her coffee, gives Nico a considering look and says, "Maybe Tennessee holds the key to your woeful wanderlust? You know, hillbillies and moonshine and… I don't know. Republicans?"

Nico barks a laugh. "I don't think that's really what it's like."

"Well, in that case," she says, then snatches his phone and types out a reply to Spencer before Nico has a chance to finish protesting, and sets it down with a decisive *thunk*. "I guess you'll just have to go there and find out what it's really like."

5

By the weekend, there's backlash about Grady's new look. Nico expected some; you can't rescue a drowning puppy without getting some blowback in this business. Nico gets up early on Sunday, goes for a run on his treadmill, showers and dresses in weekend casual wear: loose drawstring linen pants and an organic brushed cotton T-shirt. He stretches out on his couch with a smoothie that's the appetizing color of stomach bile and starts perusing all the gossip websites he usually hits after working with a client high-profile enough—or notorious enough—to land on them.

A few bloggers and articles call Grady's look an arrogant bid for attention. One blurb and subsequent comment thread theorize that Grady is making a run for mainstream success, that he's leaving country behind, and that the album he's currently working on isn't country at all, but alternative rock.

Then there's the trashy tabloid site that says Grady's haircut is obviously the first step down a spiraling path of destruction. Next to come are DUIs and jail time and a drug addiction, which is such a ridiculous leap of logic that Nico gets only halfway through the write-up before he's so annoyed that he closes his web browser.

Nico sets down his smoothie and slumps into the couch. If there's one thing he's always been sure of, it's his own creative vision. So why does he suddenly care so much what other people expect from him? Why does he try so hard to please anonymous, faceless press and people who will never all be happy? Never. Why even bother? He closes his eyes, does some deep breathing and gives in to a tug of sleepiness.

Maybe three minutes into his attempted nap the bird is back again, sitting outside the window and chirping loudly, the same trilling, loud song over and over and over. And over.

He bolts up from the couch, flushed with anger. "Shut up, you fucking demented bird!"

He needs a break. He needs… something different.

Nico grabs his phone and crams it between his ear and shoulder, waiting for Gwen to pick up as he drags his suitcase and carryon to his room. "Hey, can you take on a little more this week? Just the shoot for Zara de Olivera and then there's the fitting for Sullivan Watt. Oh and, Charlotte Victoria still needs some jewelry for that DTLA Artwalk, but I was hoping to meet with a few new designers if you wouldn't mind doing some cold calls and knocking on doors." It sounds like a lot, now that he's said it all out loud. But if anyone can handle it, it's Gwen.

"Sure thing," Gwen says, then in a quieter voice, probably to Flora, "He's totally going. I told you."

"Not too late to change my mind." Nico tosses the suitcase on his bed and then heads to the bathroom to see which travel items in the little airline-approved bottles he needs to pack: hair product and shaving cream and shampoo and deodorant and—which cologne? He holds the bottles over his suitcase, hesitating over just who exactly he's trying to smell nice for. But as he tells his clients, one can't underestimate the importance of a signature scent. He drops in his current favorite. For all he knows, Grady doesn't even like the scent of citrus blends with hints of cypress.

"Oh, don't be petty," Gwen chides. "Have fun. Relax. Just let things flow, okay?"

Nico opens his closet and considers his options with a well-honed eye. "That better not be a euphemism."

Gwen laughs warmly in his ear. "Oh it is," and before Nico can respond she says, "Okay, bye!"

He calls his parents to let them know he won't be driving up to Sacramento to visit as he'd planned, and then has to listen to them talk about his older brother's various accolades and accomplishments and how his tenure track is coming along at Cal Tech, while he folds his clothes and zips a few suits into a garment bag. He books a hotel and a rental car and since the ficus plant he thought he could handle being responsible for is dead, that's that. So much for beet farming.

He locks the door and heads to the airport with plenty of time for an extra pat-down, just in case.

When he steps off the plane several hours later he's greeted by twangy music being pumped over the intercom speakers instead of garbled announcements: It's Johnny Cash, who even Nico recognizes. The ceilings are open with huge skylights, and he passes a display of signed electric guitars from soul and R&B pioneers, a restaurant called *Tootsie's Lounge* and, just outside the exit, a young man a with guitar and an open case at his feet, crooning his heart out.

It's different. He *did* say he wanted something different.

The short drive from the airport to the hotel is maddening with traffic at a crawl down the highway for no discernible reason. It's not even that busy. There aren't any accidents. It's just slow. Nico curses and switches to the left lane, only to get caught behind someone barely going the speed limit.

"Do you understand the concept of the fast lane?" he shouts at the Chevy in front of him.

The hotel he booked near the airport is fine, nothing fancy, and sitting on the edge of the bed flipping aimlessly through the channels just makes him anxious, so Nico sends Grady a text to let him know that he's coming over, and they can go ahead and start planning.

Ok, Grady texts back. *I'm fixing to work out so make yourself at home!*

Nico squints at the message for a moment; he can hear Grady's slow drawl around the words as clear as day. The thought sends warmth right to his belly.

The drive from the hotel starts as only four lanes lined with dense trees and greenery. He passes by churches and neighborhoods, shopping centers and office complexes, scattered in clumps at first, then packed close together as he nears downtown. And then the highway expands with more lanes, the traffic gets busier and modern high rises peek out on the horizon. Nashville is bigger and more urban than he expected, with sleek skyscrapers and dense city streets, but the town clearly takes a lot of pride it its history: restored and carefully preserved old buildings of brick and limestone, pillared antebellum mansions with sprawling front porches and Victorian homes—fairytale gingerbread houses with sharply pitched roofs and turrets and lacy ornamental spindles—all set among the modern cityscape.

He finds the aesthetic immediately appealing: eclectic and charming, contemporary and iconic. He's never been to Nashville, but something about it feels familiar and comforting, like slipping into a custom-tailored blazer.

The address Spencer sent him is outside Nashville, and very quickly the buildings get farther and farther apart as he drives.

There's wide open land, then massive, brand new subdivisions with names like *Whispering Creek* and *Lochmere Landing* and *Serenity Oaks*. Thick patches of forest and farms with grazing cows and meandering horses start to appear. The speed limit decreases and the traffic goes slower and Nico gets stuck on a long two-lane country road behind an old pickup truck with a rusted muffler and broken, flapping tailgate for nearly thirty minutes.

By the time he makes it down the winding dirt path through the woods and up to the spacious cottage-style house with a wide wraparound rocking chair front porch, Nico's body is tense and his jaw tight.

"Does anyone in this entire state have any sense of urgency?" Nico demands, instead of saying hello when Grady opens the door.

Grady laughs and opens the door wider. He's wearing nothing but a pair of loose athletic shorts; his body gleams with sweat and his hair is a messy mass of damp curls. "Not really. You ain't in Los Angeles anymore."

"No kidding."

A man emerges from a hallway off the wide living room, which is painted in soft blues with a gray sectional sofa stretched across the length. He's in a similar state as Grady, sweaty and slick and barely clothed, but unlike Grady's lean, sculpted muscles, he's absolutely enormous, with giant bulging arms and a huge chest, as solid as the trunk of a sequoia redwood.

"You were great today," the man says in a deep bass, squeezing Grady's shoulders and pulling on a sweatshirt. He nods to Nico and leaves.

Working out. Right.

"That's my trainer," Grady says as he leads Nico into the house. It's beautiful, not at all ostentatious or tacky. In fact, it looks like a house out of a model furniture show room, professionally staged and pristine.

"Trainer in what, Turkish oil wresting?" Nico looks around at the kitchen, the formal dining room, the French doors that lead out to a sparkling clear pool.

Grady bursts out in a laugh so loud it's as if Nico had just uttered the funniest thing he'd ever heard, then pulls him into a sweaty hug. "I'm so glad you're here. Sit. I'm gonna shower."

Nico sits at the very edge of an overstuffed reclining chair in the corner next to a huge flat screen TV, and does not think about how it felt to be pressed up against Grady's naked, sweat-slick, chiseled torso and how amazing he smelled, even without a signature scent to speak of.

6

After a few minutes of drumming his fingers on his knees, Nico hops up to take a look around, justifying his snooping as a means to get a better handle on Grady's personality. To help with styling him. Completely legitimate, professional reasons. Grady *did* tell Nico to make himself at home, and at home he would totally rifle through all of the closets and drawers and shelves.

No matter how much he noses around, however, Grady's house remains almost completely devoid of character: clean and neat and expertly appointed. There's classic art on the soft gray walls like the kind found in hotels and upscale office buildings, accent pillows placed just so on the couch and chairs, candles that have never been lit arranged on side tables. The dining room table has a blue and green blown glass centerpiece and matching place settings for six on the table, all gorgeously hand made and pristinely unused. Nico runs a finger around the curved edges of a plate, lifts his finger and frowns at the dust he wipes from it.

The stove is state-of-the-art and spotless, no chips or scrapes in the smooth glass surface, no cooked-on stains or charred bits of food.

He walks past a library with a desk and three walls of bookshelves. It has a rustic hunting lodge feel to it—all heavy dark wood with hunter green accents, a stone fireplace, and a chandelier made, horrifyingly, from deer antlers. It also looks eerily unused. When he plucks a book from a shelf at random and opens it, the spine cracks and the pages are crisp. He re-shelves it, drags two fingers down the spine. A book of Greek myths.

There are two guest rooms with plush, immaculately made beds and plenty of natural lighting from the huge windows looking out to the wooded wild acres that surround the house on all sides. One guest room is done in all white, one in beige.

Nico follows the sound of the shower to the huge master bedroom at the end of the hallway. He finds a four poster bed and an antique armoire, an easy chair with a footstool, a knitted blanket folded over its back, a lamp behind it, a dresser. All in muted blues and grays like the living room. Even Grady's room lacks character. No pictures of loved ones, no coin collections or trophies or stack of beloved books. Not even a pile of dirty clothes or strewn magazines. Nothing that suggests anyone spends much time living here at all, let alone one of the most dynamic, talked-about performers in country music.

Finally, Nico notices something that just might give him some insight to Grady, and he's so busy being surprised and delighted by it that he doesn't notice the shower turn off and the bathroom door open.

"Well, hey there."

Nico drops the knitting basket onto the floor at the sound of Grady's pleased voice. Yarn and needles and partially finished projects bounce out at his feet.

"I'm sorry, I was just trying to get some inspiration for—" Nico crouches down to pick everything up, starts to explain, looking up at Grady: bare feet and bare legs fuzzy with light brown hair, the curve of a pale hip and exquisite cut of groin muscles and thatch of coarse dark hair and— "Oh my god, you're naked." He looks back down, his face burning and head swimming as he gathers the items back into the little wicker basket.

"I do usually shower naked. Along with some other activities."

Nico can tell he's smirking. He sets the full basket back up on the shelf, eyes kept steadfastly away from Grady. Nico can hear him shuffling around, opening a drawer.

"I'll go. Sorry." Nico walks toward the door with his head bowed and hands cupped around his eyes to keep his gaze trained forward and nowhere else.

"Now wait a sec," Grady says. A drawer slams closed. "What sort of inspiration were you looking for? Tell me about your process."

Right now Nico's mind seems to be inspired by Grady's wet, naked body. He shakes his head, blinks a few a times. Process. Right. "I uh. I just, um. Thought we should make sure it feels like you, whatever we do. I mean, we can go as out there and bold as you want, but at the end of the day, your style should represent *you*, and not what I think you should be."

When Grady doesn't answer, Nico's stomach churns at the thought that he's offended him, or more likely, pissed him off by being so nosy. Another drawer opens and closes, and Nico hears a zipper go up, so he chances a look over his shoulder.

Grady is dressed in a gray T-shirt and black jeans, looking at Nico with his eyes soft and his mouth parted and something fond on his face that Nico doesn't quite understand.

Nico turns to face him from across the room.

"Yeah." Grady's mouth tips in a smile. "Yeah, that's what I want."

They stare at each other for a long, charged moment where Nico waits for Grady to come on to him. Grady's fond expression has shifted: intent and heated, his eyelids low and tongue running along his bottom lip.

Nico has made up his mind. Grady is sexy as hell and probably dynamite in bed and was very enticingly naked just a moment ago. But for one, he really does want to be professional; Grady is a client. And for two, he has no interest in being another notch on Grady Dawson's carved mahogany bedpost on the bed that he probably didn't even pick out.

Nico clears his throat. "So, do you knit? Or is that some kind of decoration aimed at appearing homey and quaint, as conceived by your interior designer?"

"Nope. It's mine. My Memaw taught me." Grady walks to the basket and straightens the colorful balls of yarn into a neat pile.

"Memaw?"

"Mmhmm." Grady gives the knitting supplies one last wistful look before moving to the armoire to get out shoes and socks. "She was convinced that idle hands were the devil's work. She kept me busy so I'd stay out of trouble." Grady sits on the bed to pull on socks and black combat boots.

Nico watches him closely. "Did it work?"

Grady looks up with that grin again, the one that makes Nico's blood feel hot despite any reminders to himself that he's decided to remain professional. "Depends on what you call trouble."

Nico crosses his arms over his chest and leans against the door-jamb while Grady stands and stretches. Nico is keenly aware of the arousal stirring in his gut. He knows exactly what he'd call trouble.

"If you still really want to get to know me, I have a few ideas," Grady says. Nico is only too happy for the excuse to think about something else for a while.

On the forty-five minute ride farther out to the country in Grady's pickup truck, Grady wants to know everything about Nico—how he got into styling, what he likes to do in his free time, his childhood and hobbies and favorite foods. Grady drives and listens and always has a follow-up question. And another. He smiles and laughs and is charming in a way that's not at all put-upon or fake or with ulterior motives.

"My father is a barber, and my mom runs the shop, so I pretty much grew up there. Family business. It had been my grandparents' before that," Nico explains. "They don't really get the fashion thing, but to me it's not so different. Your customers—clients—want something that tells the world about them, and the smallest details are important."

"Yeah, that makes sense." Grady takes a turn, and they pass a rock quarry and then a bridge over a wide river glittering in the afternoon sun. "Were they disappointed that you didn't take over the barber shop? That you went to LA instead?"

"No." Nico looks out the window and considers. "Maybe? I get the feeling they would rather I went into academia like my brother."

Grady looks over, one hand on the steering wheel and one resting loose on the console between the seats. "Why do you think that?"

Nico scans Grady's face, his profile when he turns back to road, thrown off again by Grady, every expectation of him being self-absorbed and vain dissipating like morning fog. *Genuine* is not a word Nico employs often with the sort of people he works with.

Nico thinks about Grady's question for moment, why he feels the tug of his parents' expectations, their disapproval and disappointment, even now. "I guess because I was raised to put my head down and work hard and be successful. I don't think being a celebrity stylist is really what they had in mind."

Grady stops at a red light, ticks his turn signal down and looks over again. "You don't work hard?"

"Sure I do, but as far as they're concerned I tape people's boobs to their dresses." Nico shrugs. "Which is not entirely wrong."

Grady laughs, delighted. "Well, some boobs are pretty hard to wrangle."

The truck moves forward, and Nico grumbles, "You don't know the half of it."

A small, rural, working-class town slowly comes into view: First a storage facility and a gas station, and then as they come into town, churches and fast-food restaurants roll by, a dentist and a bank and, on the main road through town, a squat, red brick building with a combined elementary and middle school.

"So this where you grew up. Let me guess, you were like some musical prodigy, right? Playing guitar before you could crawl? Making all the church ladies swoon when you were barely out of diapers?"

"Not quite, no." Grady slows the truck, takes a side street pockmarked with cracks and pits. "I spent too much time on much less wholesome activities." The truck rattles and shakes on the uneven road, bumps over train tracks and passes rows of narrow shotgun-shack style houses with weathered chain link fences surrounding them. "But music is like a heartbeat, you know? It's always there, you just have to stop and listen for it. Once I stopped… I guess I realized I wasn't on the path that I was meant to be. Or at least, that I had a choice about where I was headed."

Nico moves his head against the seat rest to look at him; the setting sun backlights his face, that famous jawline and full pouting mouth and golden curls of Grady Dawson, the partying playboy of country music, who poses naked on the covers of magazines and gets whatever he wants. And if all that is true, then who the hell is this sweet, earnest guy sitting next to Nico in a pickup truck in rural Tennessee?

"Here we go," Grady says, pulling the truck to the side of the road.

Here is a trailer park with a clutch of a dozen single-wides scattered across a dusty dirt lot. In the center is a warped swing-set frame with a broken slide and no swings, just chains, drifting listless in the breeze. The trailers have rusted siding or busted windows or splintered wood on the porches. Some have toys and brightly colored bikes and scooters littered outside. A baby stroller sits empty on its side in the dirt.

"This is where I grew up, for the most part." Grady moves around the side of the truck to stand next to Nico against the passenger side. If any of the residents are home, they don't seem to care that a celebrity is hanging out among them. "My parents were young and into some bad stuff. They drifted in and out, you know? My grandparents raised me. Memaw put a guitar in my hands when I was fourteen after my grandfather died." He scuffs a foot, kicking up little puffs of dirt. "They did their best, but I still had all this anger I didn't understand. Demons I didn't know how to face."

Nico looks around and then at Grady, who looks drawn and sad. "I'm sorry," Nico says, not really knowing what else to say.

"As far as sob stories go, it could be worse." Grady's tone is dismissive and upbeat, though his eyes are still sad. He gusts a breath and shifts closer to Nico; their shoulders brush as he says, "Everyone likes the rags to riches story, you know? That's the sound bite interviewers like to throw out. The Cinderella story. But for a long time I was a pissed-off, messed-up kid, and I worked my ass off to overcome that." He shrugs and chuckles humorlessly. "Nobody came to save me. Fame didn't save me. Parties and being seen with the right people didn't. Music did. Hard work did. No one wants to talk about that."

"It ruins the fantasy." Nico scans Grady's face, eyes glassy with sorrow. "Everyone wants success. They don't want the work that goes into it."

"Yeah." Grady drapes himself over the truck's bed, leaning into Nico's space. "Hey, you hungry? Reminiscing makes me hungry."

Nico laughs. "Sure."

As Grady walks around the truck to the driver's side Nico wants to ask where Memaw is now, but given that they're visiting the place where Grady grew up and not the person who raised him, he has a pretty good guess.

What is it like, Nico wonders, to be loved by millions of people and still be lonely?

Grady does attract notice at the restaurant, some hole-in-the-wall barbecue place in the middle of a random strip mall.

"Now *this* is real barbecue," Grady says, sitting in a booth with torn pleather seats and a wobbly table, warped linoleum floors and the thick scent of fried food clinging to everything. "Prepare to have your life changed."

A group of young girls at the table behind them whispers and stares at Grady's back as Nico looks at the menu. Almost everything is deep fried, comes with coleslaw and cornbread and there isn't a green vegetable in sight. "I'll take your word for it."

A woman three tables down takes out her phone and clicks a picture not at all discreetly, and when the waitress come over she immediately gushes, "Oh my god, I *love* you!"

Grady laughs and says, "Well thank you, darlin'," and after that the charming, smooth, camera-ready Grady Dawson, Country Music Star, is back, posing for pictures and signing napkins until they're surrounded by a crowd of swooning fans.

By the time the crowd clears a little and Darla—their waitress and self-identified number one fan of Grady Dawson—takes their order, it's dark out and Nico is starving.

"Sorry about that." Grady reaches across the table and brushes his thumbs across the sensitive insides of Nico's wrists. Nico moves his hands to his lap before someone sees and gets the wrong idea. Darla finally brings them sweet tea in red plastic cups with a withering slice of lemon placed on the rims.

Grady may have the entire restaurant cupped in the palm of his very skilled hands, but Nico refuses to be further charmed. He is a client. He is in the public eye. His life is not something Nico wants to get enmeshed with. "It's fine," he says.

They're quiet as they wait for the food, awkward now with so many eyes watching their every move. Nico fidgets with the pepper shaker, moves it back and forth between his hands, unscrews and re-screws the top. Grady is watching him. Everyone is watching Grady.

This is the reality of Grady's life. He's on watch, even when he's just stopping to eat greasy barbecue. Nothing he does can ever really be separate from his public life. Private moments are never really so. And that doesn't stop at Grady, it ripples out into anyone he wants to be close with. Nico has seen it. Nico has watched it destroy people.

He sips sweet tea that's more syrup than liquid and feels like a living display, as if everyone is waiting for them to do something that they can *ooh* and *ahh* and snap pictures of to post on the Internet.

The food *is* amazing: rich and savory, tender and filling. Grady smiles at him and chats happily about nothing in particular, and the more he focuses on Nico while they're surrounded by people who all want him and claim to love him, the more uncomfortable Nico is with the attention.

On the drive back to Grady's house, the radio is loud and Grady sings along, his voice smooth and melodic. Nico stares out of the window at the darkness rushing by until the car stops at the end of Grady's winding dirt driveway.

"You can stay here," Grady offers, walking Nico over to his car.

"No, that's okay. I have a hotel." Nico hits the button on his key chain to unlock the rental; it beeps twice and the lights flash on.

"You sure? I have two extra rooms that are just sittin' there empty." Grady dips his head and pouts hopefully. Then says with his voice lowered and eyelashes fluttering. "I'd love to spend more time with you."

He reaches for Nico and Nico ducks away, drops into his car and shuts the door. He waves, cranks the engine and backs out of the long, dark driveway. Nico glances back just long enough to see Grady wave back at him, then head up the stairs to the porch.

The problem is that Grady keeps blurring the lines between professional and personal. The problem is that Nico doesn't know how to be close to someone who has to keep up a public persona. The problem is that Grady seems to be coping just fine with his every move being siphoned and twisted and grabbed to be turned into gossip fodder, but Nico could *never*. It's the part of his job that he hates the most. The part that makes him want to turn and run and not stop until Hollywood is just a shiny, shimmering blip in the distance.

The problem is, he wants to stay.

The next morning, Nico heads out alone. Nashville has a burgeoning local fashion scene, and he wants to find some interesting pieces to go with the suits he brought along.

He finds a boutique with a 70s glam rock-esque feel selling billowy chiffon pants, crushed velvet dresses and oversized jumpsuits in bright patterns. Gwen would go nuts for this place; he'll have to bring her here sometime. He doesn't get anything for Grady, but could easily spend hours picking through one-of-a kind items for other clients. He chats with the owner, a designer from Brooklyn who was drawn to Nashville's laid-back glamour.

"Come back soon and I'll take you up to the studio," she offers, after Nico realizes how much time he's spent in one place and thanks her for showing him around. "All the new stuff, you can take first dibs."

Next on his agenda is a store that sells Italian leather shoes, designed and crafted on site by an actual cobbler trained in Florence.

Like the last stop, the owner is friendly and helpful and thrilled to help Nico find something for Grady. "I have some in the back I think you'll like," he says, leading Nico into the workroom over scuffed wood floors and an exposed-brick interior rich with the scent of leather. "We're not quite as flashy as LA here." He nods at the minimalist metal shelves lined with men's shoes and boots, "But I like to think we have enough character to make up for it."

Nico picks a pair of hand-dyed, exquisitely detailed black work boots of buttery, supple leather, caresses them like a lover with a hitch of his breath. "And then some."

For his last stop he pulls into the driveway of a house painted purple with yellow eaves; the yard is landscaped with raised garden beds full of vegetables and herbs. Chickens scurry away as he walks to the sunflower-lined front porch, and a wind chime made of glass beads in a rainbow of colors and antique skeleton keys tinkles cheerfully in the breeze. It's the most whimsical place he's ever been.

The designer is a knitter and spinner who learned her craft in New Zealand, and who uses wool so recently sheared that bits of hay still cling to the fuzzy threads on the spindle in her workroom. Nico not only gets his commissioned piece, but learns about the lost art of hand spinning, delivered in a genuine and authentically passionate way that he can't imagine finding in LA.

"You should come meet the sheep sometime," the designer suggests. She's young and beautiful and could easily be a model or actor but looks completely fulfilled spinning yarn and knitting at her micro farm in Tennessee.

"I'd love to," Nico says, and really means it.

Back downtown Nico soaks in the vibe: dynamic and artsy and cool without the demanding rush and constant bustle of a bigger city. There's music everywhere: street performers singing on corners with hats upturned at their feet, local bands playing on patios of restaurants, clubs with their doors and windows thrown open to broadcast the wail of an electric guitar or the frantic call of a fiddle or the pulse of drums.

He eats lunch at another barbecue place. He has a very specific craving, it turns out.

Then he gets a text from Gwen.

Hey sexy mystery man.

He glares at the message and types a reply with a mouthful of slaw. *What the hell are you talking about?*

Gwen sends him a link in her next message to a tabloid website that he recognizes, and when he clicks it a tiny, grainy picture of him and Grady last night at dinner pops up on his phone.

Grady Dawson steps out with sexy mystery man near Nashville. Could this be the affair that broke Clementine Campbell's heart?

Nico writes back, *We were hungry and ate barbecue. Could not have been less scandalous. Do they just make shit up? And what does that have to do with Clementine Campbell?*

His phone rings. "He's supposedly involved with her—come on Nico, keep up," Gwen says when he answers. "The two of them are like, on-again off-again, or so the tabloids claim. And yes, they do just make shit up."

She wants to talk about some issues she's run into with getting Charlotte Victoria to agree to the jewelry she's picked, so Nico talks with her about some other options while he finishes up his lunch and shopping, then heads to Grady's house to show him what he's put together.

Spencer answers the door instead of Grady, and looks at Nico with disdain that he doesn't even attempt to hide. He sighs. "Wait here."

Grady comes up from a staircase next to the kitchen pantry that Nico hadn't noticed yesterday, even with all of his snooping. Grady is as thrilled to see him as always, and pulls him into an enthusiastic hug. Spencer exhales loudly and stands with his hands on his hips.

"He's rehearsing," he says, as if Nico is a small, slow child. "Just leave the clothes for him."

"No, no. I want you to come listen," Grady tugs Nico by the hand that isn't burdened by shopping bags. "Give those to Spencer and come with me."

He drags Nico down the stairs that lead to a dim, finished basement outfitted with sound panels and amps and microphones. Dozens of guitars of all types hang from the walls and lean in stands, and the room is cluttered with a stand-up bass, fiddles, a banjo, drums and an upright piano. Wires snake and coil everywhere, stands are set up with sheet music, and there is very little room for Nico to find a spot. Everything looks set up for a band that has yet to arrive.

Grady sits on a stool, picks up the most battered and worn guitar in the bunch and says, "If you really want to know who I am, this is the place you'll find me."

He strums a few chords, adjusts the tuning of a couple strings, and then he starts to play and sing, something slow and quiet and a little sad, singing mostly to himself but chancing a look up to Nico every once in a while. Grady performing is Grady stripped bare. Even in this dank basement for an audience of one, Grady pours his soul out.

Nico is drawn to Grady, his wide hands on the strings, and his smooth, warm voice and his face tipped down toward his guitar. His crooked grin and his easy laughter and his generous, genuine heart. The air around them hangs heavy, the soft lights glow on his skin and Nico stands frozen, suspended, breathless. He's incredible.

"Well?" Grady says, strumming the last few chords, setting the guitar by his feet, and looking at Nico with hope and a little trepidation.

"I—" Nico starts, and his voice goes rough. He clears his throat. "Good. I mean, I don't really listen to country so I don't have much to compare it to…"

Grady smiles and picks his guitar up again. "Music is music." He plucks some strings and adds, "I don't care if you like polka— when something speaks to your soul, you know."

"Yeah, I guess you do." Nico looks up to the staircase. Maybe he should go after all, give Spencer the clothes so he can play temporary stylist again and head home. He's letting himself want things he shouldn't. He knows how this will end: messy, complicated. His own name in the tabloids as just another failed Grady Dawson affair. If he leaves it would be unprofessional, but if he stays? He's not sure how much longer he can keep things between them strictly business.

Before he can decide whether to stay or go, the stairs thunder with footsteps, and a group of people files into the basement, embracing Grady and laughing and unloading their own instruments.

"This is the band that's coming on tour with me," Grady says, nodding to the group. "Billy on banjo." Billy lifts his chin in greeting and straps on his instrument. He's average height and string-bean skinny, with a ruddy complexion and a baseball cap pulled low over his buzz-cut hair.

"On drums, Brad. He's an industry veteran. A pro," Grady says, with obvious admiration for the man with kind hazel eyes and a bushy mustache and silver hair. He shakes Nico's hand with a, "How'd ya do," in a deep-South accented baritone.

The only woman in the band: "Mandy, fiddle," Grady introduces. She grasps Nico's right hand with both of hers and gives a dimpled smile. She's short, around Gwen's height, with red hair pulled into a ponytail, and an hourglass shape that Nico would love to dress.

"And Mongo. Bass." The last band member is an imposing height, towering over Nico in a way he's generally unused to at six feet even, but Mongo is round-faced, soft-bellied and a hugger like Grady. He squishes Nico into his large body enthusiastically.

Nico gives them space to get started, shuffling to a corner where he's unable to make any sort of graceful escape as the band sets up and starts to rehearse, unless he crawls under Billy's legs and manages not to take half the drum kit and Brad and several guitars down with him.

Grady isn't up for any awards at the CMAs this year, Nico had learned from his Internet journeys. Unlike last year, when he was up for best male vocalist and best new song and won neither, this year he's just performing.

Nico watches the entire rehearsal, and doesn't leave even when they take a short break. He can't keep his eyes off Grady. When he's singing, when he's discussing a key change or a tempo shift. When he's laughing at something Mongo said or even just replacing a string. Why does it matter so much if he's just another one of Grady Dawson's conquests? Maybe he can find a way to keep Grady to himself, just for a while, here in the quiet forest-topped lazy hills, away from paparazzi and Hollywood and everyone who wants a piece of Grady Dawson. Maybe no one will ever have to know.

Maybe he will have some fun.

8

After rehearsal, they all head upstairs to the kitchen, where food has appeared on the counter. The band eats from deli trays, strategizing and going over last-minute details. Nico asks them all to wear dark colors tomorrow night, if they don't mind.

After they leave Grady stands up from the counter, stretches his arms up and back, pulling his tight black T-shirt across his chest and shoulders in an enticing way. Nico doesn't dart his eyes to the side, doesn't chide himself for staring. Doesn't push back against the arousal stirring in his veins. He should. But he doesn't.

"Man, I always get so wound up right before a big performance." Grady tilts his head at Nico and lets a slow, sly grin cross his face. "Wanna help me blow off some steam?"

Nico eats a cube of cheese from a toothpick. He shouldn't. But something has shifted; he's through fighting it, tired of over-thinking it. He takes a breath, lets himself get swept away in the moment and says, "I... guess...."

Why the hell not.

Grady hits the counter with excitement, rises up on his toes then says, "Okay, stay right there."

Nico stares after him, toothpick still pinched between his index finger and thumb. Are they just going to... Like, right in the kitchen? Isn't Spencer still hanging around somewhere? Should he brush his teeth? Nico breathes into his hand and tries to tell just how strongly his breath smells of sharp cheddar, then Grady comes back into the kitchen with a pile of clothes in his hands.

Nico drops his palm away from his mouth, props a hip against the counter and hopes the clothes aren't some sort of bizarre role play that Grady is into. Not that he couldn't be swayed, just—one thing at a time.

"I hate for you to mess up those clothes that I'm sure are designer." Grady hands Nico a pair of jeans and a white T-shirt. His clothes are designer, actually—Westwood plaid pants and a button down from Marc Jacobs. He's not sure what that has to do with—"Might get muddy," Grady explains. "Come on, before it gets too dark!"

Bewildered, Nico follows Grady to the half bath tucked between the laundry room and garage in a hallway behind the kitchen. He changes, stopping for a quick pep talk in the mirror. He can do this. Fun. Exciting. One night. No one will ever know. He steps out to find Grady still waiting for him.

"I thought we were about the same size," Grady says, his gaze lingering on Nico's body.

They are, for the most part: The pants and shirt fit pretty well, but Grady is clearly more broad and more muscled; the sleeves are a little loose around Nico's arms and the pants hang baggy around his thighs.

"So, are you going to explain to me what we're doing?" Nico hopes there are no blindfolds involved.

Grady opens the garage door to reveal his truck and a classic car parked next to it: a cherry red Plymouth Belvedere. "1956," Grady says, caressing a hand down the car's hood. "My grandfather had one, his first car. This foxy thing was a rusted out shell when I got it." He leans down to rest his cheek on it. "But we fixed you up real pretty didn't we, baby?"

Nico watches him, amused. "Want me to leave you two alone for a little while?"

Grady laughs. "Nah, I'll give her some lovin' later. Right now, we're taking a spin on this." He pulls a tarp off something in the corner, back where the light from the swinging overhead bulb doesn't quite reach. Grady hits a button to roll up the wide door to the outside, and it takes Nico a minute to figure out what it is while his eyes adjust.

"A four wheeler?"

"Yep." Grady pulls two helmets from a shelf above it, gives one to Nico and shoves the other on his head. "Nothing like gettin' filthy with some power between your legs." He climbs on, then pats the little seat behind him.

"Do you dirty talk all of your automobiles?" Nico asks. Grady guns the engine in response.

Nico hesitates, shifting the helmet in his hands. That thing looks like a death trap on wheels. He's also not a huge fan of mud or of venturing into the woods as the sun is falling and darkness is spreading ominously through the towering trees. But then Grady flips the visor up, just his lovely eyes and the bridge of his nose visible, and he implores, "Please?"

"Fine. Fuck it. Why not." Nico crams the helmet on his head, swings a leg over to climb on behind Grady and grips the handles on either side of the back seat.

The ATV starts to move with a jerky start that makes Nico lose his balance, thrown backwards enough that his white-knuckled grasp on the handles isn't enough. He grabs at nothing in the air, panicked, then manages to get a hold of Grady's shirt, yanking himself back upright until he's plastered against Grady's strong back.

Grady stops just outside the garage, moves Nico's arms tight around his waist and yells over the roar of the engine, "Hold on tight!"

He takes a right off the driveway and into the yard, then down into the thicket of tall pine trees, sturdy trunked oaks and fat little shrubs with prickly green leaves. They fly over branches and ditches and bumps, and with every sharp turn and every terrifying drop into a ditch or climb up a steep hill, Nico squeezes tighter around Grady's solid torso with his chest pressed to Grady's back. Every single jostle makes Nico's pelvis grind into Grady's ass.

He tries to ignore it, worrying instead about the way he can feel the mud splatter on his back and legs when they ride along the bank of a little creek, and the fact that every time they hit a slight incline they might flip over and both be crushed to death.

At the top of an embankment, Grady suddenly kills the engine, hops off the ATV and stands at the edge of a cliff over the creek. He tears off his helmet, looks back at Nico with a wink, and jumps.

Nico scrambles off the vehicle. "Are you insane?" He shouts, lifting his helmet off his sweat-damp head. Grady is standing on the opposite shore of the creek, impish and rumpled. His answering laugh echoes through the darkening woods.

"It's fun, come on." Grady holds out his arms, as if he's waiting to catch Nico damsel-style.

The cliff is probably no more than eight feet high and it's just a few feet across to the sandy shore where Grady stands beckoning him. The creek burbles away between them over large flat rocks and sharp stones. He won't drown or fall to his death, exactly, but he could easily break something. "You're paying for my emergency room visit," Nico calls, tossing his helmet next to Grady's and taking a few steps back for momentum.

"'Kay," Grady says, a satisfied smirk already on his face.

Why, why, *why* he is doing this, Nico doesn't know. He just jumps. And in the few seconds he's airborne it's *thrilling*. Until he lands wrong on the shore and stumbles forward, arms flailing to catch himself before he goes face first into the dirt.

"Gotcha." Grady catches him around the chest and hauls him up as they both trip and sway and end up tangled together. "You did it."

They come to a stop chest to chest with Grady's arms still scooped around him, Grady's legs anchoring his own, Grady's wide hands across his back. Nico looks into Grady's eyes, blinks. Down to his mouth. Blinks. "We um—" He waits and waits for his heart to slow but it hammers away stubbornly.

Grady's head tilts and moves in. He has tiny speckles of dirt across one cheekbone. "Nico, I…" Leans in and in and—

"It's getting dark," Nico blurts. He disentangles himself from Grady's arms. Not here, not yet. He shouldn't. He wants—he shouldn't. "How do we get back?"

The ATV is still up on the embankment, which is much too steep to climb. Grady rubs at the back of his neck. "Oh. There's a bridge just over the bend."

"There's a—" Nico shakes his head. "Of course there's a bridge." Of course they had to take the pointlessly reckless route instead of the bridge just over the bend.

They take a hill and a bridge back to the ATV, and Grady heads back through the dark woods, then parks in front of the garage. When Nico gets off he doesn't kiss the ground in relief, but it's a near thing.

Grady *whoops* and takes off his helmet; his curls are matted and his face is pink. "Don't you just feel alive?"

Nico pulls his helmet off, feels as if his skull has been compressed and released again, as if his brain is loosened and free-floating. "You know what? I kind of do." It's probably just panic still coursing through his body, sizzling and skittering across his nerves like a live wire, but he's starting to understand the appeal of thrill-seeking. He feels… hungry. As if his body is yearning for another hit of excitement.

Nico combs his fingers through his hair to tame it, looks around at the unobstructed view of the dark sky and bright moon, sets the helmet on the ATV and feels more alive than he has in a long time. He's not sure if it's Tennessee or the near-death experience, or just stepping out to do something different. Or Grady. But whatever it is, he likes it.

"I really want to kiss you right now," Grady says.

Nico looks up and Grady is close, his face difficult to read in the dark, but the tension between them is palpable anyway.

Nico swallows. "We probably shouldn't." Which is not a no, not a rejection. Because he wants to, but just needs a moment for the adrenaline rush to slow, for his heart to stop being a panicked, wild thing in his chest, a moment to clean the mud off of his ankles. Grady takes it as a rejection anyway.

"Right, well. You probably want your clothes back," Grady says quietly, all of his usual enthusiasm gone.

They walk in silence into the dark house, into the kitchen with the lighting soft overhead, where they run into Spencer.

"You have sound check and dress rehearsal at noon," Spencer says to Grady, while glaring at Nico.

"Thanks, Spence. See you tomorrow," Grady says, with a smile that doesn't reach his eyes. He turns to Nico when the front door clicks shut. "I'm just gonna…" He nods to the main staircase. "I appreciate everything, Nico."

"It's my job. No thanks needed."

"It wasn't. Anyone could have done that." He looks over at Nico and it's like before, when it was just the two of them and a guitar and Nico was transfixed by him. Not the famous Grady Dawson charm and charisma and talent, but *him.* "You saw me, you took the time to get to know me. Most people don't."

Nico takes two steps forward, reaches up to get both hands twisted around Grady's hair and pulls him in to slam their closed mouths together. Grady heaves a sharp breath in through his nose, parts his lips and kisses back with a whimper, head tilting and searching beneath Nico's palms, hands coming up to hold tight onto Nico's hips. His tongue swipes across Nico's bottom lip, nudges inside. Heat gathers in Nico's belly and spreads throughout his body.

When Grady's hands move down to grab his ass and his hardening cock presses against Nico's, Nico thinks, *Oh, what the hell,* one last time, and pulls up the hem of Grady's shirt.

9

He doesn't do this, is the thing. He's put together and sensible, mature and hard working and he knows better than to mix business with pleasure, especially with the types of people he works with. He goes on dates and finds men who are mentally stimulating and serious, and it's that connection that leads to intimacy for Nico. He doesn't strip the shirt and pants off a man whose libido is more well-known than his brain or heart or music, then lick into his collarbone and up his neck and kiss him as if he's starving in the middle of his pristine, ultramodern kitchen.

He brings home a date he's gotten comfortable with over time, serves red wine in fragile-stemmed glasses, folds down the sheets and makes gentle, satisfying love. He does not sink to his knees and run his panting, open mouth from the hard bulge of a calf up to strong thighs and nuzzle with a whine along the outline of a stiff cock, without any decorum or self-control whatsoever.

"What do you want?" he'll usually say, lip-bitten nervous and coy.

Not, "Fuck, you're so hot," growled against the heavy hang of his balls. "Can I fuck you?"

This is what Grady Dawson has reduced Nico to: starving, debauched, on his knees, shaking apart with raw desire.

Nico wears clothes like armor. He tells everyone else how to see him, and then picks out the clothes that allow other people to do the same for themselves. He stands back, holds back, steps out of the limelight and into the cover of shadows where no one can look at him too closely.

Grady hauls him up and kisses him and undoes a lifetime of being zipped up and buttoned down and calmly measured. He wants Grady as he's never wanted anyone, wants him stripped bare and bent over and shattered apart as much as he is.

Grady runs his palms beneath Nico's shirt; the calluses of his left hand catch rough on his skin. Nico thinks of them moving cleverly across guitar strings, and shivers. Nico's shirt is tugged up and off, and Grady ducks to swipe the flat of his tongue across peaked nipples.

Nico cups the back of Grady's head, keeps him there as he pulls one, then the other, into his mouth and between his sharp front teeth. Nico gasps and bucks his hips and yanks Grady's curls.

Back up to Nico's mouth, Grady kisses him, hungry, and fumbles with his button and zipper, finally opens the front of Nico's pants and says against Nico's bruised mouth, "You can fuck me, but I want to blow you first. Thought about it so many times."

"Oh—Okay." Nico takes a tremulous breath. Grady drops to his knees, mouths Nico's cock straining against the fabric of his red briefs. He yanks Nico's pants down his thighs, sucks the head of Nico's cock through the fabric until it's wet and clinging, then sits back with a frown.

"Oh shit. Dammit."

Nico leans back against the solid, granite-topped kitchen counter, looks down at him with his chest heaving, nipples pebbled and cock aching, twitching to Grady's mouth that has moved frustratingly out of reach.

"What?" Nico manages to say. It's difficult to speak at all with Grady there on his knees between his legs, naked and vastly more gorgeous in person than on a magazine spread, all those sinful cuts of muscle and pale skin and coarse dark hair. His cock is thick and hard and long, rosy pink and rising up from between his legs and curving back toward his belly.

Nico's hand drifts beneath his briefs to stroke his own cock at the sight. "Look at you."

Grady licks at his bottom lip. "You're one to talk."

"Why are we talking at all?" He wants to fuck, bright sparks of need electric under his skin.

Grady shakes his head. "I don't have condoms."

Playboy Grady Dawson, who shuffles lovers as if he's playing a game of cards that he always wins, has no condoms.

Grady's face morphs as though a lightbulb switched on above it. "I'll have Spencer bring some!"

"Oh my god, no." Nico reaches for Grady's shoulder and pulls him back up. He can only imagine the look of death that making Spencer bring them condoms would cause. He'd rather ride the four wheeler without a helmet off a steep cliff.

"But I want—" Grady starts. Nico shuts him up with a kiss that's mostly tongue and curls his fist around Grady's cock. "*Oh.*"

He feels incredible in Nico's hand, rock hard and velvet-smooth and so hot, the fat head under Nico's thumb, skin soft under the movement of his hand. Grady's hips churn; his eyes flutter downward. He peels Nico's briefs down until Nico's cock springs free. They kiss and Nico strokes him, Grady's fingers run up and down and around Nico's groin in a maddening tease.

Nico jerks harder, faster, and Grady finally puts his hand around him.

Nico may have gotten there first, but Grady manages to wind him up quickly, moving his mouth to kiss down Nico's jaw and up to his ear, pulling the lobe into his searing mouth and whispering, "I want your cock so bad. Want it inside me. So gorgeous."

Nico can feel it building, his stomach tightening, his legs trembling. Grady's hand is perfect, his hard, toned body pressed up just right against him. Nico watches Grady's shoulder move, tendons twitching, watches his bicep bulge, the *tick, tick, tick* of his tricep flexing. He thinks about burying himself inside that perfect body, that plump mouth swallowing around his cock, and when Grady says, graveled and gruff, "Come on me, sweetheart,'" Nico does.

He rises onto his toes, hooks one arm around Grady's neck and pulls at Grady's cock off-rhythm and loose, and shoots up Grady's flat torso with a long moan. He hears Grady curse, watches Grady's fingers smear through the mess on his chest and stomach through hooded eyes and with his head slumped on Grady's shoulder. He can only stare hazily as Grady's hips rock and his cock pulses with ropes of come that spill onto them both.

"Mmm, you should stay," Grady says, his raspy-voiced accent gone thick, lazy and slow.

Nico nuzzles into Grady's damp neck, rests his mouth against the flicker of his rabbit-quick pulse. "My stuff," he mumbles in a feeble protest.

"Spencer'll get it." Grady runs his fingertips reverently up and down Nico's spine. His skin buzzes in their wake.

"Okay." Nico is too blissed out to argue, amazed at how quickie handjobs in the kitchen can rival the long-planned-out lovemaking that Nico is used to. Has he been doing it wrong all along? Maybe Grady is on to something with all the casual sex.

And as amazing as it was, he's only just begun with what he wants to do with Grady. Maybe the wrath of Spencer is worth a box of condoms after all. If he's going to have a stupid, brief, intense love affair, he may as well do it right.

Nico lifts his head, grins dopily and says, "Upstairs?"

10

Grady insists on going out for condoms. Nico shouts over the running water in the polished copper master bathroom sink that he'll do it, no big deal, but at the moment he's got his shirt off and his pants shoved down, scrubbing off mud, come and creek water from his skin and body and hair. By the time he finishes and changes back into his own clothes, Grady is already gone.

Nico looks around the empty house, goes back up to the empty bedroom, and casts a longing, exhausted look at the huge whirlpool tub with massaging jets. He sits on the bed instead. It's one of those memory foam mattresses, plush but firm, like a dense cloud magically morphing itself around his body as he sinks into it. It is insanely comfortable, so much so that when Nico decides to sprawl out and really test it, he nods off, startling awake only when Grady bangs the door open and rattles a plastic bag in his direction.

"Success!" he crows.

Nico sits up, blinking the confusion from his brain, looks at Grady's reddened cheeks and excited grin, at the ball cap pulled low on his head and dark sunglasses even though it's dark out and—oh, right. Condoms.

"Nobody recognized you?"

Grady pulls out a box of condoms, a brightly colored "pleasure pack"—Nico raises an eyebrow—and a bottle of lube. He tosses them on the bed, next to Nico's bent right knee. "Nobody there. Just the old pharmacist. Not sure he recognizes much at all, come to think of it." Grady digs into the plastic bag again, brandishing a sixteen-ounce bottle of Mello Yello and a sleeve of plastic champagne flutes.

Nico shakes his head, but Grady is undeterred, opening the soda bottle with a hiss and pouring bright yellow bubbly liquid in the glasses.

"I'm a little concerned that someone like that is dispensing pharmaceuticals," Nico says, warily taking the offered glass of radioactive-looking soda.

"He was really nice." Grady sits on the bed across from Nico, one leg tucked under the other, pretzel style.

"Oh well, in that case. Who cares if he mixes up a sweet old granny's heart medicine with some hyperactive kid's Ritalin, as long he's *nice*." Nico rolls his eyes.

Grady purses his lips and taps his plastic glass against Nico's. "Cheers."

Nico steels himself, shakes his head again and echoes Grady, takes a sip and immediately regrets it. "Ugh, that tastes like sweetened piss; how do you drink that shit?"

Nico hands the glass back to him. Grady shrugs, chugs both glasses and sets them down with a hollow clunk. "You are such a snob," he says, crawling closer on his knees. "With your *kombooka*. All prim and proper. But I know better."

Nico shivers when Grady moves close, brushing his lips along Nico's jaw, feather light. "It's—" Nico starts. "It's kombucha… *Oh*. And it's good for you."

"Know what else is good for me?"

Nico sighs theatrically. "You're going to say me, aren't you?"

"Yep." Grady nips at his earlobe, slots his nose alongside Nico's and catches Nico's bottom lip between his own. He gives it a soft tug, licks along the fattened flesh of it wetly and then opens his mouth to deepen the kiss. He pulls away to murmur against Nico's mouth, "I want you so much."

Nico tilts his head, flirty and beckoning. "You've got me."

When their mouths collide this time there is no teasing, no drawing anything out, just Grady pushing him onto his back and pressing down on top of him, bodies connected from their tangled legs to their grinding hips to the curve of their bellies, from the rapid rise and fall of their chests to their hungry mouths. Hands on jaws and gripping hair and kneading muscles and pulling pulling, closer and closer.

Grady feels like a guilty pleasure, like a rich dessert—something Nico knows isn't good for him, but is tired of denying himself. And, like the occasional long-awaited indulgence, he plans on thoroughly enjoying every morsel.

Nico flips them, and Grady goes willingly onto his back, hands roaming Nico's shoulders and waist and gripping tight to the flesh of his ass as they kiss. Nico pulls away and ducks his head to unbutton the hideous faux pearl buttons on the cowboy-style shirt Grady quickly grabbed before dashing out to the store. If Nico had long-term say, he'd banish them outright. So if he yanks it open a little too forcefully, it's mostly in his haste to get Grady naked again, and only partly in the hope that he'll tear off a button or two.

Nico has a brief flashback to the image of Grady after their little warm-up in the kitchen, when they'd walked up the stairs to Grady's bedroom with Grady in front, shamelessly nude, with the high, round globes of his ass shifting and rising, spilling out from his trim waist and going concave at the sides, and his thick thighs lifting from step to step. The dark look he'd tossed Nico over his shoulder was that smolder he wears on magazine covers, but more fiercely intense and in real time. If Nico had that sort of recovery period, he would have taken him right then and there on the pale, polished wood of the staircase.

Enough time has passed now and he's got Grady's ugly shirt open, his chest revealed, his eyes looking up at Nico with trust and openness. Nico runs reverent fingertips over the turn of his clavicles, around the rise of his pecs and down the definition of his abs, up to circle and pinch one pink nipple, making Grady stretch his neck out long and writhe beneath Nico's body.

Nico shifts to his side, twists his hand around to run it fingers first down from the hollow space between Grady's bottom ribs, down, down that mouthwatering trail of hair from his navel to where it disappears beneath the waistband of his mud-spattered Wranglers.

He wriggles the tips of his index and middle finger just underneath the button; fabric and metal dig into his knuckles, hot hard flesh and coarse hair are under his fingertips. Grady grunts, tips his hips up to encourage the continued downward path of Nico's fingers, but he lifts them away. Grady whimpers. Nico grins wickedly.

He wants so much, wants Grady every way he can have him and wants him now, more, everything. But he teases instead, holds back and holds back and winds him up. Rubs the tiny bumps of the stitches along one pocket, down the seam over a hip and over the stretched-tight denim high on his thigh. He runs just the pad of his middle finger along the inseam up and up, right beneath the bulge of Grady's balls and teasing along his perineum.

Grady opens his legs wider, moans and rocks his hips down onto Nico's hand, looking for harder, for more. Nico just rubs and circles, traces the line of his hard cock trapped along his left leg, goes back to circle and rub and tease.

Grady pleads, "Sweetheart, come on."

Nico nuzzles into his neck with a happy little sigh. He parts his lips and breathes him in, darts the tip of his tongue out to taste salty skin and feel Grady's pulse. He smells like the musky outdoors, like briny sweat and coppery mud and rich earth. Nico has had lovers who smelled like a carefully formulated concoction of high-end men's grooming products, had signature scents of cologne and aftershave and toner, a swirl of chemicals meant to set one apart as a classy, put-together gentleman. He'd always liked that—he owns many of those chemicals himself. But no one has ever smelled as delectable as Grady's bare skin just slightly damp with sweat.

"Mmm, you're delicious," he tells Grady, surprised that such a thing came out of his own mouth. Grady inhales sharply, tilts his head and moans in appreciation when Nico lavishes attention on the silky soft little spot behind his jaw.

He works it over with his lips and teeth and tongue until the skin there is red and wet, moves down to the knob of Grady's throat, his chest, his ribs and stomach and each sharp, jutting hip. Grady writhes and babbles and calls Nico sweet little nicknames, and by the time Nico slowly, slowly peels Grady's pants and underwear down his legs, his cock is flushed dark red, rock hard and dribbling clear fluid from the gaping tip.

Nico sits back on his heels between Grady's feet and Grady must know, certainly he knows, with the way people talk about his body as if it's public property, how impossibly sexy he is, but Nico can't help but whisper, husky and reverent and still not believing his eyes, "Look at you."

Grady's answering look seems bashful; the apples of his cheeks are red. Grady reaches for him. "I'd rather look at you."

Nico hovers up on his hands over Grady's torso, peppers a few kisses along his cheek, enjoys the catch of facial hair growing rough across Grady's skin. "How do you usually…" he says, and lets the question hang in the air.

Grady's face pulls together. "Usually?"

"Yeah, how do you like it? Usually," Nico clarifies. Grady's face shifts into something like frustration. Nico realizes he's probably spoiling the mood by bringing up Grady's past lovers, so he changes tactics. He smoothes his palm against the grain of fuzzy hair from his ankles to his knees, bends Grady's legs up and out. "Like this? Or hands and knees? On your stomach? How do you want me?"

"Any way I can have you," Grady drawls with a smirk. Grady sits up, kisses him with one hand clasped to the back of Nico's neck, rises up on his knees. "Naked would be a good start."

As Nico strips off his shirt and struggles out of his pants and briefs, Grady's eyes, unashamed and heavy-lidded, his pupils blown wide inside a ring of blue, never leave his body. It's nice to be wanted not because they've gone on four dates and get along pretty well so it feels like time, but because desire, like hunger, like madness, thrums electric between them.

Clothes discarded to the side of the bed, Grady moves closer, pulls Nico into him chest-to-chest and slips his tongue into Nico's mouth. When Nico's cock is slotted beneath Grady's right leg and nudges the rounded bottom curve of his ass, Nico realizes exactly how he wants this to go if Grady is leaving the choice up to him.

He nudges Grady off with his hands on his shoulders, moves to sit against that solid and intricately hand-carved mahogany headboard with his legs stretched in front of him. Mouth parted and fingers twitching, Grady looks at him. Nico pulls at his own cock until it's standing upright from his lap.

"Like this?"

Grady answers by clambering over Nico's legs and positioning himself with Nico's cock between his ass cheeks. Grady grabs the box of condoms, fights with the packaging while Nico opens the seal on the lube. Grady is still tearing the box open with an impatient grunt when Nico reaches around and presses two fingers where the head of his cock had just been nudging.

"Ohhhh 'kay," Grady says, losing his handle on the condom packaging and listing forward. Nico bites down hard on his bottom lip, furrows his brows and finally groans when his two fingers breach inside of Grady's body, which swallows them up in a tight, hot clench.

"Not too much," Grady says on an exhale, the strip of condoms dangling from his hand. "Wanna feel you."

Nico works his fingers inside for a moment, nods down at the condoms with his eyebrows lifted until Grady gets with the program. Finally he gets one free, tears open the foil packet and rolls it down Nico's cock.

It's bright green—so bright neon green that it looks glow-in-the-dark—with ridges down the latex in thin rings. Nico notes this with a certain level of horror, staring down at his own dick. It looks as if it belongs to an alien life form. What the hell kind of variety package did Grady buy?

He doesn't have much of a chance to dwell on it, because Grady rises up, reaches behind himself and sets Nico's cock snugly against him, keeps him there with one hand wrapped steady around the base and the other spread wide across Nico's belly, and suddenly the last thing that Nico is concerned with is what the condom looks like.

All he can think is *hot, tight, good, so fucking good.* Grady sinks down and down and Nico grips hard to his hips and pulls his lips into his own mouth and tries to not just buck up into that gorgeous body engulfing him.

And then he gets to watch: Grady's sturdy thick thighs lifting and falling, Grady's back bowing, each rib standing out in stark contrast under his skin. His broad chest expands and curls back in; each muscle in his torso clenches and rolls and tenses up.

He's so vocal, sounds so beautiful: moans and whines and curses spilling from his throat. His face is lax with pleasure and his hands are tangled in his own curls.

"So good, oh you feel so good," Grady rasps out, sinking and rising and sinking down again and again. And thank god for the added buffer of the ribbed green alien condom or Nico is sure that he would have pulled Grady down by his sharp hips and buried himself as deep as he could and come hard already.

Instead he lets it build slowly as Grady works himself, touches Grady's chest and stomach and thighs and arms and hips but not his cock, not yet. Waits until Grady is flushed pink from the top of his head all the way down to his chest, gleaming with sweat and breathless with his cock giving up gush after gush of leaking fluid.

Nico can feel his orgasm building, the telltale tremble in his legs and pooling heat in his stomach. He makes a loose fist around Grady's cock and Grady sobs in relief, curling in on himself and all but collapsing against Nico.

"Fuck me," he moans into Nico's ear, breath hot and damp and voice wrecked. "Fuck me, fuck me, fuck me."

Nico angles his legs up, sets his feet on the bed, cradles Grady's ass in both palms and thrusts up into him. Grady, limp and exhausted, cries out, plaintive. Nico does it again. Finds a rhythm and fucks him and pulls at his cock and holds off and holds off, pulls out the tip and *slams* up into him with a smack of skin and sway of balls and Grady sobs, goes rigid against him and comes with a final rise and fall to meet Nico's thrusts.

His cock is still throbbing in Nico's hand when Nico comes inside of him, hips high up off the mattress, the cushion of Grady's ass snug against his hips, comes so hard that his head snaps back against the headboard with a loud *crack.*

"Shit, are you okay?" Grady is a heavy, dead weight slumped into Nico's chest and lap.

Nico laughs, high and slightly hysterical. "I am more than okay."

Grady huffs, wiggles his ass around with Nico's softening cock still inside. "I'm gonna take *more than okay* as a compliment." He clenches and Nico whimpers. "Hmm, round three?"

Nico shoves at him until Grady laughs and falls down onto the bed. "You're gonna kill me," Nico moans. "That was your evil plan all along. Lure me to the country where no one will ever find the body and have sex with me until I die from dehydration and chafing."

Grady smiles up at him so wide that his eyes and nose scrunch adorably with it. "Dang, you figured it out before I got a chance to chain you to my bed."

Grady hastily wipes them both clean with a pillow case. Nico removes the alien condom, tosses it in a nearby trash can and settles next to Grady with one leg thrown over his hips and a contented sigh. He rests his hand on Grady's abs, snuggling down into Grady's obscenely comfortable bed. There are probably worse ways to go.

11

They doze off, wake up, doze off. Nico groggily says he should be getting back to the hotel with how late it is and how little he trusts Spencer to not accidentally toss all of his clothes and personal items in the creek should he be asked to collect them. But Grady interrupts before he can finish, sitting up with a gasp.

"Oh, I totally forgot!" He grabs for the plastic bag from the drug store. "Did you know they make white chocolate Kit-Kats?" he says with far too much enthusiasm. "And all these different types of M&M's?"

He tosses Nico a bag of pretzel M&M's. Still mostly asleep, Nico stares at the bag that landed on his chest, fumbles it open and drops candy into his mouth while reclined on his back. He could probably get away with the extra calories tonight.

They eat and trade lazy kisses that taste like chocolate, then fall asleep again among candy wrappers and condoms and flecks of chocolate on the sheets.

Nico wakes in the pitch black to Grady's head between his legs and his mouth sealed tight around his already condom-clad cock. All Nico can do is exhale shakily and float on hazy, buzzing pleasure, letting Grady suck him down to the edge of his throat and back up with his tongue flat against the shaft. Nico sprawls lazily, legs spread wide and arms flung across the expanse of the bed, Grady's head bobbing, bobbing, bobbing until Nico comes, shivering, Grady's name a whisper on his lips.

Grady stumbles to the bathroom. The light flips on, harsh and painful. Nico buries his face in the mattress, with his eyes squeezed closed while he comes down from the orgasm that has rendered his body limp and useless and his brain an unthinking lump. Grady comes back smelling like mint and soap, slips into bed with warm soft skin and a hum rumbling in his chest. Nico curls his body into him and falls back into a deep sleep.

He wakes up dreaming about it, has no idea how much time has passed, but it's still night. Outside, the sky is dark and woods darker. He licks his lips and swallows saliva and can't shake the tendrils of a dream where he'd returned the favor and sucked Grady's cock, felt the phantom heat of him on his tongue. So he sleepily shimmies down Grady's sleeping body and licks at his soft balls and flaccid dick until it's stiff enough for him to get a condom on him.

This one smells like grapes and is probably a shocking, neon purple. Tastes almost, but not quite, like a grape lollipop.

"Oh god, sweetheart." Grady fumbles around Nico's shoulders and neck until he can get a hand into Nico's hair.

Nico stretches his lips around that fat cock, widens his jaw and relaxes his throat, eyes rolling back as Grady fills his mouth and throat and hardens against his tongue.

It's not his best blowjob, half-asleep and uncoordinated and sloppy, spit dripping down his chin and moaning nonstop around Grady's cock. Still, it just might be his favorite. Grady is so responsive, hushed praise and happy sighs and fingernails scraping restlessly across Nico's scalp.

After Grady comes and pulls Nico up for a slow, sleepy kiss, Nico takes a turn in the bathroom. He rinses his mouth, smacks his lips at the lingering taste of cloying grape flavor. He uses some of Grady's mouthwash, washes his face with the facial scrub on the counter, rubs a washcloth beneath his arms and across his stomach and gently over his tender, reddened dick.

He's never come so many times in one night, not even when he was younger and didn't feel wrung out like a limp rag by each orgasm. He scans himself in the mirror. He looks totally debauched and completely fucked out: hair a wreck, lips swollen and dry, cheeks with bright spots of red, and eyes so heavy they're barely cracked open.

And yet when he manages to get back to the bed and sees Grady sleeping, turned onto his stomach with the sinuous muscled curve of his back dipping down to his round, pert ass, Nico feels heat stirring, cannot possibly get hard again and yet—it's as if Grady has gotten under his skin and into his blood and awoken some dormant, sex-crazed part of him that he never knew was there, or else tried very hard to keep in hibernation.

It's no wonder that half the damn world wants a piece of Grady Dawson.

When Nico wakes again, it's like swimming up from the deepest depths of the ocean, clawing his way toward consciousness only to be tugged down again. He finally manages to pry his eyes open, and bright sunlight hits him immediately. He stretches and yawns and turns in Grady's arms.

Grady's hands drift to Nico's naked waist and then his ass, squeezing and rubbing and pressing dryly between.

"Shit, Grady. I can't." He's sure of it. But oh, does he want to.

"Last night was amazing." Grady's voice is sandpaper rough. "I admit I haven't been to church in a while but that was a religious experience." Nico snorts and Grady's laugh puffs against his chest. "You sure you can't?" Grady's knuckles drift to Nico's stirring cock and his mouth opens against Nico's jaw.

"God, you make me stupid." Nico surges down for a sour morning kiss.

"I will also take that as a compliment." Grady's words hum against Nico's lips. Liquid heat pools between Nico's legs and he's starting to think he may at least be up for some lazy making out, when someone pounds on the door to the bedroom.

"Goddammit," Grady hisses.

"You have dress rehearsal in two hours!" That snippy, shouting voice can only belong to one person. He bangs on the door again.

"Thank you, Spencer," Grady calls, then quieter so only Nico can hear, "I know how to tell time. Fuck's sake. Pardon my language." He turns back to Nico, but Nico is already sitting up, willing his wobbly, cooked-noodle limbs to cooperate. "No," Grady whines.

"All good things must come to an end," Nico says, not at all as okay with it as he's trying to sound.

It was fun. Really, really fun. A night he will not forget for a very long time. But it's over. And that's that.

Nico hunts down underwear and pants, tears apart the covers on the bed and locates his shirt. When he looks up, Grady is out of bed and still naked, boldly so with hands on his waist and hips tipped to one side.

"You're coming tonight, right? And I don't mean as my stylist. I mean with me."

Nico presses his mouth into a tight line, looks down and buttons his shirt all the way to the very top button, tucks the ends into his pants. It's unfortunate how Grady is all too aware of how irresistible Nico finds him.

Nico turns to tell him no, but catches sight of dark red and purple marks across Grady's chest and one on that indented line between his hipbone and groin and one just behind his jaw. Marks from his mouth, his teeth sunk into Grady's skin. And Grady looking hopefully at him as if Nico's company is all he's ever wanted in the whole wide universe.

"Okay," Nico says.

Grady cheers and grins, rubs his hands together, rises up on his toes. "All right, what did you find for me?"

Nico stares at him for a moment, blank. He'd forgotten all about the clothes he brought and the items he picked up on his delightful tour of Nashville's fashion spots. The entire reason he was here in the first place. "Yes. Oh my gosh, yes!"

The shopping bags are put in the plush easy chair in the corner, and the suits in their garment bags hung on the knobs of Grady's armoire. Nico, sure of his choice, only takes out one suit and drapes the pieces over his arm one by one. Grady stands just behind him to watch, still naked, but Nico can focus instead on the perfect cut of the suit jacket, the impeccable stitching on the trousers, the obvious high quality of the materials.

"I thought, country music tends to be so hyper-masculine, and if the men aren't wearing cowboy hats and gaudy belt buckles, they're wearing boring black suits with black dress shirts. And, worse case scenario," Nico says with a glance over his shoulder, "both." He hands Grady the pieces of the suit and the shirt and belt. "So first of all, color. The slim fit of this gray and blue checked beauty is really perfect for your build. A cyan blue shirt, burgundy tie. These boots that I *covet* and am going back to get a pair for myself. The belt and cuff links are understated yet classy and..." Nico unfolds the final piece. "In honor of Memaw, a hand knit scarf to tie it all together."

Grady surprises him with a kiss, not dirty or seeking but an impulsive push forward as if he couldn't stop himself. "It's perfect. You're amazing. Thank you."

Nico steps back and smoothes the clothes against Grady's body. "You're gonna wrinkle them. I'll steam the suit and shirt and put them in a garment bag for you before I go."

He shoos Grady off to the shower and doesn't confess what's on the tip of his tongue: that Grady inspires him, that Grady has shaken him out of the doldrums he'd been itching to escape. That he's been happier here in Godknowswhere, Tennessee, more at ease, more at home, than he has been in LA for some time and he feels as though he's going back changed. Better. That he's falling for Grady despite the many, many misgivings he knows he has. Or had. That maybe, possibly, some part of him thinks he and Grady could be something. Or at least something more than a weekend tryst to remember fondly.

Nico heads downstairs and to the laundry room with a spring in his step, finds another garment bag there and an iron that he sets to steam. He hums absentmindedly as he works, and realizes it's the song Grady had sung to him and then rehearsed over and over with his band in the basement studio. He's really excited to see it live. Can't imagine how dynamic Grady must be on a stage, in his element.

Is he really doing this? Letting things between them continue on for now? Another day, another week. Longer? Nico zips the clothes for tonight into the bag, turns with the still hissing, steaming iron in his hand and nearly collides with a scowling Spencer.

Nico yelps, the hot iron dangerously close to his face. "You scared the shit out of me, Spencer." Nico sets the iron down on the board set between the washer and dryer and next to a shelf with dirt-caked boots and discarded sweatshirts.

"I came to warn you," Spencer says, crossing his arms over his chest.

"Excuse me?" Nico steps back, giving himself space until he bumps the edge of the washing machine.

"I just hate to see you get hurt, is all," Spencer says and then, with an inflection that indicates whom he's actually concerned about, because it certainly isn't Nico, "You *or Grady.*

"I appreciate the concern, but I assure you, I can take care of myself," and then adds because it bugs Nico, the way Spencer thinks he can speak for him. "And so can Grady, for that matter. So maybe it's best if you back off a little."

Spencer's jaw sets, and his eyes narrow. "And you think you know what's best for him? You don't even know him. You have no idea what he's been through. Maybe I can't dress him up and parade him around *professionally* like you can, but at least I'm not using him and tossing him aside." His face shifts from anger to pained disquiet. He adjusts his glasses higher up on his nose and his rigid posture shifts: hunched, protective. "You aren't the first and you won't be the last."

With that he shakes his head, spins on his heels and walks away.

Nico runs a hand through his hair, feels his stomach churn with regret and anger and embarrassment. He's more sensible than this. He *doesn't do this*. Because it's unprofessional. Because Grady is who he is. Because Grady's life doesn't have space for Nico. Because... maybe Spencer is right.

It's time to go home.

When he leaves, he decides it's best to leave things as they are: a pleasant memory of a wonderful night and nothing more. He doesn't even leave a note.

12

At the hotel he showers, scalding hot water pelting his skin, the hotel soap a noxious floral-scented burn. With his hair still so wet it drips onto the collar of his shirt, he tosses his clothes and personal items in his suitcase. When he checks out, pulling his wheeled suitcase behind him and speeding off in his rental car, he feels like a child running away from home after being caught stealing cookies from the cookie jar.

On the plane ride he listens to podcasts that he doesn't actually hear; on the highway he drives on automatic, pulls into his short driveway and looks around in confusion, not sure how he managed to make it home. His house is quieter and emptier than ever; his carefully procured original art on the walls, the one-of-a-kind baubles and trinkets and reclaimed vintage furniture, seem strange, as if it all belongs to someone else.

His first night home he has Gwen send him info on what he missed at work, catches up on all of that, then stares blankly at the wall with his eyes blurred and sandpaper-dry after staring at the computer screen for too long. He rubs his eyes until they water, scrubs his hands through his unkempt hair and answers emails until he can longer keep his eyelids open.

He wakes up early to work even more. It's only when his stomach growls angrily that he stops, shaking out his hand to get some feeling back into it while he waits for his smoothie to finish blending. His tablet taunts him from the table. He's barely talked to Gwen. Sent his parents a brief email to let them know he made it safely home. Hasn't checked for any industry news. No fashion sites. No red carpet recaps.

He hasn't looked up anything about Grady at all.

He eats and resists and eats and resists; finally, he pulls the tablet closer and mourns the permanent loss of his willpower.

Grady Dawson is a Winner on the Red Carpet

Grady Dawson Wows in Gucci

Grady Dawson Perfect in Trim Suit and Perfect Pop of Color A+

Grady looked absolutely perfect. As if he'd just strutted off the runway. The suit was a flawless fit and his eyes otherworldly, just as Nico had known they would look with that color shirt. He stands out in a sea of black suits and denim. But then, that has a lot do with Grady himself. He always stands out from the crowd. Nico only brought it out a little more, polished and buffed it and framed it just right. If nothing else—and really, there isn't much else for him at this point—Nico is good at what he does.

Then at the bottom of the page of the fashion site is a link to another website, a gossip blog, the one that is publishing the rumor that Grady is torn between Nico and country music's princess, Clementine Campbell. It wasn't true, not really. Not like that. If the image of his own face on a gossip site is bizarre and upsetting enough, it's even worse knowing that the nuances and complexities of people's lives and struggles and relationships just can't be broken down into a catchy blurb. He's always been aware of that, but it's one thing having some idea of it, and quite another living it yourself instead of watching it happen to someone else.

Not that it matters any more.

Whatever the article says, Nico knows better. He *knows*. Grady's name alone is enough to make him click the link anyway. He's completely unable to stop himself, stomach churning angrily, pulse thumping against his throat.

Grady Dawson Scandal!

When the page loads, it's a picture of Grady looking strung out and sad, eyes red and bruised underneath, skin pallid and face drawn. He's holding one hand out to block the picture, trying to duck into his truck outside of a hotel in Nashville with a tall, pretty brunette in a wide-brimmed hat, walking behind him with her head ducked low.

There's a video of his performance that Nico doesn't watch, but the description beneath says that it's the song Grady sang to Nico in his basement rehearsal space in Nashville: "Broken Records." It already has hundreds of thousands of hits and a long column of comments that range from: *OMG I'm sobbing I love you Grady <3 <3 <3* to *Ugh amazing* to *Grady you saved my life thank you for your beautiful voice and beautiful heart.* And there are the ones that make Nico blush all alone in his kitchen even after everything he and Grady did together.

Anyone else just want to lick his knees? Why are his knees so attractive????
LAWD the things I would do to that man.
So sexy *fans self*

Pride and jealousy war in his chest, sharp stabs of heat and ice, of desire and resistance. Those people who comment, who eat up everything Grady does, who stop him in restaurants to gush how much they love him—they don't know him at all, but don't seem to realize that. They would take whatever Grady would give them and be thrilled about it. And if Grady wants Nico, and Nico wants him, then why can't he take whatever Grady is willing to offer?

Nico clicks to read more:

Grady Dawson leaves a hotel room after Country Music Awards looking terrible. Is Grady Dawson going off the deep end like so many have speculated? Or could this just be a lover's spat gone out of hand? Dawson was spotted with Clementine Campbell outside of the hotel, neither would comment. Campbell won album of the year and best female artist at the CMAs. Congrats Clementine!

Nico flips the tablet over, slapping it down onto the table and dropping his head into his hands, sad and sick and confused. Grady probably just has a cold, or was annoyed, or the camera flash at night caught him at a weird angle and made him look exhausted and sad. It's most likely nothing.

Still. He wants to call him. He wants to make sure he's okay. He wants to go back to Tennessee and forget all the reasons why he and Grady could never work out.

But then he thinks about his own picture in the tabloids. The rumors. What Spencer said. All those people who want Grady and yearn for him and demand things of him. And is that something Nico really wants to get involved with? Is that really the sort of life he wants? Eating up whatever crumbs Grady can give him?

Nico goes back to working. He's in the middle of putting together some outfit ideas in a binder—the trip to Nashville has been great for inspiration, at least—when his mom calls.

"Are you ill? You sound ill. Are you eating well?" She takes a breath. "Are you sleeping enough? How many hours are you averaging? Dr. Oz says lack of sleep can cause heart disease."

And all he'd said was hello. "Mom, I'm fine. It's all the traveling." Nico rubs his eyes; they feel sunken and shriveled in his skull. "Why do you watch Dr. Oz, anyway?"

"He's very smart and handsome," his mom says. "Do you have green tea? And add honey, don't forget. And remember to drink a glass of water every morning, Nico. Full glass."

Nico closes his laptop and stretches his back with a satisfying series of pops. "Mom, I'm not sick, I promise."

"Okay, okay. I'll send you some tea anyway. And get more sleep."

"Yes, Mom." It makes him crazy, the way she still fusses over him, but after the last few days, it's really nice to know she's worrying about him, always there, even if she overdoes it sometimes.

"Well, if you are feeling better. My friend Yuri at temple, we do aerobics together, you talked to her at Hanamatsuri, remember?"

He talked to what seemed like hundreds of people at the last flower festival at the temple, but, "Sure, right. Yuri."

"Anyway she was telling me all about her nephew. He's an optometrist."

Nico lets his head thump to the table. "Oh no, Mom." He's already played his hand by telling her he's not sick, the only excuse she'd accept for having bad manners and refusing to meet the nephew of a woman Nico doesn't even remember. There is no escape.

Thirty minutes later Nico has resigned himself to one brief, casual dinner with Dr. Peter Ito, OD. It could be a good distraction from Grady, he convinces himself, after promising his mother repeatedly that he'll go to bed early. Peter sounds like a nice guy. A nice, regular guy who doesn't have paparazzi chasing after him or a long list of scorned lovers.

Nico doesn't go to bed early, but he does cocoon himself in pillows and scans through his DVR for entertainment to help him avoid his regrets. Walking away from Grady before the two of them were the next hot scandal-grabbing headline was the right choice. Not saying anything to Grady was… maybe not.

He finally drifts off to sleep early in the morning wishing he could shake the disappointment of Grady not making any attempt to contact him, and of how cowardly he's being by not contacting Grady first.

13

"So do I get all the dirty details or what?" Gwen says the moment Nico sets foot in the office, with the heavy front door still shoved against his shoulder and his messenger bag banging off his hip.

He strides to his office with his head held high and sits primly at his desk. "Can't you say *hello how was your trip* like a person with boundaries?" Nico pulls out his laptop, lifts the screen and waits for it to power up. "Did you make coffee?"

Gwen tips up her pointed little chin and snips, "How was my week? Oh, pretty awful. Flora's pissed at me again. Thanks for asking!" She turns on the ball of one foot, stomps to the coffee maker behind the reception desk and starts to make a fresh pot of coffee. Very aggressively.

Nico releases a breath, follows her and gently takes the glass carafe from her hands before she shatters it. "Maybe we should both start over?" He slides the carafe into the machine, flips the button and leans back against the edge of the desk while it burbles and hisses. "How was your week?"

Gwen folds down the top of the coffee bag, stares at it and shakes her head. Her nails are done in black with glossy tips, her dress is black lace with purple ribbons threaded throughout. "I got a lot done. Met with everyone, kept it organized, all events successful, no major catastrophes."

"Gwen, that's great. I knew you could do it." It was a lot to ask of her, taking on everything alone, but of course she can handle it all. She's so driven and solid and easily does the work of two people. She doesn't look happy about it, though. She continues, eyes wet, fingers twisting and twisting around a corner of the coffee bag. "I spent so much time here that Flora strongly suggested that maybe I should just live at the office. She wants some space. She still wants to move away and I'm not sure if she means both of us." Gwen sniffs and looks up. "So that was my week. You?"

Nico's shoulders drop. He'd thought she and Flora had worked it all out, but the same issue keeps cropping up. He doesn't know the first thing about fixing a relationship and he doesn't know how to help, so—

"I slept with him," he blurts.

Gwen blinks at him, and a tear slides down, smudging her heavy black eyeliner and dropping onto the top of her rouge-red lips. Then she laughs, a short burst. "What?"

Nico lifts one shoulder, tries to look nonchalant. "A few times, actually."

"Nico!" She walks over to swat at his arm and gasps. "Wow. I didn't know you had it in you." She squints one eye and looks way too much like a pixie when she says, "Or was it the other way around?"

"And that's it. No more details for you." Nico pushes off the desk and strides back to his office. She's smiling again, devilish, and it's time to get things back on the rails here. "I got a lot of work done, too. Want to see?"

He drops into his chair, scoots it closer and turns his laptop as Gwen sits in the chair across from him. He put together several look-books that first night home when he barely slept, new trends he likes and items that no one is wearing but he has a hunch will soon be.

As she looks, Nico looks with her. He hadn't noticed he was doing it, hadn't consciously incorporated those themes, but now with the scrutiny of a second pair of eyes, he sees it. Sees *him*. He's there in the colors of the gowns: rust red and hunter green and stormy blue. He's there in the golden accents of the bodice on one dress, curled in spirals and tendrils along the boning and hems. He's there in the cut of the suits, the build of the models he'd picked—not willowy and waifish, but sturdy and broad and muscled. The dress shirts he chose were made to flatter a trim waist; pants were made to draw attention to the spill of a curved lower body.

"It's almost like a violin," Gwen says of one gown, a mermaid-style dress with a rounded trumpet skirt in a pale champagne color. She traces the lines of it from curve to inward slope to curve.

"Or a guitar," Nico says, voice tight. He clears his throat.

The fabrics on the suits are plaids and calicos and the browns and greens of a pine forest. The men's casual line leans heavily on knitwear and sturdy boots and rugged touches with a feminine flair.

It's Grady. He's everywhere. Grady as a muse seems to have taken a hold somewhere deep in Nico's subconscious, dug its claws in and refused to be shaken off.

Gwen closes the computer, pats it with a definitive slap. "Inspired."

Nico isn't sure what to say to that. "Hey, do you need a place to stay for a little while?"

It's nice having a temporary roommate at first. He has company while sitting in traffic on the way home, and it's easy to fill his mind and heart with Gwen's problems and forget his own for a while. She's clean and doesn't hog the bathroom too much, and in between working at work and working at home, they mostly sleep and eat and silently zone out on their own electronic devices.

She pushes him for more info about Grady sometimes. "Is he dynamite in bed? He is, isn't he?" Or, "Did he sing to you?" And, "Are you going to see him again?"

Nico always says the same thing: "I really don't want to talk about him."

On Friday Gwen sets her tablet down, tucks her legs beneath her and says to Nico, who is reading a news article about the threat of lionfish to native species—terrifying stuff—"Do you think we both use work as a substitute for intimacy?"

Nico flicks his eyes away from the article. "Where the hell did that come from?"

"I was thinking. What if she's right, and we don't work so hard because we're trying to hustle and be better known and get A-list clients, but because for us success equals love. I mean, I know it always did in my family. God forbid if I brought home a B or lost the student election for class secretary." She picks up her tablet again. "I think we both hold back with people because we never feel good enough."

She goes back to whatever she was doing, as if she hadn't just psychoanalyzed both of them as a casual aside. Nico tries to go back to reading about the plague of lionfish on coral reefs in the Atlantic Ocean, but has trouble absorbing the story.

On Saturday his calendar pings him awake with a reminder that he has a date with Dr. Peter Ito, OD. He gets up with a very mild sense of dread, changes into sweats and hits the tread-mill. He makes egg-white and spinach scramble on sprouted grain toast while Gwen sleeps the day away, sprawled on her back on the couch with both arms flung over her head, one leg flopped onto the floor and hair standing up in haphazard platinum spikes.

While he's in the shower, she leaves to run errands; Nico sweeps, cleans the bathroom and dusts, and gives the stove and kitchen counters a good scrub down. When Gwen gets back, he heads to the grocery store.

They don't eat together, not tonight. Nico grabs leftovers and eats them standing at the sink while Gwen is still putting a salad together. A salad with a lot of bacon. He showers again, combs his hair extra neat and dresses casually: black cuffed chinos and black slouched sweater, fake-fur lined fold-over leather boots and a fringed black and purple scarf wound in a draping, carefree fashion around his neck and shoulders.

"Be safe; make good choices," Gwen says, dropping a mound of croutons and a river of ranch dressing on her salad.

Nico places a black hat at a jaunty angle on his head. "Better choices than your dinner." He tips his hat and walks backwards out the door.

Peter is… pleasant. Dressed well enough to show that he cares and has a sense of what looks good on him, in a herringbone sport coat and tan sweater with a pale blue Oxford beneath. He's wearing an expensive watch and the type of cologne that's meant to smell woodsy and earthy, but doesn't at all. Nico sips his ice water as Peter talks about... something... and thinks about the spot behind Grady's jaw that smelled the way the woods and earth really smell on a man's skin.

"So, a stylist, that's exciting," Peter says after an awkward lull in the conversation while they wait for their wine.

"It can be," Nico says and tries to smile in a friendly sort of way.

Peter tugs on the lapels of his coat. "Not judging my outfit too much, are you?"

"No, not at all."

They chuckle and go quiet once again. The wine comes and they both make bland comments about it; Peter calls it *robust with floral undertones* and says that he only enjoys Pinot Noirs when they're aged. Nico replies that he's grown quite fond of some varieties of young California Pinots.

Nico sips his wine and wants to throw it in his own face just for a little excitement. "So. Optometry," he says instead. "Do you own your own practice?"

Peter takes on the bulk of the conversation, and Nico drinks another glass of wine and feels like an asshole because of how incredibly difficult it is for him to pay attention to what Peter is saying. He's nice. And polite. And... nice. By the time Peter says something about needing to be up early tomorrow, Nico feels slow and sleepy and weirdly melancholy in the way that wine often makes him.

"This was nice," Peter says politely, walking Nico to his car.

"Yes. Nice."

They make it to the car and stand awkwardly by the open door. Nico looks at Peter with eyes that drag a few long moments behind his brain. Peter is shorter than him. He's reasonably attractive. He has a good, well-formed nose. Very distinguished. Nico can't recall what color his eyes are.

Peter clears his throat and says, "I'll be in touch," and kisses Nico with dry lips and a hand on his elbow, then heads to his car, and Nico feels nothing. Nothing at all.

14

Nico drives back to his house with the window down and radio cranked up and a route with traffic sparse enough for him to haul ass in a very satisfying way. He hangs up his hat and scarf and keys, and puts his wallet in the little catchall bowl on the kitchen counter. Only one light is on in the whole place, just the little yellow bulb over the sink. A bottle of bourbon is on the table, cap off, a shot glass next to it with drops of amber still clinging to the side and pooled in the bottom. There is no sign of Gwen.

A sob comes from the bathroom, and after that the slurred lyrics of a song that Nico can't make out. He knocks on the closed door and water sloshes in response.

"Please don't drown in my bathtub," Nico calls. "I'm not insured for that."

More sloshing and Gwen wobbles out an, "Okay. I won't."

Nico picks up the bourbon and the glass, intending to put them away, but Gwen sings again, louder, and this time he recognizes it. "Broken Records." He hasn't been able to bring himself to listen to it again. If Gwen weren't entirely twisted right now, he would bet she was doing it on purpose.

He fills the little glass to the brim, takes a shot that burns from his throat all the way down to the pit of his stomach, sets it down with a thunk and a shudder and searches the room until he spots his tablet on the little side table next to the couch. He finds the video of Grady at the Country Music Awards, takes his tablet and his bourbon and perches on the edge of the couch.

He's amazing. Of course he is. Looks amazing and sounds amazing and—probably it's just the way the spotlights on the stage are positioned—but he's radiant. As if Grady himself is the source of all the beaming bright lights. Just the tiny, grainy image of him on a screen is enough to make Nico's heart race rapid-fire and his stomach pull tight and heat prickle under his skin.

He takes swigs directly from the bottle and watches the CMA performance again. The third swallow of alcohol goes down smooth, and he has some trouble clicking the little arrow to watch the video again, accidentally scrolling down to the comments. The first one he sees says, *Who cares? He sucks.*

Nico scowls and has half a mind to respond to this, "B00BLVR5000" person. But the other comments after that are more concerning.

> *This video is great. Not sure what's happening now.*
> *I say drugs.*
> *No dumbshit. He doesn't drink or do drugs now any REAL FAN knows that.*
> *Addiction runs in families DUMBSHIT just look at his messed up parents*
> *I'm sure he's fine guys.*

I saw him in Charleston. I don't think drugs but he's off for sure.

Grady we love you please get help!!! God bless!!!!

Clementine got tired of his man-whore act that's what happened.

They are just friends how many fucking times does she have to say it?

I'm going to see his concert in Savannah wootwoot. I'll find him before the show and cure whatever ails him. *wink wink* :)))))))

Nico is way too drunk by now to figure out what is going on; he barely possesses the basic motor skills to set his tablet and the bottle of bourbon aside and fall sideways into the couch cushions.

"How was your date?" Gwen, hair wet and flat and eyes bloodshot, in baggy pajama pants and with a stretched out T-shirt drooping over one bare shoulder, drops onto the opposite side of the couch.

Nico squints at her, searching his brain for details of his date with... with... huh. "He has a boat," Nico finally recalls.

"Oh." Gwen makes a considering face. "Why?"

"For boating," Nico slurs. Obviously. "And he has a really good 401K," Nico says with a nod and then with a gasp, "Peter!" That was it. He mentally pats himself on the back for remembering.

Gwen jumps at his outburst, then reaches for the bourbon, takes an impressive swig and wipes her mouth off with the back of hand. "Nothing gets me going like a big, fat 401K."

"I'm too drunk for dick jokes."

"Too drunk is the exact right time for dick jokes." She stretches her legs out and plops her feet into Nico's lap. Nico glares down at her feet and thinks about shoving them off, but decides to leave them there. Her toenails are painted purple. It's cute.

"You're cute," he tells her, holding his thumb and index finger parallel in front of his face. "Tiny and cute, like this."

Gwen laughs. And laughs. And laughs some more until Nico starts to laugh, too. "Oh wow, you are too drunk."

Nico flaps an uncoordinated hand at her. "Gwen. Gwennie. Gwen. Why do we never just hang out? We're always working." He pouts at her. It's sad. They are both so, so sad. "Why are we so, so sad?"

"Because we work too much and don't sleep enough and then we spend weekends arguing about which organic vegetables to buy at the farmer's market and folding socks and trying to figure out why the water bill is so high this month." She sets the bourbon on the floor.

"We sound terrible. The other day the smoothie place I like started offering kelp smoothies and I was really excited. No one should be excited about kelp, Gwen."

Gwen shakes her head for an unusually long time. Nico continues, "Peter thinks my life is exciting. I want to be the exciting one. And that's why." It makes total sense to him, but Gwen gives him a funny look, so maybe not. "Grady. What if I'm the one who makes him wish he were slipping into a coma over glasses of red wine that I keep calling 'oaky yet austere'? Cause I'm boring and he's not. Who am I? Sad and boring, that's who. And everyone will be like, who the hell is that? Look at him. With his ears. Why is Grady Dawson with a *nobody* with *those ears*. *Who does he think he is?*" Nico clamps his hands around her ankles and shakes them. "Who do I think I am, Gwen?"

Gwen makes a face and pulls her feet out of his vise grip. "Who cares what people think?"

"I care." He wishes he didn't. He wishes he could just ignore it, let it go, shrug it off. He can't.

"Well, I bet Grady doesn't care." Gwen hiccups. "I mean, he thought you were exciting enough to love you down more than once, right?"

"I guess."

Gwen groans and drops her head back against the armrest. "God, I haven't had sex in so long. Tell me something about him, come on. Flora may never let me touch her boobs ever again. Let me have this."

Normally he wouldn't. Normally he'd tell her to mind her business and that he doesn't kiss and tell. But. He's had a lot to drink. He misses Grady. Fuck everything, he *misses* Grady. "His body is like—I mean. He's surprisingly humble and sweet and… clever. He's a *person*, Gwen," he chastises, more for his own benefit. "But oh my god, *his body*. His abs should be encased in marble and put on display in a museum in Rome, I swear."

"Hmm, I dunno. I'm not much of an abs person." She mutters something about boobs again. Nico zones out for a while, thinking about Grady and Grady's body and how complicated things are. But why? Why do they have to be?

When he turns back, Gwen is—

"Hey, hey, hey, what are you doing?" Nico dives for her. The phone in her hand is already ringing. He manages to grab it, ends up squished between her and the back of the couch. He hits end on a call to Flora. "She said to give her space and she'll call you." Gwen's lip wobbles and fat tears spill from her eyes. Nico shoves the phone in his pocket and holds her; her narrow little shoulders shake with sobs until she finally falls asleep.

Nico gently lays her down on her side, tucks a blanket around her, kisses the top of her head, then bumps and trips his way to his own room. He strips off his pants, struggling to get them freed from around his ankles. Gwen's phone goes skittering across the floor. When he bends to pick it up he ends up sprawled on his belly next to it.

It's fine. The floor is great. Cool and comforting under his cheek. Gwen's phone lights up with a call that goes to voice mail, and when he looks to see who it was he fumbles on the screen. Gwen's contact list pops up.

Right above *Flora Delgado* is *Grady Dawson*.

With clumsy fingers and his self-control somewhere at the bottom of a bottle of Wild Turkey Single Barrel he types, *Where are you,* pleased that autocorrect makes it look like he's not plastered and currently considering sleeping on the floor.

Grady Dawson: Heading to Georgia. Why?

Nico, tongue poking out and face pinched tight, focuses very hard on typing. *Whee are u staying?*

Grady Dawson: On the bus tonight. Tomorrow the Hyatt in Duluth, GA. Do you need to send something? Room 717.

Grady Dawson: Is this about Nico?

Grady Dawson: Is he okay?

Nico considers what to say. The apartment is growing dark around him: just the glow of Gwen's phone and this last, hopeful connection between him and Grady. He's drunk enough to forget about any rational reasons to stay away, but not so drunk that he wants to spill his soul over text message. Or, maybe just so drunk that he physically can't. Either way, he's definitely going to pass out on the floor, so he sends a quick reply; he can't bear to leave Grady hanging without an explanation yet again.

If Spencer is right and Nico won't be the last meaningless fling Grady has, then fine. So what? He can be whatever Grady needs from him. He can. Who cares? Not him.

Not ok, Nico texts back, sets the phone down and closes his heavy eyes.

15

At first, Nico thinks the urgent pounding that wakes him is his own brain rebelling, knocking against his skull and pressing at the back of his eyelids as if it would rather be anywhere but the inside of his head. He hears a noise that sounds like the bellow of a dying whale, and realizes it's his own voice. He tries to pull the covers up over his face, but can't seem to find them. It's so bright. So, so bright. Why is the world so bright? *Make it stop.*

Usually on Sundays he gets up and runs on the treadmill, cleans and does laundry, and then if he doesn't have work to keep him busy he'll call his mom. Today he wants to stay in bed, not move for an entire day and, if he's lucky, die for a little while. His mouth tastes like death, so he's probably well on his way.

The pounding starts again, only now Nico is awake enough to realize it's not coming from his own head but the front door. He takes in a long, fortifying breath, pushes up from his stomach to heave himself from the bed—then stops when he notices that he's on the floor.

Oh, right.

He slowly, slowly gets his knees under him, sits back on his haunches and brushes a hand through his messy hair, smacks his lips and then presses a fist to his mouth to stop a wave of nausea that shivers through his body. He notices Gwen's phone in its rhinestoned case, sunlight flashing off it so it's even more offensive to his senses than usual. Gwen's phone. Why does he have—

Oh, shit.

Steadying himself along walls and furniture, Nico opens the front door with one eye squinted closed and the heel of his hand on the other, realizes too late that he's wearing his slouchy sweater from his date, his coordinating purple striped socks and no pants.

"Um. Morning…" Nico says, stepping back and making a futile attempt to tug his sweater lower.

"Morning. I came to collect my wife." Flora is unruffled by Nico's sorry pant-less state, stepping past him and into the living room.

She's close to Nico's height, buxom and with round, full features, has pulled her thick black hair into a low braid, and wears a gauzy peasant skirt and billowy tie-dye blouse.

"Great." Nico backs away. "I will just… get some pants then."

He quickly pulls on the chinos that are still puddled on the floor, grabs Gwen's phone while he's at it, and when his thumb accidentally hits the home button, a message with a timestamp from late last night is on the screen.

Grady Dawson: I'm doing some local press in the am and afternoon, can you ask him to call me around 7?

Nico deletes it, and the other messages to and from Grady, before he goes back to the living room.

"So, we were drinking a little last night," Nico says. He looks horrible, and Gwen is passed out with more of her body off the couch than on. And if that weren't enough, the bottle of bourbon that used to have a lot more bourbon in it still sits on the floor like the centerpiece to their feast of mistakes. "Um."

Flora sets her hands on her hips with her jaw set and an unimpressed eyebrow lifted at him. "I gathered," she says and nods at Gwen. "She left me a message that was mostly sing-crying, and I'm pretty sure she was in the bathtub."

"She was."

"Every time." Flora shakes her head again, but this time it's with a fond smile. She claps her hands. The sound reverberates painfully around Nico's head, but Gwen sleeps on. "Did she buy bacon while she was here?"

"Like, half a pig's worth I think." Nico trails after her into the kitchen, sits at the table and presses his cheek against the cool surface while she lines strips of bacon into the frying pan on the stove.

It smells disgusting, and then amazing, and then disgusting again. The sizzling reaches a peak. Nico's stomach gurgles and roils.

Gwen sits up on the couch and mumbles, "Bacon?" Then wanders into the kitchen like a zombie and says, "Flora?" She rubs her eyes and blinks and looks as though she can't decide if she's awake or not.

Flora sets the bacon on a paper towel, presses some grease out and then slides it all onto a plate. "Eat. You'll feel better." She sets the plate down and taps Nico's head until he lifts it with a grunt. "You, too."

"Thank you, Flora," they say, like chastised children. Flora *tsks* at them, shakes her head and makes coffee.

He leaves them to talk, takes a shower—or more accurately, stands with his face smashed into the smooth tile while hot water rains down on him. At some point, he makes an attempt at shampooing his hair. The greasy food and coffee hit, finally, and by the time he pads out into the living room with bare feet on the cold wood floors, dressed in sweatpants and the thread-bare T-shirt that he only brings out when he's sick, he feels very nearly human.

He is never drinking Wild Turkey Single Barrel bourbon ever again. He shuffles around the couch, folding the blankets and picking the bottle up from the floor so he can dump the rest of it down the drain. Flora and Gwen are at the kitchen table, talking in low, serious tones with their hands clasped on the table top. Nico quietly goes back to his room.

He pours the rest of the alcohol down the bathroom sink, then starts to remake the bed he never slept in last night. The twinge in his back will be a reminder of last night for weeks, even though right now he remembers it all as a swirling haze. It comes back to him in flashes as he pulls and tugs and tucks the sheets and blankets. Every once in a while, he catches bits of Gwen and Flora's conversation.

"I missed you, too," Flora is saying, "But I'm glad we took some time apart. It gave me some clarity."

Nico folds down the top sheet, sets the pillows on top. He remembers watching Grady's video, being so moved by him and then—

"I wanted to see if I could live without you and I found out that I could."

Nico freezes at Flora's words, thin woven blanket clutched in his hands. Gwen says nothing, but Nico can imagine her face, can picture how she looks—shattered and heartbroken like last night when she cried herself to sleep.

Flora continues, "I can, but I don't want to. I want to try and keep trying, not because I *need* you but because, despite everything and even when it's hard, I *choose* you."

Chairs scrape across the floor and Gwen lets out a half-cry, half-laugh, and it goes quiet. Nico can guess what's happening now, so he snaps the blanket wide over the bed, tugs it just right and starts on the duvet.

A memory of last night comes to him very clearly: He'd watched the video and worried about Grady, because other people are worried about Grady, and maybe he does just have a cold or he's weary from touring or everyone is just overreacting. But he couldn't shake the worry last night. Can't shake it now. Can't shake Grady at all. The evidence is everywhere—he's picking out evening gowns in the exact color of Grady's eyes and texting him when he's drunk and going on a date with a perfectly pleasant doctor whose name Nico can't recall and thinking about Grady the entire time.

He gets all four corners of the duvet just right, fluffs the pillows, then ventures out to the living room, hoping Flora and Gwen are saving most of the more intimate making up for home. They're just standing close together, Flora with her hands cupped around Gwen's cheeks.

"I just need to see this face more often. I need to feel like you're choosing me too, and that we're a team."

Gwen nods under her hands, grips around Flora's wrists. "I will. I do."

He almost doesn't say it, but his defenses are down. He's hung over and worried and watching Gwen and Flora make up and vow to keep trying, *despite everything.*

"Why don't you take the week off work?" he offers. He crosses the kitchen and clears the dirty plate and mugs from the table. "Take some time to reconnect, focus on each other." He sets the dishes down, clasps his hands together and points two fingers at them. "Do—you know—stuff."

Flora gives him that unimpressed look again, and Gwen cackles. He drops his hands to his sides.

"You sure?" Gwen asks, taking Flora's hand into her own.

Not even a little, Nico thinks, but says, "Yeah, I mean. When was the last time we took a vacation?"

"Never," Flora answers for her. "Your last vacation was never."

"Well, there you go." Nico runs the water in the sink to rinse the dishes. "Better hurry up and pack your things."

He'd been hoping that all this air travel lately would make it easier, that he'd be used to the hassle, but he still has to wait too long to check in and he still gets flagged for an extra security check with that creepy scanning machine. He hates having to rush out of his shoes and take off his belt and empty his pockets, only to have to rush through putting it all back.

His seat mate spends half the trip yakking Nico's ear off about a sports team that Nico does not give one single flying fuck about, and then the other half of the flight trying to nod off onto Nico's shoulder.

The Atlanta airport is huge. He has to take a tram from his gate to the car rental area, and even with that still feels as if he's walked for miles and miles. He stops for a chicken sandwich somewhere around Gate 55. By the time he hits the parking lot, he could really use a nap.

He doesn't know how Grady does it, traveling more often than not, never settled, never really home.

It's not until he's standing in front of room 717 at the Hyatt in Duluth, Georgia that Nico hesitates, pacing and fidgeting, his palms a little damp. He knocks.

"I don't need room service right now, thank—"

The door swings open, and there he is, as radiant as ever. Nico releases a gust of air, as if he's been holding it for days and finally, finally refills his aching lungs. "Nico?" Grady's mouth hangs open and he looks both ways down the hall as if there's been some sort of strange mix-up with housekeeping. "What are you doing here?"

I can't stop thinking about you, he wants to say.

I'm worried about you.

I'm sorry I just left like that.

I miss you, I don't understand why or how this can possibly work, but I needed to see you, and by the way your assistant is kind of a weasel, you should probably know that.

Nico doesn't say any of that, doesn't say anything at all, just lunges forward and crashes their lips together right there in the open doorway of room 717.

They kiss and kiss and don't speak, until Grady scoops an arm behind Nico's back and yanks them both inside the room, kicks the door closed with a muffled *umph* and says against Nico's still moving mouth, "We should talk."

"Okay." Nico moves to devour the soft skin of Grady's neck, gets a handful of curls in his right hand, slides his left palm flat up under Grady's shirt.

Grady whines and curves his body into Nico's, then spins them, pressing Nico against the closed door. Grady's strong body moves against his, hips grinding and thigh jammed between Nico's legs. They moan and ride each other's thighs, can't get off fast enough, quick and desperate and overwhelmed.

Grady's shirt comes off and Nico's shirt comes off and they grope and kiss and curse. Nico wants him so, so much. Just being in Grady's presence is loosening the stopper on any sense of propriety, like the Wild Turkey bourbon but much, much worse.

Nico, shaking all over from wanting it the way he does, tears at Grady's pants. Grady stops his hand just as he finally gets at the hot, hard shape of him through his underwear and says at the end of a groan, "I don't have condoms."

Nico stops, can't resist a squeeze at the base of the shaft that makes Grady's knees buckle against him. He drops his head back against the door, takes a beat to breathe. "What the hell, Grady. Do you ever have condoms?"

"I didn't know you were coming!"

He could get Grady off just like this, hard as steel between the curl of his thumb and forefinger, bucking against the heel of his hand to get more friction. He wants more. "I have condoms. *Some of us* think these things through." He moves away with one last parting squeeze and says as he rummages through the bag still crossed over his chest, "Don't move."

He finds what he needs, deposits the bag on the bed, turns back to a now-nude Grady. That was fast. Nico stares long enough to preserve the beautiful image of Grady naked and heaving for breath and beautifully hard, waiting for him.

Grady leans flush against the door, watches Nico with his mouth tipped in a grin. Trusting, open, hands stretched above his head and that body laid out, skin and muscle and bone and wiry hair, cock standing at attention and the juicy-ripe sway of his testicles. *All for you,* that look says. He'll take it, for as long as possible, even with the shift of time already falling away beneath his feet; one moment strung perilously to the next is all they have to cling to.

Nico turns him around, holds his wrists above his head and molds his own still-clothed body into the curve of Grady's. He pushes hard on his captive wrists: *Stay.* Grady does.

Nico undresses in a hurry, rolls on a condom in a hurry, slicks his fingers and sinks into hot and smooth and tight right away. Grady gasps, pushes back against him, his body burning against Nico's, opening to him, taking whatever Nico offers him, giving Nico what he can in return. They don't need to talk. Not right now.

Nico grips Grady by his hips, clenches his teeth, steadies his cock and moves inside of Grady in one long, steady stroke. Grady shivers from head to toe. Nico holds his wrists again and moves and moves and fucks him and doesn't speak and bites his lip and doesn't speak and sets his mouth against the top knob of Grady's spine and doesn't say a word.

"Oh, god, sweetheart. So good, so amazing. I missed this, missed you." Grady doesn't hold back a single thing, writhing and spreading his legs wider and pushing back onto Nico's cock, so responsive and effusive with praise for how Nico makes him feel.

This would all be easier to cope with if Nico didn't constantly feel as though he was in danger of stumbling head over feet in love with him. That would be asking too much, expecting things he won't get to have.

When Grady comes it's with a throaty cry, so achingly lovely that it coils deep into Nico's belly and wrings his own orgasm from him in a cresting wave of sensation. He grinds and twists his hips throughout it, and Grady leans into him and clenches around him until neither of them can bear the weight of their own bodies.

"Nice room," Nico says, slumped and sweat-sheened and gulping lungfuls of air.

Grady looks at him lopsided and goofy, then around the room as if he's never seen the place before. "Yeah, I guess it is."

Nico stands on wobbly legs and yanks on underwear and pants. Grady sits collapsed against the door, legs bent up and casually splayed, flaccid soft cock resting almost sweetly on one hip.

"Not that I'm complaining or anything, but why are you here? You sort of disappeared on me and then reappeared, and I'm a little confused."

Nico looks down and scratches his stomach and decides to answer a question with a question. "Are you okay?"

Grady is quiet, watching Nico with his face drawn and looking anything but okay. Guilt claws its way along Nico's insides, chasing away the happy buzz of his afterglow. But then Grady's gaze travels up and down Nico's body, lands on his face and he smiles again, different. Forced. "I am more than okay."

17

"Did you eat?" Grady calls from the bathroom, the door open so Nico can see him bent over the sink in the still steamy bathroom, rubbing product through his damp hair. It's getting longer again; little ringlets spiral over his forehead, sweet little tendrils loop behind his ears.

"I had a fried chicken sandwich at the airport." Nico leans back against the headboard on the king-sized bed with his tablet balanced on his lap, pats his belly with tender affection for his last meal, so greasy and so unhealthy and so very delicious.

"Hmm." Grady comes from the bathroom in dark-wash jeans and no shirt. "We'll make a Southerner out of you yet."

"Don't get ahead of yourself." Nico scrolls through news articles. Well, "news" articles.

"You hopped on a plane, showed up in Georgia just because you were worried about me, then immediately rocked my world." He saunters over, cranes across the bed for a kiss that Nico half-heartedly tries to deny him before relenting with a sigh. "You like it here. And you like me."

Nico slides him a look as Grady pushes off the bed to pick up a garment bag hung over a chair, and to deflect just how right Grady is about his feelings, he says, "Did you want to send me a secret note like we're in middle school? *Do you like me—check yes or no?* Is that what you want me to stoop to?"

"Yup." Grady zips open the bag. "Help me pick out a shirt."

Nico holds up a finger so he can finish looking at the headlines on this site. Nothing about Grady, which is a relief. There's a picture of Clementine Campbell at a Lakers game, and the headline: *Clem Steps Out With Hollywood Heartthrob Tristan Chandler Looking Cozy!*

And a little, strange blurb about Hailey Banks: *Has Hailey Hit Rock Bottom AGAIN?* It makes him pause and continue reading. No one has seen her in weeks. It's not unusual for her to disappear for a while in a vortex of bad choices, but to go off the radar entirely? No paparazzi long-zoom shots, no "sources" popping up with sordid details, no reports of her leaving this party or that hotel? It's strange.

"Why do you read those things?" Grady holds up a plain black button-down that Nico glances at briefly before giving it a thumbs down.

Nico shuts off his tablet, scoots to the end of the bed to give Grady his full attention. "Come on, you *never* read them?" He stands, rifles through the garment bag and pulls out a red tartan shirt that he holds up to Grady's torso. "Not even in a weak moment where you just have to know?"

"Nope. I don't need to read that stuff. Lies and people tearing me down for things that aren't true." He shrugs into the shirt, and

Nico steps closer to do up the buttons for him, letting his fingers linger over his warm skin as it slowly disappears under the fabric.

Grady smiles at him, so close that Nico's eyes cross trying to look at him. "My grandfather used to say: *I'd rather be a dead pig smiling in the sunshine.*"

Nico fixes his collar, shakes his head. "Do I even want to know?"

"Ignorance is bliss, sweetheart." Grady ducks in for a kiss that gets heated way too quickly. When Grady starts to pull away Nico whines and yanks him back in by his ass.

Grady chuckles. "I have sound check. But I like your enthusiasm." He winks and moves away. "Hold that thought?"

Nico huffs and drops back down onto the bed. "Fine. Go to your legions of adoring fans."

"Come with me." Grady takes another article of clothing from the garment bag. It's a leather jacket, black leather with silver buckles going up the side. It's perfect for both Grady's frame and the new look that Nico helped him find.

Nico cinches the buckles along both sides until the leather is tight around Grady's chest and back. "Perfect," Nico declares, stepping back to admire him.

He flashes Nico that smile that makes his eyes crinkle and nose scrunch, the one that makes warmth fizzle in Nico's belly. "So, you with me? Check yes or no?"

Nico snorts a little laugh, picks up his bag and looks for an outfit of his own. "Okay. I'll go. Just to witness first hand how many people shout that they want your babies." Maybe if he laughs about it, he won't be consumed with jealousy and insecurity.

Grady shrugs. "Usually just one or two." He helps Nico out of his T-shirt and pants with an appreciative hum. "Too bad for them; I've got my eye on someone else."

Nico changes and redoes his hair and swishes some mouthwash around, follows Grady out of the hotel and to the concert venue and leaves the unspoken *"But why?"* hanging silent in the air between them.

Duluth is part of the Atlanta metro area, which is, as far Nico can tell, mostly made up of long lines of traffic, enormous shopping centers and sprawling subdivisions. He follows behind the tour bus with its trailer full of equipment and instruments in lane after lane of traffic that often stops dead before rolling to a grudging start again.

The show is at a small venue. The downtown in this suburb is a mix of a small town and new developments: an upscale mall next to the old, restored theater; tall office buildings rising up beside squat brick storefronts; an old-timey drug store and a post office slotted between trendy restaurants.

He still feels decidedly out of place in trim dress trousers and a McQueen printed shirt and a waistcoat. And the obvious lack of racial diversity doesn't help. He gets some looks, but chooses to think it's because his outfit is understated but fantastic and certainly deserving of a second look. He straightens his back and lifts his chin and crosses the street.

Dixie Land reads the sign outside; the neon letters are turned off, the windows dark. Nico passes groups of people milling around on the sidewalk outside and down the block. He's confused as to why so many people seem to have nowhere to be and nothing to do, until he ducks around a group all wearing matching shirts with Grady's face screen-printed onto the back. Right.

He maneuvers past the front of the line, where a large group appears to have been there for quite some time, set up with lawn chairs arranged in a circle, water bottles and empty food containers. They watch him approach the ticket counter.

"Um. Nico Takahashi? I guess I'm on the list?" The guy at the counter looks down at something next to the wrist bands and ticket scanner. There are whispers and murmurs behind him, and Nico's skin prickles uncomfortably with the heat of extra eyes on him. Maybe he should have worn camouflage instead. He certainly wouldn't be the only one.

Inside it's dim, but once his eyes adjust he can see a bar area immediately to his right, four pool tables to his left, and in front the empty floor area with the stage at the far end. The place seems to be wallpapered with Miller Light posters and the floor polished with molasses. Nico lifts up one loafer with a grimace. Camo and combat boots next time, for sure.

Grady spots him from the stage, beams brighter than the spot-lights around him, and starts to play as though it isn't just Nico and a few staff members out there, but a full house. Nico shakes his head, rolls his eyes and smiles. He ducks quickly backstage before they start to let people in and he's seen by the entire crowd.

"Good to see you again, man!" Mongo smacks him on the back next to a massive speaker. Nico stumbles into it, knocked off balance for a moment.

"Thanks... man. You, too."

Mongo hooks one of his meaty arms around Nico's shoulders and leans down. And down. "Don't tell him I told you, but Dude was a mess for a few days. He pulled it together, don't get me wrong. Grady's a trooper. But I'm glad you two worked things out." He pats Nico's back again and Nico stumbles again, this time catching himself on the speaker and staying huddled against it.

From here he's hidden from the rest of the venue, but can see Grady, strumming his guitar and singing a few bars, then waiting for a roadie to do some tuning and adjusting. Grady was a mess. Because of him.

From the darkened wings Nico watches Grady tune up and warm up. How hard will it hurt when they fall back down with the harsh, unforgiving reality of the inevitable end? It's not just him, it turns out, who is all too aware of where this leads.

The speaker needs to be moved, so he steps back near a spool of cables, only to have a different roadie reach around him. "Sorry, I need that." As the bustle on the stage ramps up and people start to file in, Nico can't seem to find a place that isn't in the way or won't put him on display to the crowd. Can't find a spot to watch Grady. Can't find a place for himself at all. He wanders over near the dark hallway by a staircase with an *Exit* sign lit. He pauses at the threshold.

18

The stairs lead to a balcony, and from here Nico has a perfect, hidden view of the opening band, an all-girl quartet who sing about heartbreak and loss and yearning. It's quiet up above; the floor below is now a mass of people, and the venue is filled with music. A few bored-looking middle-aged men with bottles of beer and ear plugs are scattered around the edges. Fathers, probably. Nico smiles; it's sweet. Being here so their little girls, or boys, can scream at their heartthrob in person.

And scream they do, thrilled and overwhelmed and shrill enough that Nico wouldn't mind some ear plugs. Not just the groups of teenagers, either. Grown men and women who cheer and yell and hang on Grady's every word: when he thanks them for coming, when he introduces the band behind him, when he crouches down with the microphone to hold the hands reaching for him in the first few rows and drawls, "How y'all doing tonight, Duluth?"

They sing along to every song, they dance and jump and wave and even up on the balcony, Nico can feel the thrumming energy, a living thing pulsing through the venue. Grady sings and plays his guitar and sends a joy out to the crowd that gets returned to him a thousand-fold—and looks as if he was born to do nothing but.

Grady has every single person in that place cradled in the palm of his hands, and Nico leans over the railing, forgetting to hide, forgetting everyone else; he looks down at Grady and happily lets himself be carried away.

He waits upstairs after the show until the fans drift out and the house lights come back on, a bright shock back to reality. Backstage is a frenetic after party—the band and opener and roadies and managers and the staff of the music club. Grady comes over and slides a hand loosely around Nico's waist.

"You're still here!"

"I'm still here. You were incredible."

Grady gives him a squeeze and shrugs. "It was a good crowd, and the band was killing it. I just rode the wave." Nico opens his mouth to argue, but Grady turns them both toward the back exit. "I'm gonna see if anyone is waiting. Wanna come?"

The back loading dock has a beaming floodlight that trips on when they exit the heavy doors, casting Grady in a pool of white light as he signs autographs and takes pictures and gives sturdy, full-bodied, drawn-out hugs. Nico sits back on the tailgate of the equipment trailer where it's hidden and dark. The night creeps into that netherworld of the inky early morning, when everything else is sleeping and anything seems possible, when life itself seems transitory and fleeting, suspended between night and day, between awake and dreaming.

Nico is jealous, but not of the fans. He's jealous that a man who has so many reasons to be guarded and distrustful and jaded remains so open and available and gracious. How, when he tells a hysterically crying fan that he loves her too, he really does mean it. That he can be in this moment right here and with this person right in front of him, and whatever came before no longer matters, and whatever will come next is a bridge he'll cross when he crosses it. He makes it look so simple.

"Sorry about that." Grady jogs back over, the last group of fans having been sent away with several pictures of themselves with Grady, grinning and making faces as if it isn't three o-clock in the damp, chilled morning.

Nico yawns and shivers. "It's fine."

"Come on, let's go." Grady pulls him up by the elbows and Nico sleepily snuggles into his arms.

"Leaving tonight?" Nico says after another yawn against Grady's shoulder.

"Nah, tomorrow afternoon. Got a thing tomorrow." Grady rubs his back and Nico feels much warmer settled in his arms. Grady sets his cheek next to Nico's, releases a happy sigh. "Where are you staying?"

"Mmm." Nico's eyes drift closed. "Hadn't really thought about that."

Grady chuckles and Nico feels it vibrate against his chest. "Why don't you just stay with me?"

Nico open his eyes and nods. "I'll stay."

Grady drives Nico's rental, and Nico drifts in and out of sleep, eyes flitting open to take in the dark city, the sweep of headlights, the steady, tiny beam of indicator lights in the car. Closes them again.

"I don't know how you have so much energy still," Nico says, bleary eyed and heavy limbed, shuffling though the revolving glass doors to the hotel.

"It's the buzz from a performance." Grady pushes the up button for the elevator. "Don't worry, I'll crash as soon as my head hits the pillow."

"So no fooling around?" Nico pouts, stomach swooping when the elevator starts to whisk them upstairs.

Grady holds him around the waist again, guides him to room 717 and fishes his key card out of his wallet. "Sweetheart, I always want to make love to you, but I do prefer you conscious."

The lock beeps and the little light flashes green and Grady shoves the door open, deposits Nico on the bed and then shimmies out of his clothes.

Nico snorts. "Making love. Who says that?"

"Not too tired to make fun of me, I see." Grady bends down to work on Nico's clothes; he *is* exhausted and he probably would fall asleep in the middle of it, but that doesn't stop his whole body from flushing hot with desire.

"Never." Nico wriggles into the soft bed. He needs to muster the energy to use the bathroom and brush his teeth when Grady is finished, only the longer he stays in this huge, cushy bed, the more that seems like climbing Mount Everest in a blizzard.

"Hey, Grady," he calls, sleep tugging at the corners of his mind, dragging his body under drifting waves.

"Yeah?" He's putting some sort of clay mask on his face, and that is just adorable.

"I want to stay," he says, muzzy brain insisting on the importance of telling Grady this.

Grady rubs the clay mask in clockwise circles on his forehead. "Then stay."

When he wakes up, Nico can tell without moving or opening his eyes that it's far too soon; the bright morning sun is making him feel shaky and raw like an exposed nerve. He whines and tries to burrow deeper in the bed, his nose bumping into—

He cracks one eye open. Grady's bicep. He burrows closer to Grady instead, realizes with slow, creeping awareness that he's woken up hard and ready to go. He gets a leg over Grady's thigh, some pressure against his aching morning erection, and falls asleep breathing in Grady's scent.

When he wakes again it's to the feel of something brushing up and down the length of his back. It feels so sublime that Nico arches into the touch and stretches his body from head to toe.

"Hey there, sleepy head."

Nico lifts his head from the pillow, squints and sniffs and then frowns. "You're dressed."

Grady is clean shaven and his hair has been fixed into perfectly shaped little curls springing up all over his head. "Yeah, I gotta head out in a few. I just wanted to let you know. Go back to sleep, sweetheart."

Nico closes his eyes, lets this information settle in his mind until he finally manages to comprehend it, then pushes himself up to sit. "Can I go?"

Grady is dressed simply, in a red T-shirt, which is snug across his biceps and chest and has contrasting cuffs of blue at the sleeves, thick gray twill pants wrapped tight over his thighs and calves, high top sneakers and a braided leather wrist cuff.

Nico rubs the sleep from his eyes. "You look nice."

Grady's lips curl. "So do you." He nods down to the covers tented over Nico's lap, the morning wood that seems to be undeterred by clothing or by the fact that Grady is running out the door. "Need some help taking care of that?"

Nico rolls his eyes and shifts away. "Cocky."

"Grumpy." Grady leans down a smack a kiss to Nico's cheek.

Nico slides out of bed, pulls on his underwear delicately, makes his way awkwardly to the bathroom and tries to think unsexy thoughts: Crocs, baseball, mosquitos. Parking signs in LA. Nico stands in front of the sink, glares at himself as he tries to calm down, ducks to splash cold water on his face.

Something moves behind him, pressing against his ass. "Grady," Nico warns, standing back up to pat his face dry. "You aren't helping."

"Mmm, I beg to differ," Grady growls in Nico's ear, and slides a hand across his stomach and then down inside his briefs.

Nico drops the towel, looks up to give Grady a disapproving glare in the mirror, but Grady gives him a heated look and his fingers wrap around his cock, and Nico can only gasp.

He grabs onto the counter, lets his head fall back against Grady and hums in pleasure, mouth dropping wide and hips twitching as Grady works him over.

"Don't—*Oh*—Don't we have to get going—*Fuck.*" Nico is close to the edge already, so worked up and so dangerously enamored of this man.

Grady takes Nico's earlobe into his hot mouth, sucks and bites and then pulls away to say against it, "I don't expect this to take long."

"God, you smarmy bas—*Ah.*"

Grady twists his wrist and pinches one of Nico's pebbled nipples in his other hand, whispers in his ear again, "Look at you. So gorgeous. Wanna see that gorgeous cock give it up, come on, come for me, give me everything."

In the mirror Nico's heavy eyes watch Grady—red cheeked, lips licked shining and parted softly—until he gasps, rocks up onto his toes and comes across the black granite counter in the bathroom.

Grady wipes his hand off, then the counter, gives Nico a little pat on the butt. "Come on now, we're gonna be late."

Nico grits out, "Bastard."

Grady winks and makes a *go on* motion to the shower until Nico steps in and quickly washes off, a smile stretching his cheeks. Oh, how entirely and thoroughly screwed he is.

19

"It's the fucking pedal on the right!"

Nico doesn't understand why this confuses so many people on the drive to wherever the hell they're going. There's a pedal to drive. A pedal to stop. Easy. "You go when it's green! Green light go! *Go!*" He can sense Grady smirking at him from the passenger seat of his rental car. "Don't smirk at me."

Grady smirks. "Yes, sir."

"Where are we going?" Nico guns the engine to pass a slowpoke on the right and mumbles in the car's direction, "Jackass."

Grady white-knuckle grips the armrest. "An early grave if you don't settle down."

Nico bristles. "I'm an excellent driver." He makes a quick cut in the passing lane.

"You are. In fact..." Grady cringes and grips the armrest even tighter "...I think you missed your calling as a NASCAR driver. Or for one of those monster truck rallies."

"Oh, please." Nico does slow the car a little and takes it easy on the frequent passing. "You're the one who took me speeding dangerously through the forest, if I recall."

Grady points to the upcoming exit they need. "That's different. That's communing with nature."

Nico scoffs, signaling for the exit. "So is this. It's called: the nature of driving like you know what the fuck you're doing and actually have somewhere to fucking go. Which is…?"

Grady nods to a sign placed at the end of the highway exit. "Georgia Children's Hospital."

The hospital is modern and sprawling, sunny and bright with walls of windows and a ceiling with skylights, a mural of a rainbow with happy children beneath it holding hands. The whole thing makes Nico squirm uncomfortably in the subterranean dark cave of the parking garage.

"Is this some sort of charity thing?"

Grady unbuckles and twists to grab the small instrument bag he'd tossed in the backseat. "Sort of," he says, then softer, "You don't have to come in, you know."

Nico swallows and nods. "I just hate hospitals. Full of sick and dying people." *Sick and dying kids.* Oh god, he's a terrible person. He pulls his seatbelt away from his chest, too tight, but doesn't release it.

"Not exactly my favorite place either. It's okay." Grady brushes his knuckles along Nico's jaw. Grady shouldn't need to comfort him, not here. He's being selfish. He really would have preferred if Grady were filming some cheesy local commercial for a car dealership, or doing a ribbon cutting for a new mall, or something else that Nico would find hilarious.

Nico, annoyed at himself, takes a breath and unbuckles his seatbelt. "I guess no one really likes hospitals."

Grady purses his lips and thinks. "Hypochondriacs probably do."

"Very clever," Nico mutters, opening his door so the interior of the car floods with light.

"I have my moments." Grady catches Nico's arm before he steps out, kisses him in the quiet parking garage, doing things with his tongue that leave Nico breathless and dizzy. He takes a moment to himself before climbing out of the car and following Grady to the stairs.

Inside, primary colors splash across the walls and sunlight streams in everywhere. The hospital is clean and busy and marked with signs pointing to the various departments: cardiology, neo-natal, critical care, emergency surgery, nephrology, neurology, respiratory care, psychology. So many services make Nico's head spin and his throat feel dry.

They check in. Nico quietly panics. Grady charms everyone. In the hall to the oncology department, the sun coming in behind him makes his hair look like a golden aura.

"So, uh," Nico says, clearing his sandpapery throat. "Cancer? Did you lose your grandparents to that?" Picking a cause that hits close to home makes sense and happens frequently in Hollywood.

"No, uh. My grandfather had liver disease and Memaw… a stroke." He pauses just before the U-shape of the nurses station that is the center of a steady stream of action with nurses and doctors and visitors coming in and out of glass-walled rooms laid out like the spokes of a bicycle.

They get visitor tags and wash their hands with soap that burns their skin and sinuses. As they wait for their guide, Grady says,

"If I'm being honest, this is totally selfish. Kinda puts my own problems in perspective when I see what these kids go through. If they can stay positive and keep on fighting, well, so can I. You know?"

The coordinating volunteer for the visitor program is a short young woman with soft, friendly features, and she is completely flustered from the moment Grady grins and leans toward her and drawls, "Hello, darlin'."

She stares, eyes comically wide.

"Hi, I'm Nico. What's your name?" Nico clasps his hands in hers, calming. Grounding. She shakes and stares at Grady, crushing Nico's fingers in her grip.

"I—I—" She looks at Nico in a panic. "I can't remember."

Nico twists his lips and tries very hard not to smile when he looks down at her name tag. "Jasmine?"

"Yes!" Relief washes through her face. "Jasmine, yes. Thank you."

She fans herself with her clipboard, mutters encouraging words to herself under her breath, and leads them to the first room. She tells them about the patient inside with her voice only trembling a little.

Being face to face with someone who is so obviously a fan is endearing. One on one, at any rate. Jasmine is sweet, and Grady so kind, it chips away at the cynicism that is a byproduct of the business Nico is in. It's not all skeevy alleyways and paparazzi and angry hordes just waiting for an excuse to pounce. He still wants no part of it, but Grady's determination to see the goodness of people, to ignore the bad—even just to be a witness to *Grady's* goodness—it makes Nico believe it too.

"This is Xavier," Jasmine says. She stands at the side of his bed, and Grady plops himself down in the chair next to it. Nico stays in the doorway, hovering awkwardly. He never knows how to act around kids; he's always afraid he'll forget to not curse or accidentally step on them or get something sticky on his dry-clean-only shirt.

Xavier is brown-eyed with big chipmunk cheeks, wearing a hospital gown with pastel shapes on it. He's maybe five or six—Nico isn't sure. He has an IV in one arm and a cannula in his nose; clear tubes snake back behind his ears. "I don't want to do music," Xavier says with a scowl.

Jasmine starts to talk him into it, but Grady shrugs and zips opens his music case. "That's fine. I brought this for me anyhow." It's a ukulele. A ukulele painted in neon rainbow colors. Grady strums it a few times. Xavier's smile betrays him.

Grady plays a happy little tune, leans back in the chair and says, "You don't want to sing with me, no way." Xavier nods his head vigorously. "I bet you want to—" *strum, strum, strum,* "Eat broccoli and take a nap instead, right?"

Xavier shakes his head. "No!"

The song switches to something with more complex chord changes, and Grady leans forward as he plays. "Well, if you're sure…"

Xavier wiggles excitedly in his bed. He seems to have forgotten all about his bad mood. "Sing the SpongeBob song!"

Grady sings *SpongeBob* songs with Xavier and princess songs with Hannah, some hilarious interpretations of heavy metal songs for Austin, lullabies for little Skylar who is on painkillers that make her so drowsy she can barely keep her eyes open. A medley of Clementine Campbell songs for Ada.

With every kid, Nico feels more comfortable. He goes from standing inside the door to inching along the wall to the foot of the bed, until finally he's perched on the edge of Grady's chair as he plays and makes jokes and hands the uke over for the kids to try out. Grady has the same ease with the kids that he does with everyone, listening to them and making them smile.

In Ada's room, he squeezes Nico's knee and introduces him as his "special friend."

"Your ears are funny," Ada tells him. "Did you know?" Ada is seven and in the second grade and likes horses and is missing her two front teeth, for which she claims she got twenty dollars.

"Big talk for a bald kid," Nico says.

She smiles up at him. "Rub it. It's *smooth*."

Nico scoots closer on the chair and pats her head. "Very nice." Grady plucks the strings of the uke and watches them. Nico says, "You know what I think would look even nicer?" He tugs the end of his bow tie loose, moves over the hospital bed so he can tie it on Ada's smooth little head. "There you go."

Ada touches it and *oohs*. "How does it look?"

It's a one-hundred-and-seventy-dollar silk Gucci bow tie; it always looks fantastic. But on Ada? "Beautiful."

"Listen to him, he knows his stuff. He'll tell you if you don't look good." Grady looks up, smiles and winks. He offers Ada the ukulele to play with. "And you do look beautiful, darlin'." She *beams*, holding the instrument to her chest. Grady shows her a basic chord, how to strum, then sings enthusiastically when she mangles "Mary Had a Little Lamb." The squirmy, sick feeling that had crept along Nico's spine at the mention of a hospital has disappeared, replaced by a settling warmth, an easy comfort.

Before they leave, Jasmine the fangirl-slash-coordinating volunteer asks for a picture and then grins as though her life has been made when Grady gathers her into his arms for a tight hug and says something into her ear that Nico can't hear.

In the parking lot, Nico turns to him in the dark; a yearning pulls at his chest. A week of Grady won't be enough; a lifetime of Grady won't be enough. The more time they spend together, the more reckless he is with his own heart.

"Mind if I join you on your tour bus?" Nico ventures, voice wavering as if some of Jasmine's nervous energy has rubbed off on him.

"I would like nothing more. But you are forbidden from driving. You'll kill us all."

Nico glares, but it's weak and tempered by a grin. "Fine." He starts the car, yanks it into reverse and zips out of the space. "You can't deny that I'd save us a lot of time, though."

Time is not something he can waste right now.

20

"Who's ready for Tuscaloosa?" Grady shouts, climbing the tiny staircase into the tour bus.

The band is already inside. They cheer and whoop, and Nico says, "No one ever," so Grady hooks a hand around his shoulders and plants a loud kiss on his cheek.

The tour bus is swanky yet cramped: A heavy black curtain separates the cab from the rest of the bus where leather couches stretch along the middle. Mandy, Mongo, Billy and Brad are hanging out on them playing video games on a flat-screen TV embedded in the front. There's a tiny kitchen, a tinier bathroom and six bunks stacked like cubby holes, which are closed off with more black curtains. At the back of the bus is a very large framed painting of Dolly Parton.

"Gotta pay respect to The Queen," Grady says, head bowed. The band stands up all at once, and Mongo and Billy and Brad take off their hats and hold them over their hearts; Mandy gives a deep curtsey.

"The Queen," they say in unison, then go back to blowing up pixelated people in their game.

"What in the hell have I gotten myself into?" Nico mutters.

After about an hour on the road, Nico is enamored of the entire band. They're all friendly and easygoing, entertaining Nico with their stories about life on the road: the time a fan snuck onboard in Michigan and they didn't notice until Iowa, and the road-rage incident with a trucker that involved a mooning from the entire band. Late nights and long days. How hard it is to be away from their families.

"Grady's lucky, bein' a lone wolf," Billy says, his cowboy hat tipped over his face, legs crossed in front of him. "Got no one to miss." Mandy kicks him.

Grady laughs, a forced chuckle, then howls like a wolf to keep the mood light.

They stop for sandwiches just outside of Alabama. The band stays inside the restaurant; Nico and Grady sit across from each other at the little table on the bus. Nico eats his foot-long whole wheat veggie, tuts at Grady's roast beef and cheese on white with a super-sized Mello Yello. Grady wrinkles his nose, takes a bite and says with his mouth full, "Don't worry, I'll work it off."

"I'm sure you will," Nico says with an eyebrow arched. "So. Dolly Parton…"

"Is The Queen, yes."

"Any particular reason?" Nico wipes his mouth, then holds his napkin out to wipe mayo from the corner of Grady's. Halfway there, Nico changes his mind and uses his mouth to gather the mayo instead.

"Mmm." Grady turns his head to kiss Nico properly and sighs. "Don't get me going now. I have a show soon." He leans back and takes another bite. "Memaw listened to Dolly. Dolly Parton, Willie Nelson, Johnny Cash. Loretta Lynn. All the old greats." He takes a pull of soda from the straw. "Nothing quite like Memaw singing "Folsom Prison Blues" at the top of her lungs while she dusted the trailer."

Nico picks at a pepper trying to fall from his sandwich. "I wish I could have met her."

Grady's smile turns sad. "You would have liked her. She never missed a church service and she made the best pecan pie on earth and worked hard until the day she died. She took care of me, and my grandfather when he was ill for so long." Grady looks down at the wrapper and bag from his lunch on the table. "She took it hard, my mama's... problems. Blamed herself, you know?" He looks up, eyes stormy blue and lips pulled down. "If she'd been harder on her, or gone easier on her, or kept her busier. Never gave up on anyone, Memaw. She's a hell of a lady." Grady shakes his head. "Was."

"Did she see you? You know—make it?"

"No." Grady picks at his sandwich, crumbling the bread onto the paper wrap beneath it. "When she died, I spun out. Things got bad. It was a wake-up call for me." He presses a pile of crumbs with his thumb. "One day she was here, she was all I had, and then she was just—" He brushes the crumbs off his finger. "Just gone."

Nico sets his sub down, takes Grady's hands in his. He's lost all of his grandparents, too, and even though they didn't raise him, the grief is always there like shattered glass, shards and slivers slicing through even after the big, sharp pieces have been swept away.

"In Japan," Nico starts, "there's this ceremony called Obon. We do it at the Buddhist temple my parents go to. It's this... celebration of death."

"Sounds kinda morbid."

Nico laughs. "Kinda. But it's really this time for families to come together and remember those who have passed on. There's music and dancing and these lanterns that are supposed to guide the spirits home and—I don't know if I really believe all that spirit world stuff…"

"They're still with us," Grady fills in. He strokes his thumb over Nico's knuckles. "That's the idea?"

"Yeah. They're here, because we're here, and it's all connected. All parts of a bigger picture. More than that, though, it's about honoring their lives by living yours. A joyful celebration of being in the moment."

Grady smiles. "I like that."

Nico grins back. "I thought you might." He releases Grady's hands, takes a sip of water, takes a moment to think. A moment. This moment. What else is there?

"Grady, I know this is—" *Temporary*, he thinks, but says, "New. I want you to know, whatever we are to each other, you aren't alone. I'm here, okay?"

Grady slides from his seat, is up in a flash and into Nico's space in the span of a breath. "So, do I need to smear mayonnaise on myself again to get you to kiss me or what?"

Nico kisses him hungrily until the rest of the band comes back on the bus and starts to catcall them.

Tuscaloosa is small, a bit rough around the edges and extremely proud of the local university's football program. The venue is decent, has a large stage with an open, clean floor, friendly bartenders and a cozy private seating area upstairs. The crowd is a little rowdier at this show: more college-age kids, more drinking; and Grady responds by sticking mostly to his more energetic and upbeat songs.

He's no less entrancing to Nico, who is seeing this a second time in as many days, his face aching from happiness. During "Broken Records" the lights go down, the band steps away and Grady's singing brings a hush to the entire ruckus on the floor. It spears Nico right in the center of his chest, like always. Until some incredibly drunk guy starts screaming at Grady to take his shirt off, spoiling the moment.

Not that Nico can blame him.

This show started earlier and ends earlier, so Grady finishes signing autographs and taking pictures before the wee hours of the morning. Tomorrow's show is in Baton Rouge, so Nico braces himself for a night crammed onto the tour bus with the band, but Grady surprises him with a hotel key between his index and middle finger, a sly grin on his lips, and a heated gaze in his eyes.

If Grady gets wound up before a show, he's damn near bursting with enthusiasm after. It's no wonder he has the energy to stay up all night and charm the pants off everyone. He slams the hotel door as soon they're inside, strips Nico, tips him onto the bed and goes at him, greedy and ravenous.

Nico stretches his arms and drops his legs wide and lets moan after moan spill from his throat. He's so gone, so drunk on pleasure, that when Grady lifts his head from sucking a bruising, purpling spot high on Nico's thigh to say something, Nico doesn't comprehend it at all.

"Wha—" Nico blinks away hazy confusion. This bed is smaller, the room not quite as luxurious as the last.

"I said, I'm part of this program called, *Know Your Status*. It encourages kids to get tested for HIV and other STDs. To be safe and informed and all that jazz."

He's kneeling between Nico's knees with Nico's flushed cock in his hand and his own hanging heavy and hard and tempting between his legs. He's beautiful and eager and all Nico's, and Nico appreciates his commitment to charity and social justice, but now really does not feel like the time.

"Okay..." Nico rocks his hips to move his cock up and down Grady's curled fingers.

Grady laughs, kisses just below Nico's belly button. "I'm just trying to tell you: I'm safe and I get tested every six months. Got the all clear. You know. If that's something that interests you."

"Oh." Nico drops his jaw and breathes out hard when Grady strokes and kisses, strokes and kisses. "*Ohhh.*" He slowly puts the pieces together. "I am too. I mean it's been a while, but I'm paranoid so I check anyway."

"Been saving yourself for me?" Grady says with a ridiculous wink.

Nico groans, this time in frustration, and bites out, "Can't you find something better to do with that mouth?"

A wicked lift of his lips and a, "*Yes, sir,*" and Grady's mouth sinks tight on his cock, taking him deep and holding him there. Nothing between them to dull the flick of his tongue in the slit or the smooth glide of his lips up and down and up, hot and wet and tight. Nico lets out a strangled noise, yanks Grady's curls and then cups his jaw to feel it work around his cock.

"Gonna come," he gasps after a short time. Too short. Grady hums and sucks him faster, deeper. "Wait, shit." Nico feels it build and tries to hold off. "Wanna fuck you, *oh.*"

Grady doesn't relent, messy with spit and rumbling moans, one hand wedged beneath his own body and flexing hard. His shoulder and bicep work, his mouth slides up and down the swollen shaft of Nico's cock. Nico tips over the edge with a silent cry.

He's still working out how to make his body move and his brain think when he feels splash after splash of warm come hit his stomach and chest and thigh.

"Wanted…" Nico tries, weakly grabbing for him until he's tucked warm and solid into Nico's side. "Wanted you."

"Later, sweetheart." Grady nuzzles his neck, nibbles his ear. "You have me. I'm yours."

Nico's cock gives a weak twitch against his belly and his lust-addled brain can only add, "Mine."

21

"**You cannot go** out like that," Nico hisses as Grady opens the door. He's in baggy sweatpants that hang so low the bulge of his dick looks like a tenuous hook only barely keeping them on. Nico is in his pajamas, cross-legged on the bed.

"Why? I'm just going to the vending machine."

Nico peers around him, the door open to the carpeted hallway. "There might be photographers."

Grady turns and it really would be nothing at all to nudge that waistband down *just a bit...* "At the Country Suites in Tuscaloosa, Alabama?"

"You don't know who's out there. Everyone has cameras with them at all times, Grady. Just—maybe a shirt? And shoes? And different pants?"

Grady slumps his shoulders, sighs and walks back into the room. "You worry too much," he says, but tugs on a shirt and hikes his pants up.

This hotel is standard. Bed is okay. Art on the wall is a clichéd, bland Impressionist knock-off. A TV and a kitchenette and a Bible in the nightstand.

"They had regular Kit Kats and plain M&M's. Did you want something salty?" Grady tosses the candy on the nightstand and strips his shirt off. Nico thinks about the drunk guy at the show who kept yelling at him to do just that until two bouncers dragged him away. Nico pities the man, really, eats a blue M&M and stares unabashed at Grady's delicious torso.

Grady pops open a Mello Yello and Nico shakes his head. "You have a problem."

"Well, as far as vices go, I reckon this one isn't so bad."

Nico winces and eats another candy. "Sorry. That was crass." Grady shrugs and takes several long swallows, his Adam's apple a sinuous glide up and down his stretched throat. "What is your mom… I mean is she an alcoholic, or…?"

"Anything and everything." Grady flicks the metal tab on the can: *plink, plink.*

"You don't have to talk about it," Nico rushes to say.

"No, I—" Grady flicks a look up at him. "I like talking to you. Opening up."

"I'm glad."

Grady takes another drink and scoots around so he's sitting against the headboard. "They were both really young when I came along. Hanging with the wrong crowd and just being stupid kids. They'd drop me off with my grandparents for a night, and then a weekend, and eventually for weeks and months at a time. Then longer."

Nico shifts closer. "That must have been difficult."

"You know, when I was really young I didn't mind so much. Home was crashing on a different couch every night or sleeping in a car, but at least my grandparents were stable. Memaw did her best, you know. But my grandfather had his share of trouble with alcohol and then he was sick for a long time. My mom went down that same path, never got clean and came back for me like Memaw promised she would. So I got older and I was angry and I hated my parents for never being around. When my grandfather died, Memaw's best was no longer enough." He lifts a shoulder and dips his head. "I started to self-destruct, I guess."

"You turned it around though. You chose a different path." Nico turns against the headboard, curling his body close. "That's really admirable."

"I don't know about that, but thank you." Grady gives a self-effacing little laugh, "Anyway, it's still pretty much the same story with my folks today. They show up now and then looking for money and making promises. I think it'd be easier if I didn't still have a tiny bit of hope that they'll straighten out one of these days."

Nico reaches for him then, laces their fingers together and softly kisses the round curve of his shoulder. "I'm sorry."

Grady's breath catches and he looks at Nico with so much tenderness, and Nico realizes that they've touched and kissed plenty of times now, but never quite so gently, never with so much care behind it.

"All right," Grady announces, tearing into the Kit Kat bar with a loud rustle of the wrapper. "Enough of my sob story, your turn."

He doesn't have much of one; his parents are still happily married and the barbershop has always been very successful, his dad is well respected with loyal customers, and his mom is a whiz with business and finance. He grew up in a nice craftsman-style house in an idyllic suburban neighborhood with plenty of kids to play with, went to a good school, played Little League. His brother was constantly trying to one-up him, and his parents pushed him pretty hard to achieve, but it's certainly not a sob story.

He snags some of the chocolate bar from Grady's hands. "What do you want to know?"

"Hmm." Grady takes a bite of his own and chews. "How about... Why LA?"

The easy answer would be that it just sort of happened, but Grady is being open with him and this week he wants to be with Grady without reservations. "Okay, you know how I told you before that my dad wasn't upset about me not taking over the barbershop?

"Sure," Grady says, as if there's not a single detail about Nico that he hasn't committed to memory.

"That's true. But not the whole story. He wanted me to be his partner, father and son cutting hair side by side, and then I would take over, like he did." Nico finishes the chocolate bar and licks the melted remains from his fingertips. "I was eighteen and still figuring out who I was, and I rejected his offer. At the time I just couldn't see myself working in the same place I'd spent every single day of my entire life. It was like, I looked into the future and it was this one boring, straight path that never deviated, never branched out. And I couldn't do it. LA seemed like the place to go for a kid making his first and only rash decision."

"Your brother took off, too. Didn't you say he was a professor?"

Nico nods. "I did. He didn't go far, though. And he's totally the golden boy, so he can get away with anything."

Grady drains his Mello Yello, sets the can aside and stretches out in the bed, props his head up on his fist and says, "Do you regret leaving?"

"I guess I..." Nico settles down next him, flat on his back, Grady flipped to his stomach. "I wish I hadn't left the way I did? Took off for LA and just left a note that said something dramatic like I had to chase my bliss or find my authentic self; I think I've blocked the exact phrasing out of embarrassment."

"Chase my bliss," Grady mumbles, thumbing across Nico's jaw.

"Um." Nico's skin blooms with shivery gooseflesh at the drag of Grady's fingers down his neck and shoulder and under the sleeve of his shirt. "I uh, drove there with my car packed full and no idea what I was doing. Got a job in a barbershop. Started working in a salon with a lot of celebrity clientele after that. Met Gwen there, drained my college savings account, and we went into business together. And here we are."

"Here we are," Grady repeats in a rough, deep drag of syllables.

Nico turns to his side, and when they meet for a kiss, it feels different. No less passionate, but something has shifted between them, as though the dangerous free-fall has finally snagged an updraft, caught high above the ground. It's still coming for him, the impact with the hard, packed earth. He's floating for now, holding onto the possibility that the landing won't break them completely.

22

On the way from Tuscaloosa to the next show in Tallahassee, they drive through a thunderstorm. Angry dark clouds cover the afternoon sun, sheets of rain come sideways with howls of wind, bolts of lightning crack across the sky. The driver is taking it slow, so the trip is even longer, and they're all lazing around the bus doing a whole lot of nothing.

Mandy is restringing her fiddle, slowly and methodically, plucking it and scraping across a string with an out-of-tune whine every once in a while. Brad and Billy are napping in their bunks; Mongo is staring off into space, making an annoying clicking sound with his tongue. Nico settles into a corner of the couch and watches the storm outside whenever he stops watching Grady relaxed on the opposite end of the couch, tapping out a rhythm on his knee and humming under his breath.

There's a bright flash of lightning, a boom of thunder, and Nico looks out the window, caught up in the way the whole world seems to look dark and tumultuous and crackling with furious energy.

Grady is rummaging around in a storage area above the couch, then sitting down with two knitting needles and a partially done project. Nico tucks his toes under Grady's thighs companionably, tingly-warm at the sweet smile Grady tosses him in response.

"What are you making?" Nico says, wiggling his toes and watching Grady's skilled hands quickly stitch, working the needles with a soft *snick, snick, snick.*

"Toboggan."

Nico squints at him. "A sled?" What kind of sled does one make out of yarn, exactly?

Grady laughs, and puts the unfinished patch of knitting up to his head. "No. A *toboggan.*"

"A hat?" Nico pokes him with his big toe in the meatiest part of his leg. "Can you just say hat?"

Mongo stops his irritating tongue-clicking long enough to mutter, "Yankee."

"I'm from California," Nico scoffs.

Mongo scoffs back, "Even worse," and goes back to his clicking.

Nico makes a face at him and Mongo makes one back, then Nico pushes up and moves to sit alongside Grady. "Will you teach me?"

Grady smiles. "Sure."

Two other knitting needles are located, in a different size, and more yarn, a lovely dark blue. Grady gets him started with a knot and shows him how to hold the needles, then picks his own back up. "Cast on," he says. "Just. Cast on, cast on."

"You say that like I have any idea what the hell you're talking about," Nico grumbles.

Grady does some sort of complicated over under over twist thing with his yarn and needles and looks up at Nico expectantly, as if he was supposed to learn something from watching.

"Still no." Nico holds up his sad, project-less knitting needles.

Grady shrugs and gets back to his *toboggan*. "Maybe some people are just born skilled."

Nico pokes him in the ribs. "Maybe you're a terrible teacher."

"Oh yeah?" Grady's grin goes sly and smirking and cocky. "Well maybe you'll just have to stay after class for some hands-on instruction."

Nico raises and eyebrow and purses his lips. "And maybe I can find another use for this giant metal needle, hmm?" He sets at just at the bulge of Grady's thigh and Grady gasps, indignant, and before Nico can react Grady turns, grabs his wrists and pins them to the back of the couch, hovering over him.

"What now, tough guy?"

Grady's fingers tighten around his wrists, his knees straddle one of Nico's legs, his face and chest are close, but not quite close enough. Nico looks up at his soft, plump mouth, swallows hard and licks at his own bottom lip.

Grady gives a little harsh puff of breath through his nose and kisses him. Maybe some people *are* just born skilled.

Mongo clears his throat, clicks his tongue louder.

Finally they make it to the venue. Nico watches from the balcony as Grady works his magic on stage yet again, just as he does afterward with the fans. Gets him to a hotel room where Grady strips out of his clothes and stands waiting in the middle of the dark room for Nico to finish struggling out of his.

With one arm caught in a shirt sleeve and pants pooled down around his ankles, Nico looks up to take in that magnificent, sculpted body, that hair and that jawline and that *mouth.* That thick, hard cock jutting out as if it *hungers* for Nico. But not just that, not just the superficial, but the way he's so comfortable in his skin, so sure of his own appeal in a way that always seems to toe the line between confidence and vanity, landing on charm and charisma most of the time.

"You're perfect," Nico says without meaning to say it out loud. He finally frees himself of his clothing and backs Grady up to the bed until he bumps the edge and sits down. Nico kneels between his spread legs and runs the tip of his tongue along the crown of his cock.

"No, I'm *no— Hah.*" Grady stutters, hissing when Nico sucks the tip in between his lips, tonguing around the ridge of it. "Oh god, sweetheart." Grady gasps, sets one hand on the back of Nico's head. "I'm not. Not perfect."

Nico holds the base steady with one hand, cups the heft of Grady's balls in the other, rolls and kneads, then widens his jaw and takes him deep until he hits the soft palate of Nico's throat.

Grady yelps, begs, fingers twisting into Nico's hair and hips twitching, gasping and gasping and gasping for air. Nico hollows his cheeks, presses his tongue flat on the vein running up the underside of Grady's cock and sucks up, up, up.

He flicks a glance up to Grady, lets the head slip from his mouth, a string of saliva and precome attached like a silk thread to his bottom lip. Grady's mouth is slack and his eyes heavy; his chest heaves. Nico smirks, takes him deep again and doesn't relent, not for a second; Grady's incoherent syllables and whimpers and whines spur him on. He can do this, *him,* the guy that hides in the background, waits in the wings, makes other people shine, he can reduce Grady Dawson to choked-off breathless babbling.

Grady groans, lifts his hips and pushes down on Nico's head, cock pushing past Nico's limits, making his throat flutter and tighten. Grady seems to realize this, releases Nico's head so fast he pops off and falls back onto his haunches.

"You can," Nico rasps, shocked at the wrecked sound of his own voice.

But Grady is still so tender, cupping Nico's head reverently even as he feeds his cock back into Nico's waiting, open mouth. Grady's words are awed and worshipful, watching himself disappear into Nico's mouth over and over, gasping out, "It's you. You're perfect. So much. I need. Sweetheart, please. Look at you. God, look at you."

Grady grunts and gives a warning, lets Nico pull back to swallow and swallow. Grady sobs and spurts and calls Nico's name until he's spent, then flops back uselessly on the edge of the bed and pants for air.

Nico stands, stretching his sore knees and looking at Grady and stroking his cock. Grady rubs down his own belly, his thighs, stretches his arms out to his sides and gives a happy little sigh. Nico whines, and Grady pushes himself up onto his elbows.

His grin is crooked and silly, and he drawls, "C'mere," with a beckoning finger. Nico climbs over him, straddles his shoulders and guides his leaking cock into Grady's mouth. Grady hums happily again, hands stroking up Nico's hips and the backs of his thighs and the curve of his ass. Nico's eyes slam closed from the overwhelming pleasure, letting instinct take over as he fucks and fucks into Grady's mouth, a minute, maybe two, before he's coming, can't hold back, yanks on Grady's hair and spills down his throat.

He passes out or falls asleep or just spends some time drifting through a euphoric state of unconsciousness until he realizes he's cold, and half his body is still dangling off the bed. Nico drags himself up to the pillows, stretches out on his stomach, tucks his arms under the pillow and drifts again until Grady flops down next to him. Drifts until Grady starts dotting little kisses along his shoulder blade and bicep.

Nico opens his eyes and blinks, taking in the room through the streetlights looming behind the window. "Where are we again?"

"Um." Grady pauses with his chin set on Nico's shoulder. "*Good night, Tallahassee!*" Grady says, as he had on stage to roars and cheers. "Florida."

"Huh." The hotels are already starting to blend into one another, nothing remarkable about this one, nothing that says they're anywhere in particular. It must be unsettling for Grady, to never know where he is, to have no bearings to gather.

It's quiet again, and Nico could go to sleep, just like this, Grady heavy and warm and solid at his side and draped partly over his back.

"I'm a terrible cook," Grady says, out of nowhere. "I can make three things and they all involve eggs."

"It's okay," Nico mumbles, losing the battle of wills to stay awake. "I'm not hungry."

Grady laughs into the back of Nico's neck. "No, I mean. I'm not perfect. I can't cook."

"Oh. I don't really either. Salads and smoothies and I have one of those... grill things..." He mimes closing an indoor grill, the type that are supposed to squash out fat and cholesterol from meat.

Grady peppers more kisses on Nico's back, across to the other shoulder and the first few knobs of his spine. "I suck at math. My toes are weirdly long; it's creepy. When I was a kid my friends and I would steal street signs."

"That's—dumb." Nico says, and shivers when Grady's lips reach the inward bend of his lower back. He turns his head to the side so he can see Grady. "You're right about your toes. They are creepy."

Grady responds with a bite to the right side of Nico's ass, and Nico hisses and twitches and moans just a little.

"Oh, we liked that, huh?" Grady purrs, and Nico would kick him if he could find the energy. Grady does it again and Nico grinds down into the bed. It's a slow build of pleasure the way Grady is kissing and biting and gripping at his ass, and just as the telltale heat starts to gather low in his belly, Grady stops, lifts his head and says, "I hate raisins. Not just dislike, *hate* them."

"Okay, well. That's it. I have my limits. Disrespect nature's candy and you have to go."

Nico cranes to look back over his shoulder. Grady moves, spreads his body over Nico's, front to back, half-hard cock nestling between Nico's cheeks. He runs his nose and mouth along Nico's ear. "You sure? Because I think you're gonna come for me again." Grady's voice is so deep and husky and starkly erotic Nico's cock throbs between his stomach and the mattress.

"I've never..." Nico says, pinned beneath Grady, hands clutching the fitted sheet as if it's keeping him from flying away, rubbing himself down against the sheets and up against Grady's body. *I've never...* What? Had sex this hot? Been with someone who turns him on like Grady does? Come so often and so hard? Felt like this? Connected and passionate and raw and real? The statement hangs unfinished in the air.

Grady grinds down, which makes Nico grind down. Grady is fully hard now and huge, the head of his cock catching Nico's rim, sliding hot up between the clenching globes of his ass. Grady sucks and bites Nico's ear whispers into it, "I love your ass. Your long legs and broad shoulders. I fucking love your ears." He pinches a lobe between his teeth and bites so hard that Nico cries out. Grinds and pushes, gets his hand between Nico's hips and the bed and pulls at his cock as best as he can.

"Did you know? I saw you at the AMAs. You were dealing with some model, last minute fixes I guess, and I saw you and I thought you were so gorgeous, I couldn't stop staring." He laughs, hot against Nico's skin. "Then you hissed at her to get a grip and quit whining. And *then* you told her that she was amazing. I was totally smitten."

"You…" Nico tries, has to breathe slowly to back away from the edge. "You should have come over and said something."

Grady laughs into his ear, and rumbles against Nico's back. "I was afraid I'd just fall to my knees and beg you to have your way with me."

Nico gets up onto his elbows, moves his knees wider and tilts his pelvis so Grady can stroke him easier. He gasps. "I'm gonna be honest, that probably would have worked."

Grady laughs again, and his hand slows, his grinding gets less urgent. "The point is, I look at myself and I don't see what other people see. That star in magazines. That's not me. I'm just some guy with a guitar and a lucky break, but you? Nico, you *stun* me."

He doesn't know what to say, can't get his mind around Grady being stunned by *him*. Grady's cock catches just right and his hand is tight and steady and *so good*. "I'm coming," is all he manages, cock twitching and giving up weak dribbles onto the bed. Grady follows soon after, on Nico's ass, between his cheeks, up his back.

Nico lies in the mess and can't even fathom moving, says after Grady heaves himself off to the side, "Do you think the maids will count cleaning us up as a turn-down service?"

Grady snorts. "I doubt it. But I bet if I asked him, Spencer would."

"Ugh. Spencer. He hates me."

Grady gets up and goes to the bathroom, comes back with a wet washcloth. "Nah. That's just how he is." He wipes Nico's back, then hands him the washcloth to wipe off his abdomen. He was asking about you before I left on tour."

"Like if I have any life-threatening food allergies or would notice if he cut my brake line? That sort of thing?"

They strip the bottom sheet, cover the bare mattress with a spare fleece blanket.

"Nope." Grady crawls back into bed, still naked, spreads comfortably and smiles up at the ceiling. "Fashion stuff. Like how you got into it. If internships are only in LA or New York. I guess he liked styling for me? But look, if he makes you uncomfortable I'll let him go."

Nico tugs on his underwear and sighs, "No, don't fire him." Nico ducks into the bathroom, brushes his teeth, then goes back to the bed. He doesn't want to be that asshole. Ugh, taking the moral high ground is *the worst*. "Maybe Gwen could give him some pointers. Since I really do think he hates me."

"Either way, the tour is over in a few weeks, then we can go back to Nashville and sort him out." Grady kisses the top of Nico's head and snuggles down into the covers.

Nico lets the *we* hang there unfinished as well, allows it to float, then pulls up the covers and drifts away with it.

23

Early the next morning, when the sky is a palette of pastel colors, Nico fucks Grady slow and deep and quiet. Grady's arms and legs are wrapped around Nico's body to hold him close; they pant into each other's mouths and whimper against each other's throats. It's not all-consuming fire this time, but slow-burning coals, exquisite unspooling pleasure from the clasp of Grady's body yielding to Nico's cock, to Grady's plush mouth on his, his fingers scratching, scratching, fanning out across Nico's shoulder blades.

Nico rocks into him for years, for ages, and then for no time at all; his orgasm is like a ripple on the surface of a still pool of water. Grady's cock against his belly twitches and pulses and gushes. Their stomachs and chests are a mess; Nico's come is a brand on the creamy pale skin of Grady's ass. Nico gets up to his knees, slips his hand down, and slips two fingers back inside just to feel himself there.

Grady thrashes and gasps and his cock gives up another dribble, lifting from his belly. Nico touches him inside and stares down his body, at this beautiful man and his beautiful heart.

They clean up and sleep again, and tomorrow comes too soon. They have to board the tour bus to Baton Rouge; Nico is half-asleep and dragging, and Grady has way too much bubbly energy for first thing in the damn morning. Nico grunts at him, crawls into a bunk and naps for the first part of the five-hour drive.

He wakes up somewhere in Mississippi. Grady is up and busy, involved in a jam session with the band, so Nico stays in the little bunk and turns on his tablet.

He catches up with Gwen, who is enjoying her time off with Flora, sounds relaxed and happy, and that's good—he's glad for her. He looks through his emails and checks in with his mom, takes care of some correspondence. Then he braves the gossip sites.

It's quiet, or at least as far as Grady is concerned. There is a little blurb about Hailey Banks, whose disappearance has finally been explained: She's gone on a spiritual retreat in the Amazon. That is not even remotely what Nico had expected. Of course, he should know better than to have any expectations at all concerning what Hailey will do next.

He smiles as he navigates away from Hailey's adventures in the rainforest. He does admire her zest for life. Just as the page starts to disappear he spots something, a picture of a young woman who looks familiar. He clicks the back button. It's called the *Awww Of the Day!* He finds himself staring at a picture he took of Grady and that volunteer at the children's hospital. Jasmine.

Grady Dawson Looks Adorable With a Fan, is all the caption says, but there's a link to the source. Nico follows it.

A country music fan message board loads and *Met My Hero Today,* is the title of the original post.

This is a pic of me and Grady at the hospital I volunteer at. Ignore me I look terrible, ugh. But Grady is gorgeous of course and I know this is hard to believe but you guys, pictures don't even do him justice he is SO BEAUTIFUL. Right okay, the point of this. Grady came in to visit with some of the healthier kids and it was pretty much the most precious thing ever. I got really flustered and couldn't say all of this to him like I wanted because I suck, and some of you know this already, but I was abused pretty badly by my mother who is a drug addict too. And one day I'd just had enough, you know? I sat in my room and I thought about how I was exactly as worthless as she always said I was and that maybe if I finally gave her what she wanted and disappeared she would be happy. And I was listening to the radio and just hopeless, you know, and "Broken Records" came on. I stopped. I stopped and listened and I felt like he was telling me that it wasn't hopeless. That he understood. That it would be okay. I bought the song and listened to it over and over. Whenever she got really messed up or hurt me or I got teased at school or just felt like there was no way out I'd listen to Grady's voice and I would decide to stay for one more day. One more hour. One more minute. He saved my life and I didn't know how to tell him that, but, honestly, being held in his arms was enough.

Today I'm in therapy and I've met all of you wonderful people who love Grady like I do and lift me up with joy. I'm studying to be a neonatal nurse, with a specialty in drug withdrawal. I figure I may as well start with the littlest victims. Whew, okay that was long sorry sorry! If you're still reading thank you and you should know two things: One, his boyfriend is way cute, and two, Grady whispered in my ear, "You're so wonderful. I'm so glad you're here." He was talking about being a guide at the hospital, I'm sure, but I dunno. It felt pretty pointed anyway.

It's such a poignant story and proof that there are so many positives to what Grady does and the difference he makes just being open and visible, and that's what Nico should focus on, yet his brain seizes on a little blip in the write up: *his boyfriend.*

And it's not just him who has zeroed in on that part. Reply after reply asking not about Jasmine's work or her struggle or her strength, but about Nico, who he is and what he was doing there. Jasmine has responded to several questions.

> **CntryRose:** *Wait how do you know it's his boyfriend?*
> **Jazzmin:** *They just looked like they were together. I don't know anything official, sorry!*
> **GDparadym:** *Do you at least know his name? What he looks like. OMG.*
> **Jazzmin:** *Um. Nico. Don't know last name. He's tall and fit but thin. Black hair and brown eyes and his ears are cute they stick out it's so cute. Um. He's Asian?*
> **GradysBelle:** *He could be literally anyone why are you making shit up to get attention.*
> **Jazzmin:** *Okay wow, all I did was share my story. Settle down. MAYBE I'M WRONG. He just seemed like his boyfriend they were really cute and lovey-dovey but jeez believe whatever you want I honestly don't give a shit. I met my hero and he was amazing that was the point. Go eat a cupcake or something, you'll feel better.*
> **RainbowCountryProud:** *So he's just some random nobody? Some hanger on looking for attention? Grady why?*

Jazzmin: Maybe he's known him for a long time or maybe Grady actually likes him as a person or maybe he wants to be with a random nobody or MAYBE IT'S NONE OF YOUR BUSINESS sheesh people.

Nico cranes around the curtain in the bunk. Grady and the band are fine-tuning something for the show, trying different riffs and tempos. No one has noticed that he's awake yet. He sort of has to pee, but he decides to wait. And in a moment of weakness and terrible judgment, he searches his own name in the little search bar on the message board.

A thread dedicated to him pops with post after post discussing who he is and what he's doing with Grady. Nico's stomach turns, sour and queasy, his neck is hot, his hands damp, his chest tight, and it's as if a spotlight is glaring down on him, the whole world watching him as he panics.

Found him! Nico Takahashi. Stylist based in LA. He is cute :D
WAIT WOAH HOLD IT I totally saw him at the Atlanta show after the concert. He was hanging back watching Grady sign autographs looking like a love-struck fool. I think Jazz is right. Nico/Grady I'm into it!

Meh. He's alright. What the hell kind of name is Nico? And his ears are weird.

GRADY + CLEM FOR LIFE I will never ever give up on them I don't care what anyone says I don't care about Nico or who the hell ever. GRADY + CLEM I LOVE YOU

Nico is hotttttt I don't blame Grady for jumping on that. I would. Rawr.

We all stare at Grady like love-struck fools though. We get it Nico.

I hope it's true. I just want Grady to be happy. Nico/Grady <3

Here's his Facebook page: facebook.com/Nico-Takahashi and the website for his business. stylebynico.com. Some serious yum pictures there.

But like, I can't be the only one wondering what Grady is doing with this guy??? Something doesn't add up.

Maybe he dressed Grady up and then dressed him down wink.

Yeah and maybe he gets free advertising. None of us knew who the hell he was until now, I'm just saying.

"Hey."

At the sound of Grady's voice Nico startles, fumbles his tablet facedown onto his lap and squeaks. "Hi. Uh." He lifts the tablet just enough to shut it off and tries to look as though he's not currently spiraling into a panic attack. If he thought the gossip sites were good at digging up dirt, they don't hold a candle to fan forums.

Nico hops out of the bunk, and Grady immediately moves into his space; his hands cup Nico's hips and he noses up his neck with a hum. "How are you always so damn sexy?"

They had showered and dressed in a rush that morning, and Nico was still mostly asleep when he'd thrown on the first thing he grabbed from his suitcase: sweatpants combined with a cashmere sweater. Comfy, but not quite right. His hair is messy and his face is rough with patchy hair.

Grady can do gruff and rugged. He cannot.

But Grady sucks the line of his jaw and curls his tongue around the lobe of his ear and it's easy to forget that. Easy to forget what he just read and learned. Easy to forget who Grady is and what his life is. But still it lingers, half of him with Grady and half of him on everything else: what they were saying about him and how all of his fears and worries are coming true. Just like that, the wind shifts and he goes speeding toward the ground.

24

He's wound up and off-kilter, trying to shake it off as they pull into town. Baton Rouge has an interesting vibe that Nico immediately likes: old-fashioned southern charm and cultural spots, historical buildings and theaters and museums. A lovely waterfront area with restaurants and a park and walkway, all on the banks of the slowly rolling Mississippi River.

The tour bus pulls in behind the venue downtown, and they all step off together. Nico has changed clothes—black moto jeans, a white oxford shirt with zipper details and leather high-top sneakers, then put Grady in gorgeous twill pants and a multicolor Madras patchwork shirt to match the old-school artsy feel of the city. He can style Grady. He can arm himself with a killer outfit. He can let the panic settle at the edges of his mind for now.

They have time, so the band hits a burger place and Nico and Grady wander the downtown blocks. They chat and browse boutiques and an art gallery, stroll the riverfront and take a picture on Nico's phone of their heads smushed together and too-big grins.

His boyfriend.

What the hell is Grady doing with this guy?

I'm just saying.

They find a sushi restaurant and stop to eat.

Grady pauses with the little porcelain bowl over his plate. "So." He sets it down and takes a sip of his tea. "Is there a certain way to eat sushi?"

"Yeah, you shove it in your face hole." Nico picks up a piece and demonstrates.

The restaurant overlooks the river. It's quiet on a weeknight, clean and minimalist and dimly lit. The two of them share a small table next to a huge window. Like an actual date. With his boyfriend.

Nico or who the hell ever.

Grady widens his eyes and mouths, *okay sorry,* and eats a piece. After he chews and swallows he says, "Isn't it like, your culture?"

Nico picks up a dragon roll. "Sure. All Californians know the right way to eat sushi." He pops it into his mouth. "I'm just as American as you are," he adds, not without some bite.

Grady blushes. "Sorry."

Nico gives a half-hearted shrug. "Forget it. Now, if we ordered some sake I'm sure I could show you a thing or two."

Grady looks down, touches some of his food but doesn't eat it. "I'm, um…I've been sober for almost four years, so."

"Shit, Grady. I'm sorry." He knew that. Sort of.

Grady looks up with a soft smile and eyes cast with sadness. "It seems like we're stepping on each other's toes a lot this evening."

Nico looks over his head and out at the slow-moving river and says nothing.

Some random nobody.

They eat in comfortable silence for a while until Grady says, "I wish you could come on the whole tour."

Nico's salmon roll sticks in his throat uncomfortably. He takes a sip of tea and deflects. "If you could be anywhere right now, where would you go?"

"Oh, tough one." He pokes at a blob of wasabi with his index finger. "This is pretty great right now. Me and you. I just wish it could stay like that." His eyes on Nico are too much, this is all too much. Just he and Grady, a life together, is an impossible wish and they both know it.

They finish the meal in uncomfortable silence.

There is no balcony in this venue, nowhere to hide. It's an old restored theater with slanting rows of cloth-covered seats and a little bar with stools just inside the door. Nico sets up shop there with his back to the gathering crowds, even though Grady wheedles and begs for Nico to join him backstage.

He drinks three Jack and Cokes while the seats fill, close enough to pick out bits of conversation before the voices swell into the rise and fall of echoing white noise.

The fan forum and the date that wasn't a date, the impossible imagined future, the burn of the alcohol and the chaotic chatter around him clash and twist and turn ugly on him.

He hates the way they talk about Grady as if he's a *thing* and not a person. As if they own Grady. As if they know Grady. He hates even more that people are talking about *him* like that, because at least Grady understands that it comes with the territory.

But Nico never asked for this. Never asked for any of this. Never wanted it. Never wanted anything with Grady but *him*, just him, and he can't. He doesn't get to have that, and it's not fair. It sucks. He never wanted strangers to talk about him on the Internet or gossip websites to speculate about who he is and what he's doing with Grady. Not for his whole life to be put out like a buffet for buzzards to pick, pick, pick at. To tear him down. He doesn't know how Grady does it. He doesn't know how anyone *copes* with that.

The noise and movement and wound-tight anticipation of the show gets to be too much; he's losing his grip. He needs to see Grady and calm down, stop and breathe and be in the moment. So Nico decides to go find Grady backstage after all. Maybe they can fool around, and Nico can distract himself with Grady's body and mouth and cock, and not have to fucking *think* so much.

He's dizzy and overheated and so keyed up, his mind hair-trigger anxious and body tempestuous. When he stumbles his way to the back room he bangs open the door to find the band members draped across a couch and pressed against a wall painted black. There's a photographer and Grady's manager and a beefy security guard. They turn to him and stare and Nico can't read the distress on their faces quite right and—

"Nico."

Grady is in a chair, creased black leather with stuffing breaking loose from tears, and two young girls in jean shorts and crop tops and cowboy hats are perched on either knee, one of Grady's hands set tenderly on each of their curving hips, just as he'd done to Nico mere moments before.

He hears his name being called again, more urgently, as he bolts from the room and down the dark hall where the exit sign beckons like the beam of a lighthouse at the end of a treacherous journey on stormy seas. Grady's voice calls him as the heavy door clangs closed behind him. It sounds like the tremor of a ghost—soft and thready and haunting.

He walks and keeps walking, hits the river and walks the path along that. He has no destination and no purpose, just walks with acid biting into his mouth and anger clawing his chest. He's so stupid. So stupid and naive and *of course*. Of course.

He follows the wide, lazily rolling river. *How far does the Mississippi go?* He can't remember. Could he catch a steam boat to California? Or at least the airport?

"Jesus, you're fast." Grady's out of breath and jogging just behind Nico's left shoulder. Nico ignores him and keeps up the pace. "Can we talk?"

"We probably shouldn't."

"Hey, come on. Don't be like that." Grady grabs his arm and Nico stops, wheels around to face him and everything bursts out of him, some small, lost voice trying to stop him but he never has been able to stop himself when it comes to Grady.

"*Me?*" Nico faces him, works his jaw back and forth. "Are you seriously implying that I did something wrong?"

Grady holds his free hand up, placating. "I just mean that maybe you misread the situation."

Nico laughs, a hollow tinny thing. "You know? I think you're right. I think I misread that you could ever be with me and only me. That you had feelings for me." His voice goes tight and dangerous. "That you actually wanted to be with me."

Grady's face falls and he steps forward. "I do."

"No," Nico starts and there are a few people around but he's gone now, he doesn't care. "You like when I fuck you," he spits. "Because you think sex equals love. And I was stupid enough to think that I was anything more than one in a long line of meaningless fucks that you use to validate yourself, but you obviously aren't capable of *giving a shit* about anyone. Well guess what? I don't give a shit about you either." He yanks his arm out of Grady's grasp. "Leave me the hell alone, Grady."

Grady physically rears back as if he's been hit and stumbles a few steps, his face crumpled in pain. Nico spins back around. He keeps walking.

25

Of all things, it's a phone call from Dr. Peter Ito, OD, that ends his angry march along the mighty Mississippi. He ignores the ringing in his pocket, doesn't feel like talking to anyone, but it startles him enough that he stops to look around. He realizes he's reached the end of the river walk. His mind is much more clear; the red blinding rage has bled out of his body. He's wandered onto a college campus and has no clue how far or how long he's walked or where the hell he's going.

He doesn't recognize the number lighting up his phone, as he stands on the sidewalk under the halo of a street lamp with the happy, hopeful energy of youth bustling around him. He hits play on the voicemail.

"Hello there. It's Peter. From Saturday? I was hoping to see you again this weekend. Maybe for *tapas*? You could even come to my place. I make a mean goat cheese bruschetta. No pressure though. We can keep it low-key. Give me a call when you can."

Peter. Nice, normal Peter who probably has a wonderfully dull life. They could go on his boat and drink craft beers and discuss "mouthfeel" and "thick foamy heads." Have average, satisfying sex and a steady, stable relationship for as long as they could convince themselves that it was enough. Peter probably gets excited about kelp smoothies.

Nico starts to walk again, but all the anger has been drained out of him, leaving a hollow, queasy knot in his stomach. He scrolls down his contacts list and calls the only person who might know what he's feeling.

"How do you do it?"

"Do what? Where are you? Hold on." There's noise in the background, music and conversation, the clink of silverware and rattle of dishes. Then a whooshing sound, and it gets quieter. "Nico?"

"Gwen. I don't know what—I don't know how—" And then it dawns on him that she's at a restaurant, probably gone outside alone now, and he's most likely interrupted a date. "Oh crap, you're out. I'm sorry."

"Hey, it's fine. Flora doesn't mind, I promise." She pauses and continues, "Well, as long as you hurry the hell up and get to it already."

A group of college kids in a pack passes him, and he remembers what it was like to be so confident in his choices, so sure that everything he was doing was the exact right thing. So how has he stumbled so badly with this?

"How do just put your heart on the line? Knowing how badly you can be hurt. Or how badly you'll hurt them. How do you make yourself so vulnerable?" So exposed, so bared, so close to letting himself fall while the world watches.

"Oh honey, isn't that the whole point?"

Gwen goes back to her date and her wife, and Nico wanders, so far removed from his own life that he can't seem to get a grasp on anything. He finds himself in an on-campus store, purple and yellow as far as the eye can see, stops in front of the rows of snacks and candy, sodas and energy drinks in oversized cans with names like *Monster* and *Full Throttle* and *Rockstar*.

Two paths become clear through the misty turmoil in his mind: One is Grady, and with him drama and rumors, invasions of privacy and the constant clamor of a public life for the consumption of others, of private moments stolen and hidden away like rare, precious gems. A path of distance and the ache of missing each other, of jealousy, of waiting, never settled, never simple.

The second path is the one where he walks away and keeps on walking in the same direction laid out straight and simple and unchanging.

Nico chooses two items, hands them to the yawning coed with her textbook open on the counter. He pays and leaves the store, then heads back.

Back downtown there's a park with a fountain, and behind it a decommissioned Naval destroyer. And behind that there's a bridge, which seems like as good a place as any to sit and wait until Grady's concert is finished and he's had time to greet some of his more dedicated fans. Nico plans and discards several speeches, watches the water dance and spray in the fountain. Maybe now is not the moment for perfect, planned declarations. He should maybe just start with, *I'm sorry.* And go from there.

He knocks on the closed door of the tour bus and feels silly, but also feels that every single person on this bus may want nothing to do with him. So he knocks. And waits. Stomping and shouting come from the bus, a window shade lifts and falls, and after a beat the whole band bursts through the narrow doors like clowns from a tiny car.

"Nico." Mongo gives him a hearty shoulder clap. "Told you he just needed to blow off some steam."

"Needs to blow somethin'." Billy mumbles.

Mandy smacks him on the back of the head. "Idiot."

"We're gonna hit some bars," Brad calls as they walk to the edge of the back lot. "Gotta crash on the bus tonight and I ain't doin' that without fortifying myself with whiskey first."

Nico watches them until they turn a corner, out of sight, and climbs the steps.

26

"Grady?"

The bus is dark and quiet, the TV and video game system are powered down, the driver is probably well into REM sleep at a nearby hotel, the only light is the little track along the center walkway through the couches and past the kitchen and bathroom. The curtains of the sleeping bunks are all closed.

One of the top bunks has soft light escaping through the cracks where it doesn't close quite right on the left side. Nico walks toward it, head down so he doesn't trip in the small, dark space. He clears his throat and takes a breath and says, "Grady, I'm sorry. I'm an asshole and I didn't mean what I said."

No response. Not even a grunt or a flutter of the curtain.

"I brought a peace offering." He pulls the white chocolate Kit Kat from the bag, along with the sixteen-ounce bottle of Mello Yello. He slides them under the curtain and into the bunk. Still no response. "I can just leave them if you—if you want me to go." At least he apologized. At least he came back. At least he tried.

The memory of his own angry words swells up, and he knows he needs to do more than just try. "Look. I'm an asshole, okay. In case I didn't mention that," he says to the black curtain. "It was a low blow and it was shitty and I was upset about other things and I took it out on you and—" He scrubs a hand over his face. "I'm gonna go."

Still nothing. Nico reaches for the curtain, but it slides open before he can touch it.

"Not like I didn't already know you were a flight risk." Grady is sitting up against one side of the bunk, in jeans and no shirt, feet bare, hair a bird's nest of curls. He scratches a hand through, slides Nico a look of disappointment that cuts right to the bone. "Honestly I'm surprised you hung around this long."

Nico presses his palm to the center of his chest. "Okay. I deserved that."

Grady shakes his head and looks away. "I'll be fine."

"Don't. Don't do this." Grady rolls his head back in Nico's direction with a flat look, and Nico hauls himself closer with one foot on the bottom bunk. "Don't pretend like everything is fine when it isn't."

"What choice do I have?" Grady's eyes lift up to the low ceiling. "I either let it go and move on or I mope about it, and moping never led me anywhere good."

Nico taps his forehead against the edge of the bunk in frustration; not in his entire life has he met someone so determined to turn shit into diamonds. It's as inspiring as it is infuriating. "So do you want me to get lost, or can I join you in your bunk bed, please?"

Grady shrugs, and that's good enough. Nico sets his other foot on the bottom bunk and heaves himself up and in.

Grady pulls one leg up against his chest, twists the fabric bunched under his knee. "I do know what people say about me. I try to ignore it, and I try not to care but—I know." He looks at Nico then, in the eyes, no longer avoiding him. "That's not who I am. No one gets to define who I am but me. And that includes you." Jaw set and nose flared, he adds, "I thought you were different. I thought, finally, someone who gets it. Who gets *me*."

"I do get it, Grady, that's the entire problem. It would be easier if I didn't. If I could just pretend that I don't know how difficult and ugly all of this—" He gestures to the tour bus, to the venue outside, a wild sweep of his arms to indicate the press and fans and photographers and critics and— "Your life. What it means. How impossible it is for us to have any sort of normal relationship." He drops his hands in defeat. "I know, Grady. I get it. I wish I didn't."

Grady's eyes are wet and sad and his voice cracks when he responds, "I'm falling in love with you."

"Me too," Nico replies, but not with a lightness or joy, but a deep, haunting sorrow. He never meant to. He never wanted to be just one more person that Grady loves who will leave him. "But you and I both know that it's not enough."

Grady presses his lips flat, looks up at the ceiling again to gather himself, sniffs and nods, then tugs Nico's foot closer by his ankle. "Do you think… If we'd met at a bar. Or through a friend of a friend. Or the gym." Grady's thumb strokes the tender skin of Nico's calf beneath the hem of his pants. "If we had just been two regular guys? We really could have been something."

There's a question in his voice, a hesitancy that maybe Nico would have rejected him eventually anyway. Nico scoots across the cramped bunk, crowds against Grady, shoulder to shoulder.

"Well, we never would have met at the gym because I would have taken one look at you and gone home to mourn the body I'll never have by consuming gallons of ice cream."

Grady bumps his shoulder. "Shut up, you're gorgeous." He tips his head against the wall and grins. "If I'd first seen you at a bar I probably would have humiliated myself by trying to win you over with bad karaoke and shameless flirting."

Nico's eyebrows raise. "You mean to tell me you've been holding back on me? You have a level of flirting that's even more shameless?"

"Oh yeah. You ain't seen nothin', sweetheart."

"That is truly terrifying."

Grady laughs, bright and uninhibited. Nico is so relieved to hear it, a moment of light in the darkness. Grady's hand rests on Nico's knee, Nico watches his own hand brush his fingers there, but he doesn't linger.

"We aren't, though. Just two random guys."

Grady's fingers flex, curving over his kneecap. "No."

Nico exhales harshly. "I have never wanted to be a groupie so badly."

Grady shoves at his leg. "Come on, you didn't really think that I would do that to you—"

"In my weaker, more insecure moments?" Nico scrunches his face, embarrassed. "Yeah, I did."

"You think that little of me, huh?" He says it with a teasing grin, but Nico's heart sinks.

"No, Grady. I think you're…" A million adjectives flash through his head: *beautiful, amazing, stunning, compassionate, kind, generous. A supernova.* He settles on, "Really special."

Grady gives a skeptical lift of his eyebrows. "Uh oh. I'm really special, huh?"

"I'm so so into you and it's…" He cringes at the words but it's true, "It's not you, it's me."

"Oh lord." Grady laments with a laugh. "Not that, please."

"I'm the guy on the sidelines. I'm the one who makes everyone else shine. I don't belong there, in the spotlight. I like that at the end of the day I can go home and just walk away from the cameras and the red carpets and the scrutiny. And you—you're a star. And you can have *anyone*."

Grady turns, the cramped space of the bunk making his limbs bump and nudge and curl around Nico's body. During Grady's shows, in the moment just before he starts singing the opening line of "Broken Records," there's this pause, this moment suspended in the air when the audience is silent and waiting and doesn't even dare to inhale because in that moment, Grady's soul is laid bare. He looks at Nico just like that, and Nico can't breathe around it.

"I don't want anyone," he says, voice low and serious. "I want you. How do you not get that?"

On a wavering breath Nico answers, "I'm trying."

Grady slides a hand along Nico's jaw, tilts his face up. "I know how complicated this is. But if you want to try—I just need you to know that I'm all in, okay? I'm yours."

And there it is, Grady's heart, so easily given but no less valuable because of that. It would be nothing for Nico to take it and keep it and damn the consequences. If Grady gets his heart broken, well, that's the risk he's taken. But Nico can't. He can't be so flippant about it. Grady's heart is an offering, but that doesn't make it Nico's to take and bend at will.

He won't be just one more person who breaks Grady. He refuses.

Nico swallows and nods. "I want to be the person that stays, Grady. So badly." He leans his cheek into Grady's palm. "I think I just—I need time to figure out how."

27

"**Now what?**" **Nico** says, pulling away; the air stuffy and thick between them.

Grady shrugs and shakes his head, fidgets and wriggles as if he needs to do *something* with all that frantic energy he always has. He thunks his head back against the hollow walls of the bunk, *thunk, thunk, thunk.* Then surges forward and kisses Nico.

"I'm sorry, I had to. I can't just sit here with you and do noth—"

Nico yanks him by the curls and kisses him back. Grady bites down on Nico's bottom lip, sweeps his tongue across. Nico groans and grips his biceps, kissing him so hard their teeth catch and their noses smash together and his jaw pops.

Grady's hands move around to grip onto Nico's ass, yanking him closer as Nico climbs onto his lap, bumps his head on the ceiling and laughs before he's settled, can feel Grady's cock swell and fatten under his ass as he kisses him. Cups his face and grinds down on his lap and opens his mouth to kiss him harder.

Things are messy and unfinished, and he doesn't know where they go from here. He can't focus. Or speak or form a coherent thought when Grady slides his mouth up his jaw and to the sensitive lobe of his ear. He will never ever think another bad thing about his own ears with the way each bite and lick and suck makes his cock stiffen in his pants.

"Come with me." Grady shoves Nico's shirt up to his armpits, doesn't even wait until Nico has it all the way off of his head before mouthing across his chest and swirling his tongue around a nipple and says hot into Nico's skin, "I'll give you space. We'll keep things professional."

"I somehow doubt we can manage it." As if he hasn't been trying to do just that.

"I am pretty hard to resist." Grady yanks open Nico's belt.

Nico moves up on his knees, hits his head again and helps Grady get his pants quickly undone. "Smug bastard," he says, belt clanking and zipper humming.

Getting naked is a struggle. Cramped and twisted, Nico nearly elbows Grady in the nose, and Grady gets one leg caught in his underwear for a long, but hilarious, moment. Then Nico has to hop down and navigate the bus naked, in the dark, hoping that no one can see in, to grab lube and a condom from his bag.

Nico hoists himself back into the bunk. "This is so awkward."

"You want to stop?" Grady flicks the bottle of lube open, settled back on his knees, cock standing out from his body, hard and flushed.

"God, no."

Grady pitches forward to kiss him again, cradling Nico's jaw in those talented, callused fingers. Nico lets it wash over him, everything he feels for Grady, everything he wants with him. Kisses his mouth and nose and both silky eyelids. His temples and his rough cheeks, his jaw and his throat and his shoulders.

"I want you to fuck me," Nico whispers.

Grady's hands squeeze Nico's hips. "Okay, sweetheart." Before Nico can crawl back into his lap, Grady stops him, a hand pressed flat to the center of Nico's chest. He looks down, licks his lips and then back up. "I wish you would stay."

"I know. I'm not disappearing, not again," Nico babbles. "It's not a no. I'm not leaving. I promise. I just need some time. I need to figure out…" He shakes his head. "Everything."

"It's okay." Grady pulls him in for a kiss. "I get it. I do." Slick fingers nudge between his cheeks, and Nico sucks in a sharp breath at the feeling. Grady rubs in gentle circles, rubs and rubs and pushes one fingertip inside. "Just like this?"

Grady's legs are still crossed, knees lifted to make a cradle for Nico's body to settle inside, Nico's legs set on either side of Grady's body on the thin foam mattress. Their cocks slip and slide against each other as Nico twitches and trembles with two fingers inside.

It burns, and at first it's too much, all stretch and intrusion and Nico fighting the urge to pull away, get it out, make it stop. But Grady strokes Nico's cock with his other hand, kisses his ear and sighs and whispers sweetly in Nico's ear about how amazing he is and how good he feels and how happy Nico makes him. Nico stops fighting it, allows the feeling to take over and the pain edges to pleasure, pleasure into hunger, and soon he needs more, feels empty and open and yearning.

"Do it," Nico says on a gasp, back bowing when Grady's fingers brush a sensitive spot inside him. "Oh fuck, baby, please."

Grady smirks at that, and Nico can't even roll his eyes because the blunt pressure of Grady's cock feels like every nerve catching fire, like lit matches flaring to life across his body. It's so much and so full and so big. Nico whines and sinks down and holds tight to Grady's strong shoulders until he's settled down in his lap, Grady around him, Grady in him, Grady everywhere.

"Just like the first time, remember?" Grady pets at his back, face screwed tight and chest heaving and voice strained, staying still, waiting for Nico.

"Technically the second time," Nico points out, barely a whisper. He lifts a little, falls back down. "That's—oh, that's good."

"It's like a song." Grady gasps and grabs hard to Nico's ass, helping him rise and fall again, a little higher, and little faster. "Intro," Grady explains. They both moan. He grits out each word one by one when Nico drops down with Grady fully sheathed inside him. "Verse. Chorus. Verse. Outro." Pleasure blooms from where Grady moves in him, where he touches and kisses Nico's skin. Sex with Grady will never be just satisfying, will always be Nico willingly going under, a riptide, an irresistible force. "Full circle."

Nico rises and falls until his legs shake and his knees hurt and his lungs burn. Then Grady lifts him, puts Nico on his back and covers his curled body and pounds into him with Nico's hands in his curls, knees over his shoulders.

"Harder, fuck. Harder, harder." Nico doesn't know where it's coming from. Some primal part of him wants everything Grady can give him, the power in those thighs and the ripple of his abdomen and the piston of his cock. "*Harder.*"

Grady holds him and fucks him and kisses him and moves his hips as fast and hard as he can, until he comes, every muscle and tendon snapping, Nico's name a chant from his lips, spilling and spilling and coming inside him.

"Stay." Nico gasps, holds Grady close, writhes on his slowly softening cock, fumbles for his own.

Grady gets there first. "I've got you." Head on Nico's shoulder, shuffled up a little on his knees to tilt Nico's hips up, jerks his cock a little loose and sloppy, but it's perfect. He's still stretched open on Grady's cock, Grady's hand is flying, and his orgasm hits like a kick to the gut, knocking the breath out of him, pulling him down and down until he's nothing but drifting pleasure and soft affection.

Lying together in the bunk is not without its issues, but they manage, curled together tightly. Grady's breathing is slow and steady against the nape of Nico's neck.

"Maybe it's the…what's the part where the song goes from one section to the next?" Nico asks, sleepy and sated and slow.

"The bridge?" Grady dots little kisses on his spine.

"Right. That." Maybe the song isn't over, but transitioning. If only Nico had some idea of where the other side might be.

"I hope so," Grady says.

Then they have to break apart, get cleaned up and dressed quickly because the band is back and being excessively loud on purpose to announce their arrival. Nico doesn't get a chance to say, *I hope so, too.*

28

Nico looks up a cab company, calls while Grady stands shirtless against the bathroom door, can of soda in hand. Nico needs to focus and gather the few things he has in various places in the tour bus: his tablet; an extra toothbrush; some protein bars in the cabinet over the microwave. It's impossible to pass Grady in the tiny hallway without brushing solidly against him.

Grady grins, still flirting, even though Nico knows his heart must be cracking apart with little fissures, too.

"Sure you can't stay?"

Nico lifts his eyes from the half-closed zipper on his suitcase, up Grady's tight jean-clad legs to his bare torso to his smirking half-grin. He does make a compelling argument.

"I already called a cab," Nico says, as if it's some irreversible decision. He has a life. A home. A job. Things and people he can't just walk away from without a glance back. He needs time. He needs clarity. He needs Grady's life to be something else.

Nico heaves his bag off the bunk and onto the ground, rests it against his knee and leans forward, barely a breath of space between him and Grady. Grady reaches out to set his hand on Nico's hip. He misses Grady already, and he's not even gone yet.

"Are you…" He looks down, away, pulls the suitcase handle up and clicks it into place. "Are you sure you're okay?"

"Don't you worry about me." Grady crooks a finger under Nico's chin. "I'll land on my feet. I always do."

Nico brushes a kiss to his lips, so fast that he's already moved away before Grady can kiss back. Turns around and walks away, suitcase loudly rolling behind him.

The Baton Rouge airport is a ghost town this time of night. Most of the stores and restaurants have their metal gates pulled down, and there's just the occasional echoing announcement and the fast clip of Nico's shoes on the tile floors echoing through the terminal.

His flight isn't for hours, which makes his sudden decisive departure from the tour bus seem a little silly and dramatic in retrospect. Nico sits at a burbling fountain, surrounded by waxy foliage—wispy little trees and thick ferns and colorful flowers. He leans back, stretches his legs and crosses his arms over his belly. A leaf tickles the back of his neck.

He doesn't know where to start. He could make a chart with pros and cons, or list all the reasons it's best to make a clean break from Grady, but he can't even come up with bullet point number one without coming up with an argument against it. Nothing about Grady or being with Grady is sensible or practical. It twists and twines, tangling his thoughts, and he can't figure out how to untether it all.

Nico sighs and sits up, runs both hands through his hair and grunts at how unkempt he's let it get. He needs a haircut.

"A haircut," he says, *Eureka* style, his voice bouncing around the empty terminal corridor. He stands and walks briskly back to the ticket counter, suitcase repeatedly banging into his Achilles tendon.

"When is your next flight to Sacramento?"

He manages to get on a plane quickly, but with two layovers on a red-eye it still takes forever. When he lands late the next morning, he's so exhausted he feels as if he's haunting his own body, an apparition drifting alongside himself. He finds an open spot of wall to lean against in the baggage claim and calls his mom.

The first thing she does when she finds him is cup his face in her hands, frown deeply and say, "Are you ill? Nicolas, just tell me. Give me the bad news, I can take it."

She's almost an entire foot shorter than him, with black hair cut in a bob around her worried face and lines of wrinkles around her small dark eyes; she's wearing a pink cardigan and pressed khaki slacks.

Nico pats her hands. "I'm not sick. Just tired."

"You always say that," she tuts. "Maybe you have sleep apnea. I read about it in *Reader's Digest*."

Nico smiles and follows her out of the airport as she rambles on about the many conditions that could be causing his fatigue. Anything other than his own stupid choices.

He falls asleep in the car almost immediately, then wakes up when they pass the water tower with *Welcome to Sacramento: City of Trees* in broad black letters. They head down familiar streets and past shopping centers and neighborhoods. It's comforting already.

"Want me to drop you off at home?" They sit at a red light, the radio chattering with commercials between popular songs. *Has she heard of Grady Dawson?*

"No," Nico says and yawns, only remembering to cover his mouth when she purses her lips at him. "I came for a haircut."

Lips still pursed, she admonishes, "Nicolas, I don't understand you."

"That makes two of us."

His father looks older: his little round potbelly more pronounced, his black hair going silver at his temples and hairline, face creased with more lines. He still holds himself proudly, tall with his back straight, squared-jawed and handsome, with the same dark eyes and high cheekbones that Nico inherited. He's finishing a trim on a man who doesn't have much hair left to trim, but he's focused and genial as he combs and clips and chats.

Nico's mom goes around the other side of the counter, checks the customer out once he's finished, then says over her shoulder, "Ken, he came for a haircut, he says."

"Can't find anyone in LA who can cut hair without adding a peacock feather or purple dye, I bet." Nico sits in the chair; the tight cinch of the cape low on his throat feels like settling in at home. His dad brushes through his hair, checking the length, bringing it forward into his eyes and then back off his face.

"You keep it so long." He brushes it all forward again.

Nico shrugs, and the nylon cape swishes and flutters. "So cut it short." Maybe he isn't through making rash, reckless choices.

His dad picks up a sterilized comb, mists Nico's hair and starts to trim. "When you were a little boy, you used to sit here and tell me all your hopes and dreams." He lifts a lock between his index and middle finger and cuts. Hair falls to the floor, a stark black splash on white tile. "You talked about getting a dragon a lot."

Nico looks at him in the mirror and smiles at the memory. "I'm still not quite over finding out they don't actually exist."

"It was a sad day for us all."

Maybe not for his brother Lucas, since he'd so eagerly told Nico the truth and crushed all of his innocent little-boy dreams.

Nico watches his dad work, bit by bit snipping away the haircut Nico had chosen to hide his flaws. "Does it bother you…" he asks as another customer comes into the shop. The front door rings cheerily; his mom greets him like an old friend. "That this wasn't my dream?"

A snip over his ear. "Does it bother *you*?"

Nico considers this, and his dad evens out the other side. "It feels like something I should have wanted."

He switches to the electric razor, a tickling, rattling buzz up the back of Nico's skull.

"Should have. Your generation gets too caught up on *should have* and *what if*. What happened to doing, hmm? Whatever happened to *being*?"

Nico keeps quiet about all the *doing* in his life lately, but the point stands. He's bogged down by what he wants and what he thinks he wants and what he should think he wants and what other people want and think. No wonder he's tired all the time.

"So how do you just—do, and find peace?"

His dad crouches in front of him, trimming his bangs and closely checking the evenness. His father has had a good, simple life. A successful business owner, a healthy family, a part of a community. All the things Nico's grandparents had hoped for them, and his parents for him.

Couldn't he just have that? Isn't that what he wants?

"I am an old man, Nico. So I'll give you old-man advice." He stands, knees popping with the effort, touches Nico's forehead with one finger. "If you aren't at peace here, you will never find it anywhere." Taps and taps at his head. "You don't search for peace. You are peace."

29

It's a slow unspooling then, what he'd thought he wanted, his worries and fears slipping loose from the spindle. He goes home with his parents when the barber shop closes, wheels his suitcase past his old room that is now a crafting room for his mom and into Lucas' old room. Technically it's a guest room now, but it still has trophies and ribbons and plaques with Lucas' name on the bookcase with all the books that Lucas didn't bring with him when he moved out. Nico props his suitcase in a corner and goes outside.

For as long as he can remember, there's been a hammock stretched between the two sycamore trees in the center of the backyard. Not always the same hammock—so many have been worn out by weather and two active boys and their friends using them as a spaceship or time machine, or just to launch themselves as far and dangerously as possible.

This one is a double hammock, blue and green striped with two little pillows. He smiles, imagines his parents out here, cuddled together and enjoying a few moments of peace on the rare occasion they aren't working or otherwise keeping busy.

Nico eases himself in, loses his footing and ends up unattractively flailing his way to the middle of the hammock. He manages to settle, though; he sways in the sun and tries to channel his inner peace.

He falls asleep instead.

"Nicolas."

"Nico."

"*Nicolas!*"

He wakes up completely out of sorts, with no clue where he is at first. "Five more minutes," he grumbles. Then his mom's frowning face comes blurrily into view. Then the backyard that's gone dark and cool.

"Shit, what time is it?" he sits up and grips the hammock as it sways.

"Eight o'clock."

Nico rubs his eyes and heaves himself, wobbly and awkward, from the hammock. "Why didn't you wake me up?"

She tosses her hands up. "You're always talking about how tired you are!"

"Well that doesn't mean I want to sleep in the backyard!" He follows her inside. The kitchen is dark, and his dad is in the den, watching a rerun of *The Daily Show.*

He remarks without looking up from the TV, "In Sweden, people let their babies sleep outside."

Nico has missed their slightly off-kilter advice and support. "Right, okay. I'm gonna go get some stuff done. Love you guys."

He climbs the stairs, smiling. His stomach growls. His mom calls after him that she left some dinner in his room, and he smiles again to see a plate with a peanut butter and jelly sandwich and a glass of milk.

It's good to be home. It's nice to know he can have these touch-points where he can go and feel settled—a safe place to fall.

He answers emails and sets up meetings in a near future when he'll get back to the life he built for himself. But it feels different. Will he want it still? Will he want the safety of the sidelines, or will he want to share his life with a man who lives in the center of a raging storm?

He finishes his sandwich and milk, settles on his bed with his tablet and phone, in shorts and no shirt; it's always so hot upstairs in this house.

> **Nico:** Ready to get back to work?
> **Gwen:** I already have been.
> **Nico:** Uh-oh.
> **Gwen:** No it's good. Me and Flora. We're good.
> **Gwen:** But after a while it's just kind of like: I love you. Now please go away.
> **Nico:** Absence really does make the heart grow fonder?
> **Gwen:** Sometimes.

He powers on his tablet, then thinks better of it; no peace can come from the rabbit hole of despair that is Internet gossip. But then there are people like Jasmine, who love and admire someone they don't know to the point of feeling rescued by them, and how can that ever be a bad thing? He wonders how the kids at the hospital are doing. About Hailey. About Grady, who is probably on stage at this very moment, singing and playing his heart out.

Is it all the same thing? Coming from the same place? Passion. Love. A hunger to make a life count for something. *Doing.*

He sends him texts, even though Grady won't see them for a while.

Nico: Have you ever been to Sacramento? I think you'd like it.

Nico: I can take you to Lake Tahoe. And if you're here in the spring there's this festival at the temple. Hanamatsuri. It's like… the Buddha's birthday celebration. Sort of. You'll lose it at all the food.

Nico: Just in case you thought Southerners had the market cornered on deep fried delicacies.

Nico: I know you aren't really okay.

Nico: Confession time. I pretend to love healthy foods, and traditional Japanese food is my soul food, but my very favorite meal is a peanut butter and jelly sandwich on Wonderbread, no crusts.

Nico: My mom would really love you, I think.

Nico: I'm not okay either.

He goes to the bathroom with his bag of travel toiletries, does a double take at his own reflection; his shorn hair and very prominent ears make him stop and touch his head and squint at himself. When he pinches his earlobe between his thumb and forefinger, it thrills down his spine. If he closes his eyes he can pretend it's Grady's soft lips and blazing hot mouth and sharp teeth tugging at the lobe instead.

He goes to bed, restless and turned on and the opposite of peaceful.

The single text waiting for him the next morning is cryptic.

Grady: Stay.

Nico rubs the sleep from his eyes and blinks at the screen until his mom calls him to come down and have some toast. He sets the phone down and gathers an armful of laundry.

"I didn't buy enough food for you," she says by way of greeting when he comes down the stairs. Nico loads his clothes into the washer and glances over his shoulder at her.

"It's okay, I'm not staying long."

She sighs. "Let me at least cook lunch for you today."

The washer lid clangs closed. He's down to jeans and one back-up T-shirt. "All right, but I'm coming to the store with you."

"Morning, Amy!" The manager of the grocery store waves as they enter. "And... Nicolas, right? The one who hangs out with movie stars in Hollywood."

His mother chats and Nico's ears burn. *Wow, it's nice to be back in suburbia.*

She used to send him and Lucas on scavenger hunts in this store when they were little, which Nico now understands to be a last-ditch effort to get them to behave while she shopped. Lucas always had to win, racing off and grabbing the wrong brand or size in his carelessness. For Nico the challenge was carefully selecting just the right thing at the right price. The Honey Nut Cheerios are $3.49 for seventeen ounces, but the original flavor are $3.98 for twenty-one ounces. The crackers they like are on sale, but the store brand is even cheaper and just as good. The tortillas are always better from the "ethnic foods" aisle, which is also the best place to find the good rice. Outside of an Asian supermarket, anyway.

It didn't matter how much Lucas bragged about finding his items first, Nico tried the hardest; he cared the most, and that was more important to him.

His mom pushes the cart and Nico picks up and puts back down tomatoes and green beans, finally selecting the juiciest, plumpest heirloom variety and the crispest, greenest beans. They pick out cuts of strip steak and a new bottle of olive oil, head down the drink aisle to pick up the seltzer water his dad likes. The bottles of soda lined up in their little slots there send a silly pang of sadness through him.

She pauses at the end of the aisle. "Anything else?"

Nico knows the confession will only reaffirm her worries about him, but he's yearning for comfort and peace so he says with his gaze shifted away, "*Okowa?*"

That's the sticky rice with vegetables he liked to eat after a tough day at school or a breakup or just when Lucas was being extra insufferable. She frowns and then reaches up to grasp his chin and lifts up on her toes to kiss his cheek. "Of course, my darling."

They sit outside on the patio, under the shadow of the gabled awning of the back porch. Nico mixes chunks of his steak and his green beans with the *okowa*. It reminds him of his grandmother's house. He misses her. He thinks about Grady again.

"You aren't leaving too late are you?" His mom asks. Nico tells her he's planning on going once his last load of clothes is finished in the dryer. The drive is just long enough to qualify as a road trip, so he'll pick up the rental car he reserved and hit the road soon.

"How's Lucas?"

"He published a paper. In… a business journal," His dad says, cutting his steak and skipping the rice.

"What was it about?" His mom chimes in. "Market sharing? It's all very complex. Don't you talk to him, Nicolas?"

Nico shrugs and swallows his food. "We play online chess."

Nico's mom sets her fork down and folds her hands together. "I worry about him," she says and Nico chuckles to himself. Of course she does. "He works and goes home to his empty apartment and works more. He's not like you, Nico. Always doing things and meeting people. You should call him."

Nico scoops more food and promises he will. He's surprised, though. He'd always thought of Lucas as the one who had his life all figured out.

Does anyone have it figured out? Is that what the lesson is? Just taking leap after leap, and never knowing what waits at the bottom?

"How is work?" His dad holds his fork out with a chunk of meat speared on the end, pointed at Nico. "Is that what you're running from here?"

"I'm not—" Nico starts, then closes his mouth at the look his dad levels at him. Nico takes a breath. "I'm just not so sure that the things I want are the things I want anymore," he says, and hopes that makes even a little sense. "I thought it would be fun and interesting. I didn't anticipate all the difficult parts."

"Hmm." He bites his steak off the fork and watches Nico while he eats it. "Do you know how many bags of hair I throw away?"

"Yeah, you used to make me tie them up and take them out to the dumpster. It was horrifying. Still kind of haunts me to this day." Nico moves his food around and shudders at the memory.

"Well, there you go," his dad says. His mom nods.

Nico smashes a pile of rice with his fork. "Look, I'm not the son with the PhD. Could you explain that?"

His dad stabs another chunk of meat. "Everything has bags of hair, Nico. I would suggest that you don't think about it so much."

30

He's sipping terrible coffee at the car rental place, waiting for Andrea to finish processing his paperwork and rental charges, leaning one elbow on the counter and staring off into space when his phone vibrates twice in his pocket.

> **Grady:** If you ask me to I'll walk away
> **Grady:** If you ask me to I'll give you

Nico swipes across the screen to unlock his phone, hits the message icon to respond.

"Mr. Takahashi? I'll get you all set up if you'll follow me to the parking lot," Andrea says, all politely efficient.

He listens to the usual spiel about the car's specs, possible fees, the return policy. Looks over the car for scratches and dents, and Andrea writes them down on her clipboard. By the time he's in the driver's seat breathing in the caustic scent of Armor-All and

Scotchgard, he can no longer recall what he was going to say to Grady.

He looks at the texts and decides that maybe he'll let Grady say what he needs to.

Stay

If you ask me to I'll walk away.

If you ask me to I'll give you

He cranks the engine of the little red Dodge Neon and putters out onto the street. When Nico stops north of Harris Ranch to get a snack and use the bathroom, then fill up the tank since he's already at a gas station, there's one more text.

Grady: Everything.

He comes out of the dark, piss-stained gas station bathroom, buys a bag of Combos and a bottle of water.

"Do you ever stock Mello Yello?" he says to the clerk in her red smock, as her nicotine-stained fingers scan his items with the sort of angry disinterest that can only come from working the counter at an Exxon station in Los Banos, California.

"Do what, now? That'll be four seventy-two."

"Mello—" Nico starts, then takes his cheese-filled pretzel snacks and so-called spring water. "You know what, never mind. Have a nice day."

Harris Ranch is usually where he gets anxious and restless, ready to be back home. It's even worse this time because this car is smaller than his and harder to keep at a consistent speed with its wimpy little engine that's terrible for gunning past slowpokes. Finally he gets a break. The left lane clears, leaving nothing but open highway ahead of him. He cranks the engine, mashes the cruise control button and sets his mind on racing to his destination as quickly as possible.

A white minivan with one of those cutesy-obnoxious sticker family decals on the back window drifts into his lane. Nico curses under his breath, taps the brakes, but stays close.

"Take a hint," he snarls. Whatever calm he had achieved at his parents' house evaporates like the fragile wisp that it always was. His shoulders pull in, his jaw clenches, impatience and frustration rise like a churning tide. Why does he have to fight so hard to have anything? Why does he feel as if he's constantly running in place, swinging his fists and landing on nothing just to get a little peace, a little comfort?

His ass is numb and he's been on the road too long and he misses Grady, is no closer to figuring out how to be with Grady, where to be with Grady, what minuscule part of Grady's chaotic life he could possibly cram himself into, and he just wants to get home. So for fuck's sake, *move*.

It happens too fast. The minivan slams on its brakes, and Nico is too close, can't see the bumper, just a flash of red lights and a happy, frolicking sticker family. He stomps on his brakes but it's not enough, he's still moving too fast. He swerves, and his car goes into a tailspin.

None of his driving experience kicks in, none of the knowledge gleaned from Department of Motor Vehicles handbooks or driving lessons with his parents or trial and error pops up in his brain. The car spins and he—does nothing. Watches it as if he's outside of his body, can't stop it, can't fix it, can't influence the outcome, good or bad, so he just sits in the center of the spiral and waits for things to sort themselves out one way or the other.

The little Neon screeches to a halt, facing backwards and crooked on the shoulder of the right lane. The left headlight bangs into the guardrail. Hands death-gripped to the steering wheel and foot still jammed on the brake, Nico stares unblinking and unseeing out of the windshield.

A truck comes by, has to swerve around him and blares its horn. He startles. Gasps a breath in and wheezes it out. Heart knocking against his ribs and adrenaline spiking his blood, he puts on his emergency flashers, pulls the car out into the empty right lane, waits for a clearing in the left lane and turns around. He's very thankful that he bought the extra insurance when the tail light falls off behind him.

Pulled to the side again, he takes some deep breaths. "It's okay, you're okay, everything is okay." He rests his head on the steering wheel, then picks up his phone when his hands stop shaking. Maybe it's just the adrenaline rush, or the near-death experience, but everything suddenly seems so much clearer.

"Gwen, listen. I almost got into a terrible car accident—"

"Oh my god, are you okay?" Gwen says, and then with the phone pulled away from her ear, "Nico was almost in an accident... I don't know, I literally just asked him that... Well, it was only a matter of time; he drives like a maniac... *Okay*." And then at regular volume, "Flora wants to know if you're okay."

"I'm fine, I—" Wait. He checks himself all over, pats his head and face and chest and legs. No blood, nothing hurts. "Yeah, I'm fine."

"He's fine," she says, tinny and far away, to Flora. To Nico, "Do you need us to come get you?"

"No, no." He leans back in his seat, looks up into the vast, clear blue sky. All this time, he's been looking everywhere else and it was right here all along. "Gwen, listen. Did you know that the strongest part of a hurricane is just outside of the center? Like I thought that was the safest part, that I could hide out there. But all along I've been battling against gale force winds, trying to avoid getting impaled by a fence post, when I should have been right there in the center!"

He flings his free hand out to the side, laughs high and giddy and *yes*. It makes so much sense.

"Nico, I—" Gwen starts. And sighs. "You know, this isn't a term I like to throw around lightly, so I'm sorry to level such a serious accusation at you, but you sound coo-coo bananapants right now. You sure you didn't hit your head?"

"I'm sure." He smiles despite her teasing. A puffy white cloud loafs by, traffic rushes past, the highway stretches back behind him where he once was, in front of him where he will be. Home is LA and home is Sacramento and home is a generic hotel room in Tuscaloosa or a cramped tour bus or the muddy woods behind a secluded house in Tennessee. Home is here, in this car just outside of Harris Ranch. Home is everywhere, home is everything.

"It's *kensho*," he explains. "A moment of understanding, enlightenment. It's like, as the car was spinning out, everything fell away. All my worries, all my stress. I don't need to run to the edges to find peace. I have to stand in the center and be still."

"Mmkay… I swear most of the time you're a wishy-washy agnostic and then you spend a few days with your parents and you sound like Siddhartha or whatever."

Nico snorts. "Not quite." There is something to it, though, making his thoughts quiet, letting his worries go and his ego drift away. It's what his dad was trying to say, with his gross bags of hair analogy: Just be. "I just think I… keep looking for the right path and the right choice, and maybe I just need to let things sort themselves out instead."

"Well, you are definitely going to fill me in on all the details here because I'm still confused. But I'm glad you aren't." She pauses and her voice goes a little thick. "And I'm glad you're okay; please get back safely."

Nico grins to himself. "Aw, you love me. We're totally bonded."

Gwen scoffs. "Yeah, you wish. Now get your perky ass back here. I'm tired of picking up your slack."

"There she is. See you soon, Gwennie."

Just as he pulls back onto the highway, he gets two texts from Grady, pinging his phone one after the other.

> **Grady:** If you ask me to I'll give up
> **Grady:** Anything

The next morning he discovers that the deranged bird has been waiting for him, and has only gotten more deranged in Nico's absence. *Chirp, chirp, CHIRP, CHIRP, TWEET* starts at six a.m. and doesn't let up for an hour. Nico takes it as the sign from the universe it obviously is: a mockingbird shouting at him to get out of bed and get back to it. No more texts from Grady overnight, and still none as he gets ready with plenty of time to spare, not rushing out the door frazzled and halfway dressed and exhausted already.

It's amazing how the traffic doesn't bother him when he's early. And how he miraculously finds a space on the street, waves to a cute couple walking a bouncy little Yorkie, glides up the steps and gets to the office first.

He unlocks the doors, flips on the lights, sits in his chair and spins it back and forth. He looks out the little window at the wisteria trees, the palms, the happy skitter of purple flowers on the sidewalk. He's missed this. He's happy to be here. He and Gwen really have built something special. They've got a good thing going. He's proud of what they've done.

He feels... peaceful.

The office phone rings.

"Style by Nico, this is Nico speaking, how can I help you?"

The other line cracks and fades and seems to go dead. Nico starts to hang up, when a voice finally comes through.

"Nico? Are you there?"

Then something screeches and howls like—like a monkey?

"Yes. Hello?"

Crackles and rustles and he can't make out what they're saying and then finally, clear as a bell: "Nico, it's Hailey."

"Hailey?" There's an animalistic howl again, demonic and threatening. Nico sits up straight in his chair and takes a breath. "Okay, whatever trouble you've gotten yourself into, just—just give me the address and I'll figure something out. Can you get somewhere safe?"

She laughs. A free, boisterous thing. Nico has never heard her laugh like that. "No, no. I'm fine. I'm great."

More howling and the line crackles in and out again. Nico presses the phone tight to his ear. "Are you really in the rainforest? And is that a monkey?"

"It's... actually a person."

"Oh god, that's worse." Nico groans. Just what sort of terrifying situation has she gotten herself into now?

"No, no. Listen. I went on this spiritual retreat and Nico— It's like I'm a new person. It's amazing."

She says something else but it cuts out, and in. Something about hallucinogenic tea and shamans and, possibly, a *cleansing bowel purge.* He pretends that he misheard that and pushes it right out of his brain.

"You're okay though?" He finally says when she slows down, leaning back in his chair in relief.

Gwen comes in to the office then, cocks her head at seeing him slumped in his office chair. He waves at her reassuringly, and she shrugs and goes to her office.

"I feel like I've been awoken," Hailey says. "Like I was fast asleep in the middle of my own life and I've finally opened my eyes. Like for the first time I can *see*, like suddenly everything makes so much sense and I know that sounds crazy, but—"

"It doesn't," Nico tells her, imagining her in some jungle hut made of palm fronds, surrounded by lush green trees and wild animals and people who sound like wild animals, this Hollywood star turned disaster turned lost girl—finding herself in the most unexpected of places, peace after looking so hard in the wrong directions. "That may be the most sense you've ever made, Hailey."

"I knew you'd get it," she says. "Anyway, the reception out here is shit and it's almost time for the ceremonial drum circle, so I wanted to see if you were interested in helping me with a new look still? I'm ready to step out on my own terms. Decide for myself who I am, you know? So like, can we meet when I get out of here and back to some fucking air conditioning and flushing toilets. I mean, the spiritual journey has been great, but I'm shitting in a hole in the ground here."

Nico tips his head and smiles. That's the Hailey he knows. He's glad she didn't purge everything. "Of course. I've got some ideas already. I'll put together a few things for you to look at."

"A week from now?" Hailey hedges. "I have to go by like, dinghy to a fucking mule-drawn wagon and an airplane that was made from old tin cans, I swear to fuck."

"Fun." Nico laughs. "I'll see you then."

"Hey, thanks Nico. For being one of the few people to give a rat's ass."

"Giving a rat's ass is what I'm here for." The phone cuts off on Hailey's end.

He wants to hit some boutiques before hunting items down online, so he pockets his keys and snags his sunglasses. Gwen calls out as he's crossing to the door.

"What was that?"

Nico spins his keys on his fingers, slides his glasses up the bridge of his nose. "Peace."

It's as if he's in a state of suspended animation. He shops for Hailey, meets with her and takes her to some design studios. She's foul-mouthed and bursting with snapping, impatient energy, as always, but she's happy. Excited for Nico's ideas, radiant in boyish cropped trousers and wide collared shirts with ballet flats, confident in simple white or black dresses with a winsome woven hat or bold statement jewelry.

At lunch after a few successful fittings, Nico and Gwen sit down with Hailey on the outdoor patio of an organic vegan restaurant in Venice. Hailey looks gorgeously casual and cool in a wide-brimmed straw hat, shorts, and a loose poplin tunic with simple flats.

Nico lays out the rest of his plan over butternut squash risotto, hempseed pesto polenta and bottles of kombucha. Hailey has managed to snag an invite to present at a daytime television awards show, and this is their in to get Hailey featured in the right section of celeb mags and websites. *Style* instead of *Scandal.*

"A simple off-white gown," Nico says. "Elegant, classy. Makeup will be understated." Hailey nibbles her salad. Nico nods at her current outfit. "This is sort of what you should be doing for everyday wear. The idea here is, everyone's talking about you going off on a spiritual quest."

"Everyone is talking about how she went off the deep end and ran away to the rainforest to trip on hallucinogens," Gwen interrupts. They both look at her. "Just making sure we're all aware."

"We are," Nico says with a fond smile. Hailey shrugs. "But we can work with that. We'll turn into it instead of running from it. So, your look is chic bohemian meets earthy meets casual."

Hailey arches an eyebrow, so Gwen adds, "Distressed jeans and jean shorts, fringed tops, kimonos, lace dresses and shirts, sandals. Easy and breezy."

"And..." Nico spreads his palms flat on the table and leans in. "We dye your hair. A soft red, like the morning sunrise, style it in long layered waves."

"So like..." Hailey pokes at her food with disinterest. "No big splash, no *hey everyone I'm back, bitches?*"

"Nope. You are going to do your thing and be your incredible, magnetic self and let everyone come to you. You are Zen. They are chaos. Let them swarm around you while you live your life how you want."

Gwen says, "It's his new thing."

"I like it," Hailey replies.

Nico folds his hands together on the tabletop, satisfied and calm, and dips his head. "I'm also really into rompers right now, add those too."

Then he's on the hunt for the perfect dress. Still, in quieter moments, Nico allows himself to miss Grady. He lets it wash over him, acknowledges it and lets it wash out again like low tide. He doesn't feel any more confident in his choices, and it doesn't ache any less, being without him these past weeks. But he's able to pack it away in a box, keep busy with Hailey and other clients and just not think about it.

Until he's in downtown LA, picking up Pacific blue mabe pearl earrings, waiting at the front of the store while Gwen gets a few alternative sets just in case, when he hears it. The words that he's looked at over and over and never figured out what they meant and what to say, crooning over the store speaker system in that voice that filled entire venues with reverberating ease, that curled in sultry drawling whispers against the shell of his ear.

Stay
If you ask me to I'll walk away
If you ask me to I'll give you
Everything
If you ask me to I'll give up
Anything

He's frozen. He can't manage to draw a simple breath, standing pinned against the wall next to the door of a tiny family jewelry store, as people go in and out the front door with a happy chime of bells. Grady's voice, and Grady's words and Grady's heartbreak are taking hold and grasping him tight.

It's a song. It's a song and it's a song about him, about them. The peace and calm he's been clinging to fall from his grasp. Nothing has been sorted. Nothing has changed. Only now he knows that

Grady still yearns for him just as he does for Grady. And just like that, he's lifted from his feet again, swept away by Grady, spinning headlong into the hurricane.

Gwen finally finishes, walks up to him chatting away about the earrings. The words die on her lips as she sees his face; she sighs.

"All right, time to get wasted. I'll call Flora."

That's Grady Dawson and Clementine Campbell on the surprise collaboration they dropped onto iTunes just a few days ago. Already number one on the country charts and rapidly climbing the pop charts. Crossovers are nothing new for Clementine; however this is a first for Grady. Now this may be controversial, considering his fans' affection for "Broken Records," but I like "Stay" even better. All the raw emotion and brutal honesty, with a more mature musicality. Of course, Clementine's harmonies don't hurt. You're listening to the weekly top forty on KISSFM. LA's one-stop pop radio destination.

The song is everywhere, day after day. Playing on the radio and in stores and restaurants and gas stations. Snippets of it stream from the open windows of a car passing by or are caterwauled at max volume during karaoke night at the bar next to the one where Nico is currently not nearly drunk enough. And every time, it knocks him sideways. He has no equilibrium, no peace and no idea what to do.

"I can't escape it." At the bar, Nico drops his head in his hands, twists his fingers tight in his hair.

"Is it better or worse that she's butchering it?" Gwen shouts over the off-key yowling next door.

He's honestly not sure. In the week since he's heard the song he's felt like an exposed nerve. Flora and Gwen are doing their best to keep him distracted. They're wonderful. But they aren't the distraction he wants.

"Have you talked to him?" Flora asks, steals some of Gwen's fruity concoction and finds it more to her taste than the beer she'd ordered. She switches their drinks.

He's picked up and put down the phone so many times. "No."

Gwen takes a pull of the beer and says, "Maybe you should go see him, tell him how you feel. Try not to fuck his brains out instead."

Nico stares at her with his mouth open.

"You get graphic after about the fourth drink," Flora says, giving him a comforting pat on the back.

Nico drops his head to the sticky bar top. "It doesn't make any sense." He drags his cheek against the bar top as he turns his head toward Gwen, then Flora. "I can't figure out how things could possibly manage to work between me and Grady."

"Love doesn't make any damn sense, Nico." Gwen says.

"Yeah it's… not the most reasonable endeavor," Flora adds gently.

Gwen stretches her hand out to Flora. "It's stupid, is what she means."

Flora takes her hand, grasped tightly in front of Nico's scowling, smushed face. "So stupid. And yet we keep doing it. Over and over again."

Nico hides his face in his arms. "Go be adorable somewhere else; it's depressing me."

They're right, and once Nico can separate out that pure, glimmering thread of truth, that quiet place in the center, what he knows without any doubt or confusion or conflicting thoughts is that he's in love with Grady. And maybe…maybe it is enough.

Sunday night he sits in bed, holds his phone and tries to decide what to say. He doesn't even know where Grady is right now. If he has a show. If he should call, or go find him. Should he wait until the tour is over? Should he wait for the right time? What is the right time?

Then he gets twisted all around in his own head again, paralyzed with indecision. He rubs his hands down his own arms and a pleasant memory of Grady's muscles shifting and trembling under Nico's fingers flitters through Nico's brain. Being with Grady was always easy. Thinking about being with Grady is always so complex.

He moves his fingers to his forehead, tap, tap, taps. *Be.*

Nico: When can I see you again?

The reply is immediate, but vague.

Grady: Soon.

On Monday, he's late to work after running into construction traffic twice, all the while muttering under his breath about the city of Los Angeles paying their workers to stand around blocked-off lanes of traffic eating sandwiches and staring like morons at unmoving bulldozers and pavement rollers.

Gwen is with a client, an R&B musician looking for something with a bit more edge to set her apart in subtle ways. Nico pulls a few samples.

Gwen comes in after the meeting with notes, plops down at his desk. "Did you call him?"

"Kind of."

Gwen smiles knowingly. "Sexted him, right?"

"Gwen, no. Why do—" And then he pauses, because Gwen spots something behind him that can only be an alien or a ghost or Vivienne Westwood herself come to offer Gwen free range of her show rooms whenever she wants.

Gwen gasps and her face goes pale and then red, her mouth flaps soundlessly and she sputters out, "Clementine Campbell..."

Nico straightens and spins around, and sure enough, looking as though she just stepped off the pages of a magazine cover and was followed here by a wind machine and a chorus of angels, is Clementine Campbell.

It isn't the first time Gwen has gotten a little star-struck, and it's not as if he's totally immune, but she visibly struggles to get herself together enough to stand, trailing Nico as he walks to the front of the office.

She is absolutely stunning in person: statuesque and regal, chestnut hair in waves spilling past her shoulders, classically beautiful and styled exactly right. A soft baby-blue vintage-style dress shows off her long legs and lovely shape, her nude heels, her makeup in soft browns with a burst of pink lipstick.

"You're Nico?" she says, her accent like Grady's but with a sweet, bouncing lilt. She shakes his hand and tips her head, sweeps Nico up and down with a scrutinizing gaze. "That boy may be a handful, but he does have good taste." She drops his hand and looks around the office with that same shrewd eye.

"Um. This is my partner Gwen."

Clementine turns back and tips her head the other way to look at Gwen, whose cheeks are bright red and eyes wide. "Partner partner or business partner?"

"Business," Gwen says, just a little too loudly. "I'm married. I have a wife. He's not. No."

Clementine grins. "Gotcha." She shakes Gwen's hand and Gwen takes a harsh, rattling breath as Clementine continues, "So nice to meet you, hun. I *love* your hair. I could never pull that off."

"You can pull off anything you want," Gwen says on a gust of air. Then claps both hands over her mouth and giggles.

Nico lifts his eyebrows, but Clementine laughs. "I'll keep that in mind." She turns to Nico then. "I was hoping to talk to you, specifically. If that's okay, Gwen?"

"Yeah, of course, yeah, yes." Gwen walks backwards, trips and giggles again and finally makes it to her office.

"I'm sorry, she's normally not like that. At all, actually." Nico gestures to his office.

"That's okay, she's adorable." Clementine sits, crosses one long, toned leg over the other and puts both hands around her knee.

Nico sits at his desk, clears away some of the embarrassing clutter that's been slowly taking over the surface: magazines and boxes of jewelry and makeup samples, random scribbled notes on scraps of paper that only make sense to him. "So what can I help you with?"

"Oh, I think you know."

33

After Clementine leaves, Nico sits at his desk staring blankly at the wall, head spinning. In a lot of ways, what she offered changes everything. And it solves a lot of problems, but then it also creates new ones. One thing is for certain, he decides, putting the boxes of earrings and necklaces and bracelets in a desk drawer, piling the magazines into a stack and moving them to a shelf. He has to talk to Grady about it.

And Gwen. And Flora. And all of the clients they have here. And the landlord for their office. His other landlord for his house. Nico breathes out a stream of air, shuffles all the loose papers on his desk together and throws away some granola bar wrappers that had been buried beneath them.

Under a printout of his car rental information from the Nashville airport and a phone number he can't place on a scrap of paper, is the magazine that Gwen had dropped onto his desk the day he'd met Grady.

Nico traces fingertips over Grady on the front cover, bared as he so often is, and he misses that body and that smile like a physical ache. This time he lingers on the picture; he knows so well the kindness in those eyes, the sweetness of his quirked lips, the confident curl of his fingers around the neck of the guitar he's holding: how careful he is with them, how skilled, how much he means every touch.

Nico sits, polishes off a cashew-honey bar that he's unearthed, and reads the article he never got around to looking at the first time.

Country Music's Bad Boy Grady Dawson Opens Up and Strips Down
By: Hannah Jordan

Grady Dawson's reputation precedes him: Bad boy. Playboy. A free spirit who defies easy classification. And everyone knows Grady has charm and charisma to spare. But what most don't know is how generous he is, with his time and with his easy, crooked smiles and warm, genuine hugs. I met Grady at the iconic Arnold's Country Kitchen in Nashville for some fried chicken, collard greens, mac and cheese and, of course, banana pudding. After we stuffed ourselves with down-home country cooking, he invited me to a rehearsal with his band, who, he claimed, were the true musicians that make him look good. This reporter can say from personal experience, however, that Grady Dawson does not need anyone's help in looking good.

You grew up in Tennessee, you've paid your dues in Nashville and yet industry buzz is always about your crossover potential. Do you see yourself leaving country music behind someday?

Like you said, country is what I've been nurtured with, it's what I've been around my whole life. There isn't any real effort on my part to turn my back on that, but at the end of the day I have to make music that feels honest to me. I refuse to do a paint-by-the-numbers sure-fire country hit. That's disingenuous and people can tell. As long as it comes from my heart, I don't really care what label gets slapped on it.

Your music tends to defy genres, going from traditional country to rock to folk to even some punk riffs here and there. Is this intentional?

I mean, it's my influences showing, certainly. I listened to the old greats growing up: Johnny Cash and Dolly Parton and Willie Nelson and Loretta Lynn. But I found artists like Bob Dylan and Emmylou Harris and Jimi Hendrix, then bands like Social Distortion and Los Lobos and The Clash. I don't know that I actively try to defy people's expectations...

But you do try to defy people's expectations?

(laughs) Exactly.

And on that note, let's talk about you being openly bisexual. Has it been a roadblock for you? The South isn't exactly known for its progressivism.

It sometimes can feel like a no-win situation, sure. In some ways I'm held up as this ground-breaking role model, which I'm not. And then on the other hand, I'm lambasted for being immoral and dragging country music through the mud. People think I'm confused or I'm greedy. I feel like I'm never quite welcome, no matter what space I'm in. I don't know. I just try to do my thing and not sweat what other people think my values should be.

Which are?

You know, be good. Do good. Try to put some happiness back in the world. God knows it's miserable enough without adding to it.

So as far as your reputation for causing trouble and playing the field... is that completely unfounded?

I'm not perfect. I've never claimed to be. That said, what makes a good headline or click bait is very often far from reality. Day to day, I'm honestly kind of boring. I want boring things. A home and a partner and a life filled with laughter and love. Maybe I've hooked my wagon to the wrong person on occasion, done some things I'm not proud of, but I don't think that means I can't have the same sort of future anyone else would want.

So the hard-partying playboy is gone?

That's not what I want to be known for. I've made mistakes, but I am not my mistakes. I think every person has the ability to do better, to get back up and try again. That's all I can do, really.

Before we talk future, how about we discuss the past a little. You've also been open about your parents' struggles with addiction, your own struggles. Being raised by your grandparents, your grandfather's past with alcoholism and his illness and death and how hard your grandmother's death was for you. How has all that impacted you? Or has it?

Sure. I mean, yeah sure it has. But you know, there's this saying: "Let go or be dragged." I can't let it drag me, I've got too much on the line. I do think it's made me realize the importance of just going for it. Whatever it is. I've lost enough in my life that I don't waste my moments. A lot of bad things can happen, but as long as I'm here, as long as I'm trying, a lot of amazing things can happen, too.

What's an amazing thing you're looking forward to?

I want to fall in love. Not that hot flame burning fast and leaving in a puff of smoke. Long lasting, this is the person I want by my side in this crazy life type love. I'm ready for that. I hope I find it soon.

34

Getting Hailey ready for the daytime television awards show is as much of an ordeal as getting Hailey ready for anything always was. She still needs a lot of hands-on attention, still second guesses everything Nico plans for her. He gets now that it's less about him than it is about her, so he lets it roll off him, doesn't consider running to a shack in the wilderness or a hallucinogenic jungle retreat at all, and it ends up being kind of fun.

He still gets home at an ungodly hour, still falls into bed fully dressed, still wakes up and wishes more than he has ever wished for anything that he was not awake. So when his doorbell rings at eleven thirty, he hauls himself out of bed, rubs his eyes and stubs his toe, accidentally jabs one eye with his thumb, answers the door limping and cursing and squinting, his hair sticking up on one side as if a Jersey heifer snuck into his room in the middle of the night and licked it all into one unattractive clump.

"Grady?"

He'd expected a delivery, or a Mormon, but not Grady, standing on his porch looking as casually sexy and disarmingly sweet as ever.

Grady grins his lopsided grin. "God, I forgot just how gorgeous you are."

"That's a joke, right?" Nico says, snuffling and sleepy. "It's too early for joking."

Grady shifts closer, leaning with one hand on the doorframe. "Not a joke. And it's nearly lunchtime. Late night?"

Nico grunts. Stands blinking dumbly at Grady. Grady, Grady, Grady is here. Here. At his house. "Oh. Shit." Nico steps back, stumbling again. "You're here."

He doesn't understand what he does and says to get Grady to look at him like that, as if he's the sun and the stars and Grady could just stare and marvel at him for hours, but that's exactly what he does.

"Can I come in?" He tilts his head and drops his eyes, down Nico's body. Up Nico's body.

"Yeah. Sorry." Nico shakes his head to get some sort of coherent thought process going, watches Grady push off from the door frame and slink inside. "I—um." Nico steps back and steps back, hits the wall between the living room and kitchen. "I need coffee."

He carefully scoops the beans into the grinder, watches them get shredded into fine grains, pours that into the coffee maker. Fills up the tank, listens to the burble and hiss of the water, watches the drip, drip, drip of the coffee into the carafe. Gets a mug, pours. Milk, sugar. A few sips to test it and—

"We should talk," he says over the top of the steaming mug, acknowledging Grady again after several minutes of pretending he didn't feel the heat of Grady's eyes laser-pointed onto his back the entire time he was making coffee.

Grady leans over the kitchen island and says with a slow curl of his lips, "Okay. But you should know that I desperately want to kiss you right now."

"We probably shouldn't." Nico takes a too big, too hot gulp of his coffee.

"Remember what happened the last time you said that?" Grady's eyebrows lift and fall.

"Vividly," Nico chokes out. He takes more sensible sips and is immensely grateful for the solid mass of the kitchen island blocking their bodies. Grady looks for all the world as though he wants to devour Nico, and Nico wants very much to let him. Instead he says, "Stop looking at me like that."

Grady frowns and pouts. "Okay." Dips his head and looks up at Nico through his eyelashes, full pink lips wet and downturned.

"Nope, that's worse."

Grady laughs, and Nico smiles and drinks his coffee. The chemistry is still there, still easy. Falling into Grady's body and Grady's touch was always easy. Easier than Nico ever wanted it to be. But this is hard, this part, and it has to be done.

"Can we just talk?" Nico says with considerable effort, his voice a little gruff. "Somewhere else?" Preferably somewhere without a bed. Or a couch. Or a kitchen counter. Or walls.

Grady knocks on the island twice and stands up tall. "As a matter of fact, I would love to."

Nico showers quickly, locking the door behind him to avoid temptation, ignores the swell of interest in his cock with Grady in his house while he's naked. Then he starts to not ignore it, gets irritated with his own lack of self-control when it comes to Grady and turns the cold water on full blast.

"You okay in there?" Grady says through the door after Nico yelps from the blast of icy water.

"Fine!" Nico hisses and hops, but the water does have the desired effect. "Can you wait out by my car? Be out in a few."

He dresses down, black acid-wash skinny jeans and a snug screen-printed white tank. Okay, maybe not *totally* casual. His hair is easier to style now— a quick run through with some pomade and he's good to go. Grady is leaning against the passenger side of his car with a picnic basket in one hand, his face tipped up to the sun, curls catching the light and his neck stretched long. Nico locks the door and jogs down the steps.

Talking. It's time for talking.

"I'm really enjoying your haircut, by the way," Grady says as he buckles his seatbelt. He reaches over and brushes his fingertips over the closely shaved hair on the side of Nico's head, fingertips skimming the top of his ear.

Nico cranks the engine so hard that it makes a god-awful screeching noise.

Talking.

"So. Uh." Nico puts the car into gear and backs out of the driveway, glances down at the delightful way Grady's thighs are stretching out his jeans. He glances up again just in time to notice the stop sign he very nearly ran through. He looks up at the roof of the car for a long moment. "Are you done touring?"

There. Conversation. They know how to do this.

"Yeah, for now. Got a press tour next and then I have to pre-record some *Christmas in the Country* thing that my manager convinced me to do." He stretches his arms behind him, grips the seat back, biceps bulging.

Do not think about his biceps. Do not crash the car into that tree.

"Good. Good. That's good." Nico says.

The picnic table is marked with cigarette burns and carved with initials and swear words, stained and dirty and wobbly at one end. It sits beneath the shade of an old-growth oak tree, with a perfect view of a lush grassy field, winding dirt trails and colorful pops of flower buds climbing the hills surrounding them.

"I love this," Grady says, unpacking sandwiches and a bottle of sparkling grape juice.

"I thought you would." Nico unwraps a sandwich: peanut butter and jelly on Wonderbread. "You remembered."

"Of course I did." Grady reaches out to grasp Nico's hand, but Nico drops both into his lap. Grady pulls his hands away and unwraps his food. "And I remembered that you needed time to figure things out. So…"

It's a moment, and Nico gives it some space to sit unopened while birds chatter in the tree above them, a drum circle thumps away off in the distance, bright sun beams and leaves dance in the warm breeze. Easy or hard. Safe or risky. Think or do.

Nico takes a breath and sets down his food. "I have. Figured it out."

Grady looks up, locks eyes with him. "Before you tell me, I just want you to know that I'm announcing my retirement on the press tour."

Nico tilts his head and narrows his eyes and is sure that he misheard. "What?"

"I'm retiring. From music. For us, Nico."

"For us. Grady that's—" His mouth moves uselessly. Insane? The worst idea ever? Wonderful?

Grady stands, moves around the table and scoots across the bench where Nico is sitting. He takes Nico's hands from where they're clenched in his own lap and holds them up to his chest. "I meant every word that I sent you. In the song." Nico nods and blinks and nods. "I've tried being without you and I can't. I think about you all the time, I've never felt like this about anyone. I can't just let you go, I can't. So I'm giving it all up: the touring and the crazy fans and the press and the gossip. All of it. For you."

"Grady, I—Wow, you really do not do things halfway, do you?" Nico shakes his head. "You can't do that. Not for me. No."

And oh god, oh no, the way his face crumples and his shoulders bow in, as if he'd make himself disappear if he could. Grady starts to pull away, swallowing and swallowing and his eyes wet with unshed tears. "Okay. That's fine. Okay, then." Nico can see him pull back, shut down, bury it all away. He gives Nico a wobbly smile. "I tried, right? It's fine."

"Wait. Let me finish." Nico slings one leg over the bench and moves in, touches Grady's knee in a quick brush. "Grady, I've seen you, up on a stage. You are lucky enough to have found the thing that you were born to do. You have a *gift*. You've made a difference in people's lives. You give them hope and joy and you…" He spreads his fingers across Grady's knee and watches his fingers squeeze there, looks up into Grady's vivid blue eyes. "You, Grady Dawson, are something special. What kind of selfish asshole would I be to take you away from the world just because I can't deal with sharing you?"

"I'd give up anything for you," Grady says on a quavering breath.

"I know." Nico touches his thigh, his waist, his back, his arm. "I know you would." He ends with his fingers twisted into the soft curls at the nape of Grady's neck. "And that's why I think we can do this."

Grady scans his face and turns his body, and Nico twirls and twirls and twirls a tendril of hair around one finger. Grady's eyebrows pull together. "Help me out here. Do what, exactly?"

Nico laughs, can't stop it from bubbling up. Grady frowns. So Nico cups his face and smooths away the wrinkle of confusion between his eyebrows. "Be together. Choose each other. Even if it's hard and it's crazy and chaotic. I want to be right there, in the middle of all that, standing by your side."

Nico can feel the upward shift of Grady's cheeks beneath his palms. "Be together?"

Nico nods and laughs. "I want to try. Yes."

"Oh my, are you—" Grady clutches a fist to the center of his chest. "You nearly gave me a heart attack, Nico, good Lord in heaven. Could you have started with that part maybe?"

Nico slides his hand back to Grady's neck, pulls him and purrs, "I promise I'll make it up to you."

The kiss is quick and closed-mouth and not enough, not even close, but Grady's lips smile against his smiling lips and his chest and heart feel light and free, loosened from the knots of all the *what ifs* and *if onlys,* all the *shoulds* and *coulds* and *can'ts.*

Grady pulls away, puts a very bold hand high up on the inside of Nico's thigh and growls out, "How do you feel about sex in public?"

Nico hops up and rolls his eyes at Grady's pout. "It's like you're *trying* to make the front page of the tabloids."

Grady shrugs impishly, rises up from the bench and moves into Nico's body, whispering against the shell of his ear. "Gotta give 'em something to talk about."

Nico gasps and shudders, then Grady ends the sentence with a nip to Nico's earlobe and that is *absolutely the final straw.*

"Pack up that picnic and get your ass in my car, right now," he orders, tugging at the bottom hem of Grady's T-shirt.

Then suddenly the heat and press of Grady's body is gone, leaving Nico swaying unsteadily as he sits back down.

"First we have to enjoy this picnic I lovingly prepared for you. I went shopping all alone and made it myself and everything." Grady tilts his head and winks, patting the seat next to him.

Nico glares. "You smug little shit."

"Oh, we are gonna have so much fun."

35

Not only do they have a picnic, they hike and go up to the observatory and look over the balcony at downtown LA and Hollywood.

"It's beautiful," Grady says, leaning over the railing with one arm slung low on Nico's waist. "Not really what you'd expect, huh?"

Nico leans into him. "Yeah. Kinda takes you by surprise."

Grady gets recognized after that, and even though the two preteen boys who stare at him while trailing their parents around the deck never come up to him, Grady insists on waving and asking if they'd like to take a picture. They nod, goggle-eyed and pink cheeked. Nico snaps the picture and completely understands that look of wonderment on their faces.

"How much do you love making people swoon over you?" Nico says, after yanking him in for a hard kiss back in the car.

"Gotta shake what your mama gave you." Grady's fingers trip-trap up the inside of Nico's right leg, knee to groin. Nico shifts and wriggles in his seat.

"Take me home?" Grady says, all soft and hesitant and devoid of his usual sure charm. Nico cranks the engine.

They've done fast, they've done desperate, they've done *can barely get their clothes out the way fast enough to get at each other.* They've done intense and longing and aching, but never this. Where they kiss in the center of Nico's living room for so long that his head swims and his lips are raw and his jaw is sore, his cock is a persistent pulse of want, and his belly tugs warmly with devotion to this man and his happiness.

He keeps his hands firmly on Grady's back, feels the shift of shoulder blades and churn of muscles under the thin cotton barrier of his shirt. Grady's fingers tighten and release and tighten and release against his hips.

Grady drops a kiss against the corner of Nico's mouth and across the sweep of one cheekbone, down over the hinge of his jaw and rests his panting mouth there. "I'd quit my job today just so I could spend every second of my life worshipping you."

The room spins, the tug and push of heat and desire, still Nico breathes out a soft chuckle. "That won't be necessary. But I do appreciate the sentiment."

For the first time, he wants Grady without the clawing, screaming desperation of an hourglass stealing all of their moments together, as if every time was their last time, as if Nico had to glut himself on Grady so he could hold on just a moment longer. He wants him now, just as much, but he could hold his rough-shadowed jaw and kiss him and kiss him and nothing else. Because they have so many moments left still.

Grady starts to kiss down his neck, one side and then the other, his breath coming in humid puffs against his skin. Nico swallows and says, "I love you," with Grady's teeth against the knob of his throat.

Grady pauses, and Nico waits for him to stand up with a crooked grin and say something like, *I know* or *Well, it's about damn time.*

But he cradles Nico's head in both wide hands, scrapes his fingertips against Nico's scalp. He whispers on an exhale, "I thought I'd never find you."

They kiss and kiss until Nico feels bruised by the press of lips and the curl of tongues. They shed clothes with heated looks and soft laughter and quick inhales. Nico turns Grady around, places Grady's hands against the back of the couch, touches the stretched taut expanse of his pale skin, brushes his lips and tongue down each protruding knot of his spine, crouches and spreads his cheeks with both thumbs and licks against the tight, clenching heat of him.

"*Jesus,*" Grady yelps, his hand flying to his cock. Nico pushes it away, puts his hands back on the couch, leaves him bobbing hard and full and heavy in the air.

"Let me," Nico says against the luscious curve where ass meets thigh. "Let me show you how much."

Grady grips hard, widens his stance and leans over. Nico gentles him soft and relaxed and open with his tongue and a finger, sharp bitter tang flooding his mouth, Grady's moans and gasps and curses spurring him on. Two fingers and the speared point of his tongue between, and Grady cries out a high note, churns his hips and chants Nico's name.

"Nico, Nico, oh sweetheart, Nico I need—I'm gonna—"

Nico stands then, knees protesting with a creak and face filthy and wet. "Hold that thought." He rushes off to the bathroom where he hastily wipes his mouth and digs in a drawer for lube, hissing when his arm brushes his own steel-hard cock.

Grady hasn't moved, draped like a sacrifice over the back of Nico's couch. "You are…" He starts and then doesn't know how to finish it, he just knows that he can longer fathom not being with this man who traps his breath in his lungs and sets his world spinning in directions he can't understand. They'll spin together.

"Everything," he says.

Nico slicks his cock and nudges up between his cheeks to grasping, grabbing heat, slides in and in and in, runs both hands up Grady's chest to pull him close.

Fingers spread across Grady's neck and jaw and chin so Nico can kiss him at an awkward angle over his shoulder, open panting mouths and messy, messy, off-the-mark and perfect. Nico holds him tight, back to chest, ass to hips, thigh to thigh. Long, slow, even strokes inside, and if he could he'd melt into him, twine around him like crawling vines, not close enough, never close enough.

When Grady starts to whimper high in his throat, his knees giving and body slumping back against Nico's, he snaps his hips harder, fumbles for Grady's cock and lets the movement of their bodies push and pull the shaft through his fingers. Grady comes in hot, slippery gushes over his hand, a tight clench on his cock to the beat of Grady's heart, Grady's release like a song in his ear and Nico sinks his teeth into Grady's shoulder and comes so hard his vision whites out.

They slide to the floor, gulping air and grinning like fools.

Grady gives a soft *whoop,* runs a hand through his curls. "Yeah, it's settled. I'm retiring just so we can do *that* all the time."

Nico shakes his head and blinks up at the ceiling. "I don't think we'd survive it."

He looks over at Grady and there's that cocky grin he loves so much. "But what a way to go."

Their senses and the steady use of their limbs come back to them eventually. Nico stands and reluctantly dresses, and Grady stands and cleans up and doesn't. The irony of him ending up with someone who often prefers no clothes at all. Nico watches him walk to the fridge for water and return, all those gorgeous cuts of muscle, his cock soft and pink now, his pale skin ruddy at his chest and cheeks and the back of his neck.

Nico is madly in love with every single inch.

As much as he enjoys the view, it's not ideal for the one last card Nico has to lay on the table—his whole hand, nothing held back now. It's a big one, and a choice he can't make without Grady's input.

Grady offers him some of the water, and Nico takes a long gulp, hands it back and says, "So Clementine came by to see me."

36

Grady sets his hands on his naked waist, pops a hip out to one side. "I didn't even know she was in LA. What did she want?"

"Well, she—" Nico starts. Then gets distracted by the bulging vein that travels like a winding brook down Grady's groin. "Could you maybe put some clothes on for this conversation?"

"Uh-oh." Grady bends to pick up his underwear and pants, wriggles into them then stands and waits again.

"Shirt, too," Nico says with a flick of his finger.

Grady tuts in annoyance but picks up his shirt too, and slips it on. "Better?"

"Yes." Much less distracting. Although Grady's biceps do stretch the sleeves of that T-shirt so nicely. "Are you hungry?" Nico blurts. "I'm pretty hungry after that."

Grady sighs, scratches the back of his neck. "If we eat something, will you tell me what the hell is going on?"

There's a cute cafe not too far from his place that makes really excellent smoothies and interesting salads and has a wide selection of teas. He brings clients here often. Explaining to them why they made a worst-dressed list (he did tell them to ditch the side bow) or that the designer they wanted to work with said no (laughed in Nico's face) goes down a little easier in such a bright, charming atmosphere. Who can get angry over rooibos tea and a selection of colorful summer veggies?

And they have a decent-sized free parking lot.

"What is that?" Grady whispers a little too loudly while they wait in line to order.

Nico follows his confused stare to a table in the corner where two women are eating. "Um, a raw gluten free vegan pizza."

Grady's eyebrows pull in more and his mouth goes flat. The line moves and Nico browses the chalkboard menu. He *is* pretty famished.

"You can't just mash lettuce into a pizza shape and call it a pizza," Grady mutters next to him, shaking his head. "That's not how pizza works."

The person in front of them finishes paying and they move ahead. Nico rubs Grady's back comfortingly as he places his order. "You don't have to get the pizza."

Grady frowns at the menu. The guy at the register with blue hair and tattoos covering his arms frowns at Grady and taps his finger on the cash register.

"Sorry," Grady says with a little crook of his mouth. "I can't decide." Then he leans forward over the counter, rests his chin on his fist and looks up at the guy with pleading eyes. "Can you help me out? What do you recommend…" He flicks his eyes down at the guy's name tag. "Trevor?"

A blush spreads across Trevor's face and he stutters breathlessly, "Uh—I—What do—um—"

Nico rolls his eyes, smiles and shakes his head. "Grady, stop bewitching the guy and pick something." And to Trevor he says, "I'm sorry, he can't help himself."

Grady stands and flits his eyes flirtatiously in Nico's direction. "I'll just have what he's having."

A decision Grady regrets once they get their food and sit on the outside patio. "This is the sort of stuff my trainer makes me eat." He pokes at his kale salad with petulant little stabs of his fork. "So, you gonna finally tell me why we're having a business lunch and what you and Clem talked about?"

Grady sets down his fork and raises his eyebrows and Nico nods, takes a breath. "She told me about the tour."

"How can I help you?"

"Oh, I think you know."

Nico's stomach twisted sickly, and his fingers clenched tightly on the desktop. Clementine watched him, head inclined just so, elegantly propped in the chair across from him.

"Grady," Nico said, and not as a question.

Clementine uncrossed her legs and leaned forward. "I care for Grady very deeply, and I want you to know first of all that I have his best interests at heart."

"So do I." Maybe it didn't look like that at the moment, but he'd walked away from Grady knowing that he could never be someone else in Grady's life that he couldn't count on to be there. Someone else selfishly flitting in and out. Someone else who couldn't deal with the hard stuff and would never come back for him.

Clementine dipped her chin and luminous locks of hair fell around her face. "Good. That makes this much easier, then."

In his office Clementine stood, went to the little window in the corner, and, just standing there, looked like a fresh-faced model who'd just stepped from the pages of a peppy, playful teen magazine photoshoot.

"Grady's reputation is overshadowing him. And I don't think I need to tell you that he can be so much more than playing dinky clubs and feeding the rumor mills. He's special."

"I know." God, did he know.

Clementine turned with a look of triumph. "I got the idea when we collaborated on the song he wrote for you." Nico's stomach tied itself into more and more complicated knots. "I want to do a tour with him. I'm talking sold-out stadiums and major press and Grady's name on every media outlet from class to trash."

"Okay," Nico said slowly. "So why are you telling me?"

She gave a little one shouldered shrug. "He said no."

In the cafe, Grady blinks and flattens his eyebrows, then shakes his head. "Nico that tour is a year. Three months of which will be out of the country. You and I are just getting started. It'll kill us dead in the water."

Nico sets down his own fork and reaches for Grady's hand. "I told you, I won't ask you to give anything up for me."

"No." Grady crosses his arms while the chatter around them fills in the heavy silence at their table. "I'm not doing it."

Nico squeezes his hand, just once. "Look, I can't promise you much. But I can tell you that I'm not going anywhere. No matter what."

Just for a fleeting moment, Grady's resolve cracks with a flicker of warm affection across his face.

"So you want me to convince him?" Nico said.

"Yes and no." Clementine sat on the edge of Nico's desk and Nico spun his chair to face her. "Grady leads with his heart, and his heart is with you."

The knots in his stomach loosened their hold a little. "Mine too," *he said shakily.*

Clementine smiled. "I'm glad to hear that. And listen, before you think this is just me being completely over-invested in Grady's career and personal life, there's a benefit for me. I want to be taken seriously. As a businesswoman, as an artist. I'm tired of being styled to look like I'm Alice following a bunny rabbit to a magical tea party. A tour with Grady positions me with a wider audience." *She set her jaw, and her eyes flashed.* "Do you have any idea what my net worth is? The deals that I've brokered all on my own? No one has any idea of what I'm capable of. I am building an empire here, and I'm done with being treated like a little girl playing dress-up."

Nico scanned her look. The blue sundress was whimsical and lovely, but didn't exactly say business professional, it was true.

"Okay. So I'm still not sure why I should convince him to leave for a year." *He was just starting to think they could make occasional short tours and press junkets and a semi-long-distance relationship work somehow. But this?*

"Well," *Clementine started with a sweet smile,* "I figure if we convince him first, you'll be easy."

"Wait, she wants you to do what?" Grady says, scooting his chair around the table closer to Nico.

"Take over styling her. Me and Gwen. Full time." Out of the corner of his eye he spots a man across the street taking pictures of them with a long-range camera lens. Great. "Here and in Nashville. On the tour."

"Exclusively," *Clementine finished, after laying out all the services she'd want from them. Styling her and the entire band, the dancers and the backup singers on the tour. Red carpet events and photo shoots and interviews and magazine spreads. Press stops in LA and New*

York and Nashville, any other appearances on the road or at home.
"And then I'd like you to stay in Nashville when I'm off, for everyday
styling."

"That's..." A dream come true, a game changer, a huge, major life
decision. "I'd have to talk to Gwen."

"Of course."

"And Grady."

"You'd better."

She stood and Nico stood, and they sized each other up for a
moment. Nico was rather immediately taken with her; he could cer-
tainly understand why Grady enjoyed her company so much.

"You know I'm gonna make you change your hair, right?"

Clementine gave a surprised burst of laughter and shook his hand.
"I think the two of us will get along just fine, Nico Takahashi. How
about you call me when you're ready to say yes."

She started to leave with a swish and swirl of her dress, and Nico
called, "Wait. You and Grady... I mean you never..."

She looked over her shoulder and replied, "Don't believe everything
you hear, hun."

In the cafe, Grady gives the same sort of laugh, a hiccup of
sound from his chest. He grabs Nico's face and plants a hard kiss
on his mouth. The creepy paparazzi in the bushes snapping photos
of them probably just wet himself.

"That's amazing, why didn't anyone say?" Grady kisses him
again, then pulls away with a look of sudden terror. "Wait, did
you tell her no? Is that why we're doing this in a neutral location?"

"Sort of... I wanted to be somewhere else when I told you so
you could feel free to say no. This is new, the two of us, and I know
you're used to being on your own. I don't want to crowd you. And
I wanted you to know that I'm all in, either way."

"Good Lord, you make me crazy." Grady pecks his lips and nips his jaw, then drops a hand to his thigh.

"Grady, public."

"Fine," Grady says, pulling away with a dejected sigh. "What do you say we get out of here and order some real pizza and eat it in bed?"

"Yes, please." Nico covers his kale salad with his napkin, drops a wad of bills on the table and takes Grady's hand. "Naked?"

"Is there any other way?"

Gwen texts him a link to a gossip site later that day when he's still in bed, still naked, with Grady's head resting on his stomach, his fingers carding through Grady's hair. Nico can only laugh now. These sites aren't even trying to be accurate.

Gwen: I'm looking forward to living in the boonies more and more every day.

Gwen: You two do look awfully happy though :)

GRADY DAWSON ENGAGES IN VERY PUBLIC DISPLAY WITH ONE NIGHT STAND. WILL THIS BE THE FINAL STRAW FOR CLEMENTINE?

37

He wakes to sunrise in brilliant glinting gold on a blue, blue sky, a bed so comfortable he burrows inside of it like a piglet in hay, the clock on the nightstand lit up with 7:40 in floating green digits and a chipper, cheery voice in his ear saying, "Morning, sunshine."

Nico closes his eyes, smashes his face in his pillow and grunts into the plush downy softness. "Fuck you."

His body curls up behind him, warm bare skin and scratchy hair and a hand sliding over Nico's hip, up his chest, open lips on his neck. "Sounds like somebody needs some sugar."

"God, you're worse than that fucking bird." Nico spoons back into him. He's wearing pajama bottoms and socks, but Grady sleeps naked even when the temperature drops to freezing overnight. Then again, Grady reads naked and knits naked and vacuums naked and burns food naked, and the day that he splatters hot grease onto his crotch is the day Nico is going to put his foot down about it. Probably.

He starts to drift back into sleep, twenty minutes, just twenty more blissful minutes, but Grady's fingers pinch his nipple and his cock nudges insistently along the small of Nico's back just over the top of the loose waistband. Nico grunts, pushes his ass up and in against his hips, and Grady gives a breathy little moan.

Time is not something they have to spare today, or any day, but Nico lets the arousal unwind slowly, stretches and sighs and lets Grady grind and grind and grind against him.

Ten minutes.

"You still going by the office today?" Grady says, then tugs Nico's pants down, over the curve of his ass and down to his knees, leans away and comes back with the cold, hard edge of a bottle set on Nico's ribs.

"Yeah, I—*Oh.*" Cold, slick, then warmed by his body and the movement of Grady's fingers inside. His eyes fly open, his right leg moves to give Grady more space to touch and stretch and move. "And my place." He hisses and pants. "To pack."

The room is different now. They've gone together to flea markets and swap meets and antique stores in cities that have congealed over time into one mishmashed cityscape. Some days he'd turn on the TV in his hotel room first thing in the morning just to figure out where the hell they were.

Today in Grady's room there's an old Gramophone record player, complete with a polished brass horn, pinewood box casing and original hand crank. They found that in... Grady's fingers twist just right and Nico takes a sharp breath and can't remember if it was Milwaukee or Madison.

Grady's fingers slide out and Nico waits as he scoots in and positions himself, darts his slowly focusing vision to the banjo made from a cigar box they bought in Denver, the collection of folk records from Seattle arranged on the wall, the hand-carved dulcimer from Chicago. Photos in frames line the shelf and the top of the dresser: the black and white one of Grady's grandparents that they unearthed from a storage unit, the photos of him and Grady in Nashville and LA and New York, and the one of the two of them sweat-rumpled and laughing and clinging for dear life to the railing of the Sydney Harbor bridge.

Blunt pressure, heat and fullness. Nico's mouth drops open and his eyes clamp shut again; he reaches back and gets a fistful of Grady's hair, pushes his ass back and twists his torso forward while Grady inches in with choppy thrusts.

Five minutes.

"Fuck, Grady, come on." He moves his own hips in opposite time, shoves back when Grady snaps forward, then forward until just the tip of Grady's cock stays in. He fumbles down to jerk himself, fucks himself on Grady's cock, fast, fast, fast, no time no time.

"Wish I could just fuck you all day," Grady says into his ear, bites the lobe then curls his tongue around it.

"Might—Uh. *Mmm, that's good.* Might make the plane ride a little awkward." Grady chuckles and then moans gruff and deep and— oh, Nico has developed a very visceral response to that particular noise, which is a problem when Grady does it onstage. But now it takes him right up that perfect, wonderful edge of bursting pleasure. "Close, close, fuck me please, please, baby please."

He's pinned to the mattress, face down with Grady's weight over him, his knees spread wide and Grady moving with a purpose. The bed squeaks and shakes, the frame batters the wall, he manages to get a hand shoved between the mattress and his body and pulls on his cock while Grady fucks and fucks and—

The alarm goes off just as he starts to come with a muffled shout. Grady finishes with a full-bodied shudder, moves inside of him until his cock softens and slips free and Nico snorts and flips over.

"That was impressive timing, well done."

Grady hums smugly and leans down for a quick kiss. "We've had lots of practice at making the moments count."

They do have to take what they can get and make the most of it. Despite Nico being on tour with him for a year, there were always shows or interviews or photo shoots. Nico's priority has to be Clementine, and Clementine's life tends to weave in and out of Grady's. Sometimes they had days together, and then they'd go weeks without seeing each other at all, and the frantic, frenetic reunions almost, *almost* made up for it.

Then he was in LA and Grady was in New York, then he was in New York and Grady was in Nashville, then *he* was in Nashville and Grady was in LA and then finally, two months ago in the dead of winter, things came to a grinding halt.

They didn't quite know what to do with all the time together, until they did, and now Nico goes weeks without seeing his own apartment in downtown Nashville. His ficus tree is probably dead. Again.

"Okay." Nico stretches, a different type of satisfying ache in his limbs, and forces himself from bed. "Stuff to do, red-eye flight, then the big day."

Nico showers, shaves, fixes his hair with a quick comb-through of pomade. It's still short and closely trimmed on the sides, swept up and away from his face. He dresses in a thick red cable-knit sweater, wool pants and brown wingtips.

He hustles downstairs to the kitchen where Grady is cooking fried eggs and warming up biscuits and is actually dressed. Nico pours himself some coffee to go, gets his coat and hat and scarf from the hall closet and bundles up, while Grady wraps an egg biscuit in a napkin for him.

"Hmm, what handsome and multitalented fellow hand-knit this beautiful scarf for you?" Grady holds out Nico's to-go breakfast and winds the scarf carefully around his neck.

"I think his name was Greg or Gary?" Nico carefully pushes down the lid to his coffee cup, squints one eye in mock confusion. "He was okay looking, I guess. Weird toes, though."

"How you sweet talk me." Grady gives him a pinch on the ass and a kiss on the cheek, says goodbye and calls after him, "Love ya!"

"Love you, too." Nico smiles and winks. When he opens the door, he shivers and pulls his scarf up higher. He loves Nashville, really does feel settled here, but he is happy he'll be back in California soon.

As he walks to his car clutching his warm coffee cup, Billy and Mongo pull in. Nico waves them over. The band is meeting for very preliminary third album talk, which mostly means jamming, which means Grady being so caught up in music that he forgets to eat or check his phone or show up to the places that Nico needs him to show up to.

"I need him at seven o'clock, no later guys!" Nico climbs into his car and turns it on to warm it, a billowing exhaust cloud filling the air around him.

"You got it," Mongo says.

"We don't want him any longer than that anyway," Billy adds. Nico beeps the horn just as Billy walks by, *totally by accident.*

He'd like to say that the nearly two years he's been more or less settled in Nashville have mellowed him, that his near-accident has made him more cautious, but old habits die hard, and he still finds the commute from the outskirts of town into Nashville immensely frustrating. It's why he'd decided on an apartment right downtown. He likes the vibrant hip atmosphere there, too, but mostly—

"Come on, Jethro!" he shouts, tailgating and then backing off with a frustrated groan. At least it's not as bad as the day he got stuck behind a tractor going five miles an hour for at least ten miles. That turned ugly.

Their Nashville office is in an old brick building above a bakery in the historic district; it's retro-cool and always smells delicious. Even though Clementine has them contracted for any occasion she may need them, and compensates them very well for it, they have enough of a handle on things now to take on different clients here and there at their own pace. On the door to the office their new logo is stenciled in a contemporary square font: Nico + G Style Studio.

Tonight Clementine is being featured at the Grand Ole Opry in a showcase of the top female country artists, and Nico has to be sure everything is set to go before he takes off.

His usual greeting of, "Morning," is met with the usual scowl and second cup of coffee. He goes to the row of garment racks first to check that the three gowns are ready to go, and greets Gwen, who is setting out earring options.

"That Spencer really brings a certain something to the office atmosphere, doesn't he? Like a raincloud, but filled with deadly poison instead of raindrops."

Gwen laughs, and holds up dangling black pearl earrings. "You have to admit, he's always on top of things and we've never been more organized. He's certainly made my life easier."

"Mmm," Nico answers noncommittally. Stupid Grady and his stupid heart of gold convinced Nico to give Spencer a shot at being their intern after he promoted Gwen to full partner. "I guess. I could really do without the constant hatred, though."

"Aw, I think Spencer kinda likes you." She picks up a pair of teardrop onyx and diamond earrings. "The other day he said that you sometimes didn't have terrible taste."

"*Wow*," Nico says with an eye roll.

"I know, right?"

Before he heads to his desk to confirm with hair and makeup, Nico stands against the open door to the closet. "How is Flora liking this winter? I know it's not quite the East Coast. Still, a big change from Southern California."

Gwen closes the lid and puts the box away. "She loves it, really. It's been good for us, being here, you know? Holding down the fort where things are a little..."

"Slower?"

"Yeah. But in a good way? We've even been talking about buying a place. Kids maybe?" Gwen says with a wrinkle of her cute snub nose.

"Wow," Nico says, genuinely surprised this time.

Gwen grins and shrugs. "We'll have to name it BillyBob or LouAnn, but oh, well. When in Rome."

"Right. Hey thanks for taking over tonight, by the way."

"Sure. I know what a big deal tomorrow is for you." Big. Possibly the biggest hurdle they've had yet. That's *if* Grady makes it to the airport in time.

38

The only constant in his and Grady's relationship seems to be the unstoppable sands of time slipping through their fingers. There's never enough of it, and they're always racing against it: appointments and interviews, charity events and hospital visits, award shows and studio time and fittings and photo shoots and strategy meetings and—how the hell are they supposed to be in New York and LA and camera-ready and rested all at the same time?

When things slowed down in Nashville after the tour—and all of the interviews and appearances after that—there was an adjustment period. Grady's constant impulsive energy had gotten exhausting, and Nico's caustic gibes sometimes veered into cruelty.

So try and try again, and they aren't perfect, things will never be perfect. But the way Nico's whole body hums and vibrates when Grady hustles down the aisle of the airplane just minutes before takeoff—relief and gratitude and adoration flushing his veins—Nico knows it's worth every argument, every stressful event, every moment of jealousy that makes his insides feel rotted-black and sickly. And it's worth every worry that it's too much. That they can't.

They can. And they are.

"By the seat of his pants, as usual," Nico says, leaning for a kiss on the cheek.

"Thinking about my ass, as usual," Grady replies, lips against his cheekbone. "Sorry. Lost track of time."

"It's okay," Nico says and means it. He's here now, and that's what matters.

The flight attendant starts the safety demonstration, and they both buckle up and get settled in their chairs; first class, wide and comfortable and roomy, a perk Nico does not feel the slightest bit guilty about. Screw economy.

"So did Clem wow 'em like always?" Grady asks, while the air masks are being demonstrated.

Nico checks the time on his tablet. "We'll find out soon. How did the session go?"

"Ah, we mostly riffed, but I think we may have a few little kernels that could be something." He watches the demonstration finish, lips pulling down and fingers strumming on his knee. "Maybe."

"Well, I wish I could have been there; I love watching you on stage, but there's something about when you just play for yourself." The plane starts to creep out the gate and onto the runway. "That first time you played for me in your basement, that was when I knew I was falling for you."

Grady turns to him, the plane speeds up, and a knowing look spreads slyly across his face. "That was definitely my plan."

Grady is quiet through liftoff and ascent, through food and beverage service, and when the seatbelt light flicks off. Nico turns on his tablet and scrolls through sites to see if anyone is talking about the exquisitely detailed Marchesa gown Clem wore, and thinks about what a change it's been having designers knocking down his door to work with him instead of him begging someone to take a chance.

Clementine Campbell looked stunning at a Grand Ole Opry event honoring the accomplishments of female artists in country music. The Grammy-winning singer showcased yet another win in a floral-accented gauzy hunter-green Marchesa gown. The swathed material and strapless bodice gave Clementine a very flattering womanly shape, and the sleek bun, red lips and diamond studs brought a slight edge to the otherwise winsome gown.

Click through to see our favorite Clementine looks so far this year.

Nico clicks through, and next to him Grady sighs and frowns and fidgets. The endless expanse of sky outside the airplane window grows darker with a somber, muted blue.

"Doing okay?" Nico asks offhand.

"Yeah. Just nervous." He tucks a leg beneath him and rests his head against the window beside him.

"They're gonna love you, don't worry." Nico looks up and pats his bent knee. "Everyone loves you."

"Not everyone."

"Okay everyone who isn't a petty, jealous, vindictive Internet troll loves you."

Grady *tap, tap, tap-tap-taps* on the armrest between them. "I know but this is—I mean it's different when I'm on stage or being recognized for my work, because that's beyond me. That's other people with me. This *is* me. Just little ol' me."

Nico turns, twisted uncomfortably in his seat. "Are you saying you're more nervous about this than you were about playing a sold-out show at the Staples Center or winning a Grammy award?"

Grady frowns and crosses one arm over his stomach. "Yes."

Nico's heart flutters and he lifts Grady's skittering, nervous hand to kiss his knuckles. "Mmm, I think I like you all nervous and timid. It's cute."

Grady runs his thumb along Nico's bottom lip, ducks his head and says in that gravel-rough voice that sends heat jolting to Nico's groin every time, "How do you feel about joining the mile high club? That would really relax me."

Nico ignores the pulse of his dick and goes back to scrolling on his tablet. "We've managed to stay out of the tabloids lately, let's keep it that way." He follows a link to another website and speaking of…

Best Red Carpet Couples:
#7: Grady Dawson and boyfriend, stylist Nico Takahashi, in coordinating slim-fit plaid Moods Of Norway suits brought a pop of color and pattern to an otherwise drab black and gray showing at the MusicCares charity concert in Los Angeles last May.

"Oh, I like this picture." Nico uploads the image to make it his tablet background photo. They look good together, and it's a great shot.

Grady looks over. "Just don't read the comments."

"Too late." Nico goes from pleased to annoyed to pissed off and back to pleased. He shrugs them off. It's beyond them, as Grady said. It's not them, and he's able now to let it swarm around but never touch them.

They manage to sleep in fits and bursts, Grady's head on his shoulder, snoring softly in his ear, Nico sideways in his seat with his feet in Grady's lap, both of them slumped and bent and contorted.

They yawn and stretch and stumble off the plane, stop in the bathroom before getting their luggage.

"Why do you look all sexily disheveled and I look like a cult leader on the lam?" Nico says, squinting into the mirror over the sinks.

"No." Grady waves his hands in front of the automatic paper towel dispenser. "You look incredible, as always." He sighs when he says it, though, instead of smirking or smoldering or coming onto him.

"Are you—" As Nico glances at him in the mirror, Grady whips his shirt off.

"Trade with me," he says. "I came right from the studio, I'm a mess." He drops his shirt onto his carryon bag. "Come on, gimme your sweater, I wanna look nice."

A toilet flushes, Grady holds his hand out and Nico—just stares at his bare torso unmoving. He shakes his head. "Grady, put your shirt back on. Wait—" Drags his eyes back up and down his chest once more. "Yes, put your shirt back on."

"But—"

Nico holds up his hand. "You're wearing rust colored pants and my sweater is red. No." Grady's shoulders slump. It's adorable how badly he wants to make a good first impression. "Okay, fine. You can wear the button down I have on underneath."

Nico has his sweater hanging over the edge of a sink, his navy and red checked shirt open to his belly button; Grady's shirt is still off and his pants are unbuckled and unsnapped when the occupant of the closed stall comes out, stops dead and gapes at them.

"Morning," Grady says, breezy and pleasant. He looks right at Nico as Nico pulls his shirt off all the way. "Beautiful day, isn't it?"

The man from the stall grunts, washes and dries his hands quickly and leaves in a huff.

Grady shrugs, takes Nico's shirt and asks, "Tucked, right?"

Nico clicks his tongue. "A shirt tail flapping around is a good look for no one. Not even when they look like you."

Grady waggles his eyebrows. Nico sighs and rolls his eyes and puts his sweater back on. It's a more casual look without the collar and rolled cuff of the contrasting shirt underneath, but the plush knit of the cotton feels wonderful on his skin. He helps Grady get tucked in and smoothed out. It is certainly not the strangest, or filthiest, place Nico has ever had to do an emergency improvised quick change for someone.

Grady turns this way and that way, sizing himself up in the mirror, looking for flaws and imperfections. "I don't know…" He grimaces and sighs.

"Enough." Nico grabs him by the shoulders. "Get a grip, quit fussing." He presses a dry kiss to his lips and smiles. "You're beautiful and amazing. Go knock 'em dead."

Grady's body shifts into his, he smiles and rubs their noses together. "I really love you."

Nico closes his eyes, takes a moment to be. He's going home. He is home, right here. In the airport bathroom. He opens his eyes, cringes when he remembers where they are and steps back. "You ready for this?"

Grady nods, turns to lead the way out of the bathroom. Nico grabs his ass and laughs when Grady squeaks in surprise. Nico smiles and says, "Let's go find my mom."

His mom hugs them both, and Grady responds so enthusiastically that he lifts her off the ground while she squeals. She insists that Grady sit in the front seat and gives him the driving tour of Sacramento, asking him repeatedly if he's tired or hungry and if she needs to stop by the store for anything.

At the house, she's stocked the fridge with Mello Yello.

Grady and Ken talk cars, while burgers char on the grill outside and Grady mentions that his first major purchase after getting a record deal was a Dodge Viper that he promptly totaled.

"More dollars than sense," his dad grumps.

"Back then I didn't have the good sense that God gave a goose," Grady says gravely.

Nico munches on potato chips, watches them get on like old fishing buddies.

Lucas regales them all during dinner with the details of his latest published article about, "Price reaction to information with heterogeneous beliefs and wealth effects," that Nico barely stays conscious for and Grady follows closely with a furrowed brow and serious nodding.

Grady takes a drink of soda and says, "So basically *believing* something has value means more than it *actually* having that value?"

Lucas pauses. "Well, that's simplifying it but, more or less, yes." He looks impressed. Lucas never looks impressed. Nico bumps his knee against Grady's beneath the table.

When it gets too chilly outside, they go in for pie and coffee and play Trivial Pursuit and they all get too competitive, as always. Grady looks a little shell-shocked, so Nico forfeits, even though it wounds him to lose to Lucas on purpose, and heads to bed early with Grady.

The bed is made up with extra pillows and extra blankets and warm slippers down at the end for Grady that his mom informed them were, "Just in case he didn't bring any."

Nico showers and comes back to Grady holding the slippers to his chest and staring blankly at the floor. Nico ruffles his curls, kisses the top of his head.

"I'd forgotten what it was like," he says thickly.

Nico crawls on the bed next to him. "I know it's not the same, but I want you to think of them as your family, too." Grady nods and Nico pulls back the covers with a yawn. "And if you want I can call my mom whenever you're sad or sick or tired and she'll care about you so aggressively you'll suffocate."

Grady gives a shaky laugh. "I would love that."

By the time Grady comes back from a shower and slides into bed, warm and sweet smelling, Nico is already drifting hazily. He moves toward Grady's body like the tide pulling toward the moon, sets his nose against Grady's neck and sighs.

"*You put me together stitch by stitch,*" Grady sings, softly and airily, throat vibrating against Nico's lips. "*I feel you there inside, I hear your voice say mine. Stay.*"

If Grady ever sings their song to him during the day Nico *tsks* and calls him overly sentimental and schmaltzy, but right now he's tired and too happy to be anything but grateful that Grady has never been afraid to offer Nico his heart again and again, trusting Nico of all people to keep it safe and whole.

He tries.

"You should move in with me," Grady says, rubbing circles on Nico's back. "That big ol' house feels empty when you aren't there."

Nico tries to answer *maybe* but only manages a contented sort of snuffle.

Grady lifts the back of Nico's shirt, scratches his fingernails against Nico's skin, leaving a trail of goosebumps in their wake. "Then we can do this all the time."

"Mmm." Nico curls and stretches and shifts against his touch.

"Living together. A future, just you and me, sweetheart," Grady says.

Nico snuffles against his chest. "Slow down. I didn't say yes."

He can't see it, but he knows anyway, that smug, self-satisfied grin is firmly in place when Grady nudges Nico onto his back, gets a thigh between Nico's legs and replies, "You didn't say no, either."

The End

ACKNOWLEDGMENTS

This book is, first of all, a love letter of sorts to the South. I may love you in a bewildered, often frustrated sort of way, but you're home and you're an important part of who I am. Thanks, as always, to the Interlude Team: Candy, Lex and Annie. Your support, encouragement and hard work is humbling and inspiring and immeasurable. To Becky and C.B. and Victoria S. for their beautiful artistic vision and talents. To my family and friends for being my touchpoint, my safe place to fall, and my dad in particular for gifting me with an appreciation for all music. And I mean *all*. To my readers: Thank you, thank you, thank you. Thank you. Finally, to everyone who has ever loved and lost a Memaw or a Nana or a Gammy or a Gran or a Grandmother, who knows the loss of a constant loving presence, the extinguishing of a warm hearth, the vanishing of a soft embrace, this is for us. And one last shout-out to anyone out there making a jumpsuit work. Rock on.

ABOUT THE AUTHOR

Lilah Suzanne has been writing actively since the sixth grade, when a literary magazine published her essay about an uncle who lost his life to AIDS. A freelance writer, she has also authored a children's book and has a devoted following in the fan fiction community.

Her novella, *Pivot and Slip*, was published in 2014 and her novel, *Spice*, was published in 2015—both by Interlude Press.

Broken Records Discussion Guide

1. LA and Nashville are completely different. How so? How does each setting affect the way Nico feels and behaves?

2. Describe Nico's process for styling Grady. How does it contribute to the misconceptions he has of Grady? How does it affect his ability to connect with Grady?

3. In chapter six, Grady tells Nico "Music is like a heartbeat... It's always there, you just have to stop and listen for it." Explain how Grady's philosophy relates to the way he lives his life, and the way it affects his and Nico's relationship.

4. Hard work saved Grady from the mistakes he and his parents made. What other rags to riches stories are based on hard work rather than luck or connections?

5. There are so many cues Nico missed that could have cleared up his misconceptions of Grady's reputation. Look for them. How might he have changed his thinking if he had noticed them?

6. Spencer's jealousy and Nico's misconceptions combine in the worst possible way. How could that have been avoided? What part does Grady play in that situation?

7. How much of Nico's insecurity comes from the tabloids? How much from his perception that his parents' love was conditional? What else in his life might have made him so insecure?

8. How does "fan culture," possessive or crazed fans feeling entitled to the private lives of celebrities, contribute to Nico's insecurity? What makes Grady let it go so easily, where Nico can't?

9. At the end of Chapter 28, Nico's father tells him, "You don't search for peace. You are peace." How does this life lesson apply in Nico's life? How does it apply to the world at large?

10. Nico's road rage often reflects his inner turmoil. Compare how the two appear in his life. How does he find his way to ameliorate both problems?

—*AC Holloway*

BURNING TRACKS
by Lilah Suzanne

Gwen Pasternak's life seems to be perfect: She has a job she loves as a stylist to the stars, a beautiful wife, Flora, and a wonderful house in the heart of Nashville, Tennessee. It's everything she's ever wanted. The only problem is that the more time she spends working with country music's princess Clementine Campbell, who is dynamic and fascinating and bold, the less Gwen is sure of her commitment to a life of domestic stability. Meanwhile, her business partner Nico Takahashi is now happily settled down with musician and reformed bad boy Grady Dawson. Until Grady discovers that Nico may not be as committed as he seems, and Grady falls back into some dangerous old habits. Will Gwen ruin the amazing life she's built with Flora for something new and exhilarating? Can Grady be convinced that Nico is really in it for the long haul before it's too late? Burning Tracks is a story of difficult choices, taking risks and the pressures of living life in the spotlight.

On the drive out to Grady's house—or, Grady and Nico's house—or, like, sort of Grady and Nico's house, Gwen is on Nico's side of the issue. The place is way out in the boonies, just farms and forest and the occasional gas station and lonely curving street with squat brick houses. She understands why Grady would want to be secluded, somewhere with a little solitude and peace and quiet, but—

She always half expects to be hauled off by some banjo-playing redneck who emerges mysteriously from the woods and disappears just as quickly. No offense to banjo-playing rednecks.

She drives all the way over the river and through the woods, down the winding dirt driveway to Grady's huge country cottage set on acres of trees, and he's not even there. The house is dark and locked, and when she peeks in the windows of the garage, all of his various vehicles are parked and silent and covered. The space for his pickup truck and the spot next to it for Nico's zippy red Miata, are both empty.

Gwen hops up on the hood of her orange Mini Cooper, thinks and then calls the one person who will know where Grady goes when he doesn't want to be found.

"Listen. I'm pissed at you, so let's just put that out there. A heads-up, maybe? I thought we were semi-acquaintances who mostly tolerated each other, Spencer. You don't just throw that away. I'm hurt." She kicks her studded combat boots against the front bumper and switches the phone to her other ear. "But this isn't about that. I was hoping you could help me find Grady. He's... upset about something. I can't find him. Just call me back, I guess?"

She hops down and opens the car door. Maybe Grady went to Nico's apartment? Probably not.

"Oh, and by the way," she adds before cranking up the engine and ending the call. "I was just about to teach you about how the Industrial Revolution was a total game-changer for fashion, and about the complex feminist history of corsets, so I hope you feel bad about missing out. Because you are."

She's on the highway just a few exits from the center of downtown when she gets a text, interrupting The Lunachicks blasting from her sound system.

Spencer: Try Ray's in Edgefield

Ray's in Edgefield is a rough-looking gray cinderblock dive bar in an even rougher-looking part of town. Half of the windows are covered with plywood, the dirt parking lot is riddled with potholes, and the walkway is cracked and weed-lined. A neon sign reads OPEN and under that, handwritten on a scrap of cardboard, is CASH ONLY. Inside it's dark and the floors are brown-stained cement. There is no stage, no music, just one TV loudly playing Sportscenter. It reeks of cigarettes and sour beer and is the sort of place Nico would purse his lips and drolly call "charming."

Yet, with his back turned to the door, hunched at the bar with a sweating clear glass in front of him, Grady doesn't look out of place. It's as if he spent a lot of time in places just like this once. Before he was famous, before he was rich, before he met Nico. Before he turned his life around. The bartender is no doubt the leader of a biker gang; big, bald, bearded and tattooed.

"What do you think would happen if I ordered a Cosmopolitan?"

He turns to face her as she hops on a stool with her legs dangling high off the floor. His face is still drawn and sad, but less angry now. Resigned.

"Can't be worse than trying to drown your sorrows in a club soda." He picks up the glass and shakes it; ice cubes tinkle and condensation drips onto the scuffed surface of the bar.

He's not drinking alcohol. Gwen's shoulders relax. The bartender comes by, and she orders a club soda with lime, partly in solidarity, and partly because she's never had a great grasp on how to deal with the minefield of recovery and sobriety and addiction. Gwen sips her drink and ignores the sportscast, looks around instead.

It's fairly empty, still the early afternoon on a weekday. There's a guy at the far end of the bar about their age, a group of college-age girls playing pool at the one warped pool table and a man in his seventies—possibly younger plus decades of hard living—who keeps unsuccessfully hitting on the girls.

Gwen sends a look of disgust his way—he could be their grandfather for fuck's sake—before turning back to Grady.

"For what it's worth, I do think he intended to tell you."

Grady spins his glass in damp circles. "You know what they say about good intentions."

Squeezing lime juice into her club soda, Gwen says, "Wait, I know this one. It's something related to penis size, right?" She watches Grady bite down on a smile, and knocks his knee with her own. "I may be mixing my idioms."

The joke seems to work; Grady's protective posture opens a little, the crease disappears from between his eyebrows and he sits up taller. "You know, I never really understood that one. I mean, if the road to hell is paved with good intentions, then where do bad intentions lead you?"

Gwen takes a sip of her drink and jerks her head in the direction of the creepy old guy openly leering at girls who are barely of legal age.

Grady glances over, scowls and says, "True." He takes one last swallow of his drink, then pushes it away. "Okay, this place is too depressing sober, let's go."

As they leave, Gwen slows, worried about the young women. She's sure they're smart and capable and perfectly fine, but a weird nurturing instinct takes over and she can't help it. She just wants them out of there and safe. So she makes a detour to the pool table, leans close to the girl with shoulder-length brown hair and takes a chance.

"Hey, do you want to meet Grady Dawson?"

The girl just looks at her blankly, and okay, not everyone knows Grady. Not even in Nashville, and that's probably the anonymity Grady was hoping for here. But then the tall one with curly black hair smacks the short one with long brown hair and hisses, "I told you that was him!"

By the time Grady is finished chatting and charming and taking pictures in the parking lot, the creep is gone and all three girls head home safe and swooning. Gwen gets in her car and is pleased enough with herself to indulge in saccharine pop radio. Then

Grady leans into her open window and asks, "Have you ever ridden a dirt bike?"

She has not ever ridden a dirt bike, and apparently never will. After a dozen attempts and a dozen graceless tumbles into the dirt, Gwen gives up and sits on the bleachers to watch. Too bad, the steep hills and sharp turns and constant roar of engines appeal to her inner Evel Knievel. She could also create some interesting looks with the brightly colored leather and heavy black padding.

Grady is indistinguishable among the other riders, taking the cliffs and turns at increasingly risky, breakneck speeds. When he nearly wipes out after flying off the highest hill, Gwen decides to call for back up. She's out of her depth with Grady. They're friendly; they have a solid working relationship. But Grady came into her life via Nico, and that's how she thinks of him, mostly: one half of Grady-and-Nico.

Gwen takes a short video, sends it to Clementine with a message: Should I be concerned about this? She doesn't hear back until Grady has blasted around the course three more times, so recklessly that it may be time to give in and call Nico. It's not worth giving Grady space from him if he's going to break his neck in the process. Clementine gets there first.

Clementine: Maybe. Where did you find him? I got the 411 during fitting.

Gwen texts back, a bar, and the reply is immediate.

Clementine: I'll be there just as soon as I'm done with this meeting.

6

"Hey, G. Would you mind stopping by the store for a loaf of bread? Something crusty, you know the kind."

Gwen hesitates. "Well, I can."

Flora's frustrated puff of air crackles through the phone. "Are you not coming home for dinner? Because I made pot roast and I hate when you don't tell me in advance—"

"No," Gwen interrupts, before she can get too upset. "I just..." She turns away from the back corner, to the folding chair where Grady is being treated for scrapes after an epic wipeout, where Clementine hovers over him fussing about the gash next to his eye.

"Your face, Grady. Of all places."

Just outside of the closet-sized first aid slash concession stand slash gear shop, stands Clementine's enormous and ever-present bodyguard Kevin. Inside it smells like motor oil, popcorn and antiseptic; it's cold and dirty and cramped. And yet. Not the weirdest client situation Gwen has ever found herself in. Close. Not quite.

Grady is more than a client though, or he should be, and not just to Nico.

Gwen turns back to the corner. "How do you feel about having a guest for dinner?"

She just can't shake the feeling that Grady shouldn't be alone, even though he claims to be fine and is clearly annoyed at Clementine's worried fluttering about. She tried to get him to call Nico, but no dice, so she feels a little guilty about contacting him, but if she were Nico—

Gwen: Found him. Thought you would want to know. He's okay.

Nico: Thanks, Gwen. Where are you now?

The metal folding chair squeaks and scrapes across the floor as Grady stands and brushes a cascade of dirt from his racing jersey and pants.

Gwen: Dirt bike track.

Nico: Thought he might be there. Or out in the woods.

Gwen: Come to my place. 45 mins?

"Do you want to fill me in here?" Flora asks, taking the bread that the whole caravan stopped to buy with Grady's truck and Clementine's Town Car and the black security SUV all parked in a circle around her tiny car like a celebrity seance ritual.

Only Gwen had gone inside, fidgeting in front of the bakery shelf with her phone ringing and ringing in her ear. What kind of crusty bread did Flora want? And will she care if Clementine tags along? And Nico shows up later? Does Clementine's bodyguard sit down to eat? Is he a cyborg as Gwen suspects?

Flora never picked up, probably let the battery die on her phone again and forgot about it, so surprise asiago cheese bread and two more extra guests it is.

Gwen stretches on her tiptoes to get out five bowls and five plates, and says in a quiet rush before Grady or Clementine come into the kitchen, "Nico didn't sell the apartment, but told Grady that he did, and Grady was at a bar but not drinking and then at a dirt bike track, which is potentially worrisome? And then he crashed and looked like an injured sad puppy, like look at him, and Clementine—"

She snaps her mouth closed when Clementine glides into the kitchen and gushes, "This place is just darling!"

Flora dishes out a serving of pot roast, rich and steaming and mouthwatering. "Thank you." She smiles at Clementine, then gives Gwen a wide-eyed, this-is-seriously-strange, look.

"And look at you two, in your precious little kitchen." She claps her hands. "Oh I just adore it."

Gwen wonders when superstar Clementine Campbell was last in a regular home with a regular kitchen. Judging by the way she's exploring the photographs of Flora's nieces Nyla and Evie on the fridge, the whiteboard with reminders about vet appointments and bills due and the number for a plumber as if she were an anthropologist discovering an unknown primitive society, probably a long time.

"Uh. Let's eat." Flora says, after filling up the bowls and a basket with slices of asiago bread. "Should we wait for—" She glances down the hallway, where Grady is sitting slumped at the table, and mouths, Nico?

"He's tied up with a designer right now, it's fine." Gwen leans up for a kiss. "This smells amazing, Flor. Thank you." She's laying it on thick to make up for the celebrity guests, and they both know it, but Flora indulges her with a smile and a kiss, then instructs Gwen to get everyone something to drink.

"So, how did y'all meet?"

Grady has been quiet, polite and sweet, but sullenly tearing off chunks of bread and swirling them around the thick gravy in his bowl for the most part. Clementine has been chatty, wanting to know what Flora does, then talking excitedly about her own favorite teachers, the ones she had before her first hit single at fifteen. Then she had favorite private tutors.

"We met in college," Flora answers vaguely.

"At a party in college, the week before I dropped out," Gwen adds. "One of those dorm room gatherings where you just sit around getting high as a kite." She winces. "Sorry, Grady."

Grady swirls his bread and sits with his cheek smushed on his fist. "I've been high as a kite plenty of times. Don't bother me."

"Anyway. At a party..." Clementine says, moving the conversation back to safer topics.

Gwen takes the prompt and squashes a carrot into mush with her fork. "I couldn't stop staring at her. I mean, can you blame me?"

Flora scoffs at that, shakes her head and stares at her bowl.

Grady pipes up with, "She's right. You're an incredibly beautiful woman, Flora," in that gravelly purr of his. Flora's cheek burn a deep red.

"But," Gwen continues, giving Flora time to recover, "She had a girlfriend. So I didn't talk to her at all. Stared at her like a creep instead. We had some friends in common though, so I'd keep seeing her at gatherings, at bars, at parties. Always with the girlfriend. What was her name, Flor?"

"Imani."

"Imani, that's right. She was this brilliant, dreadlocked goddess, double majoring in—"

"Philosophy and literature—poetry."

"And here I was. A college dropout who looked like I'd just busted out of eighth grade detention—"

"She had blue hair and a tongue ring," Flora says, a soft smile meant only for Gwen. "I noticed her. So when Imani and I broke up and I ran into Gwen, I... I guess I was intrigued."

"Yeah, by my tongue stud." Gwen gives her a smirk. She had some good times with that tongue piercing. "I chipped a tooth with it right after we started dating, so it had to go."

"And I stayed."

"And then they lived happily ever after." Gwen tucks a lock of hair, loose from her braid, behind Flora's ear.

"Awww." Clementine's cooing breaks Gwen from a spell; she'd almost forgotten other people were in the room with them.

She'll never forget that night, when shy, quiet Flora had approached her, looked at Gwen with those round dark eyes, with her hair a curtain of black around her face and down her shoulders and a summery blue dress clinging and hugging every gorgeous thick curve of her body, and haltingly and breathlessly asked if Gwen wanted to hang out alone, and Gwen went dizzy with rushing blood.

"She was way out of my league," Gwen says. They're fast approaching a decade together, and Flora makes Gwen tilt-a-whirl woozy still. "She still is."

Flora frowns at that and shakes her head, and Clementine says, "Hey, don't sell yourself short. You're hot. Like a hot little pixie."

Before Gwen can begin to process that, there's a knock on the door. Nico calls out, "Can I come in?"

Grady goes stiff. Clementine hops up to kiss both of Nico's cheeks, and Flora stands, picks up the only plate still full of food and goes to the kitchen. "I'll heat this up for you."

"Grady, I—" Nico stops, halfway into the chair on Grady's right side, then grabs Grady's chin and frowns. "Your face."

"That's what I said," Clementine tells him.

"He wiped out." Gwen makes a dramatic wipeout motion with both hands.

Grady jerks his chin away. "It wasn't that bad."

It looked that bad; he hit the ground after flying off a hill so hard his helmet popped off, and he went skidding like a rag doll across the dirt. Gwen didn't remember getting up, was at his side in a flash to make sure he was okay with every instinct bubbling up, sudden and urgent. Not even Clementine had gotten there as fast as she had.

The dining room is silent and terse. Flora is taking her sweet time heating up that pot roast, and the rest of them are finished with their food and with something, anything, to say. Gwen shifts in her chair, Clementine glances unfocused around the room, Grady scowls at the floor and Nico frowns at Grady's scowling.

The microwave beeps, and Clementine's phone chirps with a reminder. "Shoot, I'm sorry, y'all. I have a phone interview soon. I forgot."

"No problem." Gwen hops up, relieved at the excuse to scurry from the dining area and walk Clementine to the door. Behind them, Nico and Grady start talking in terse whispers.

"Keep an eye on him for me, okay? And tell Flora I apologize for eating and running and that I thank you both for the dinner. My place next time?"

"Sure." She'll find some way to cope with eating a professionally catered dinner at Clementine's mansion. Somehow.

Clementine hugs her. Her body is slim and rounded with pert, toned curves. She always smells so good, too. Like honeysuckle.

Looks like a model, sings like an angel, smells like a flower, nibbles pot roast like a hummingbird.

They say goodnight, and then Kevin the bodyguard appears to walk Clementine to her waiting Town Car. She really is something else.

The door clicks closed, Gwen stays facing it, and the conversation in dining room steadily increases in volume.

"... has nothing to do with wanting to be with other people, Grady," Nico is saying. "As if you're the one who should be worried about cheating."

"The hell is that supposed to mean?" Grady says, voice verging on a shout.

She doesn't want to hear this, she doesn't, she—there's no escape. The foyer leads to the dining area on the left and the living room space on the right and then kitchen and staircase behind that. The open floor plan between the dining room, living room and foyer that they loved so much when they bought the place means there is no way to get anywhere unnoticed. Maybe she could creep along the far wall and dash up the stairs. They're so creaky, though. Why does this house have to be so old and open and creaky?

"I didn't mean it that way," Nico says, backpedaling. "You know I— The bi thing doesn't bother me, you know that."

Grady gives a humorless laugh. "The bi thing."

Nico groans in frustration. "I mean that I— I am here, for you. I left my family and I left my career in L.A. I moved to your house in the middle of fucking nowhere, Grady, in some nothing town well past any sort of civilization where I'm afraid to stand too close to you in the grocery store because this godforsaken state has to be dragged kicking and screaming into the twenty-first fucking century, for you. I came here for you. I am sorry that I didn't tell you about the apartment. I just didn't think it was that big of a deal."

There's a long beat of silence, and maybe it's okay, maybe they're hugging or kissing or gazing lovingly into each other's eyes, or making out on the table. At this point Gwen would be happy with any of those. She breathes out and pushes off the door. Then Grady speaks again.

"Well, if you're so miserable, maybe you should leave."

"Leave what, Grady?" Nico's voice sounds thin, helpless. "This house? Your house? The state? You? All of it?"

"Yes. No. I dunno." Grady mumbles, just as lost as Nico.

"Okay. I will be at the apartment then. For when you do know."

At the sound of rapid footsteps, Gwen jumps, picks up an umbrella from the stand by the door and pretends to be really enthralled by the Velcro strap keeping the folds tightly closed.

"Thanks for dinner, Gwen. See you tomorrow."

"Goodnight!" She calls, with way too much enthusiasm. Nico gets in his little sports car, guns the engine, peels away so fast his tires screech, and then he's gone.

This is not good.

And still, even with the palpable hurt on Grady's face that makes Gwen's stomach sink and the way he lets himself be gathered into Flora's arms when she rushes back into the dining room— Still, Gwen gets where Nico is coming from.

To give someone everything and still feel as if it's not enough, as if nothing will ever be enough because you are not enough. Gwen knows what that feels like.

To be continued...

also from
lilah **suzanne**

Spice by Lilah Suzanne

As writer of the popular "Ask Eros" advice column, Simon Beck has an answer to every relationship question his readers can throw at him. When it comes to his own life, the answers are a little more elusive—until computer troubles introduce him to the newest and cutest member of his company's IT support team. Simon may be charmed by Benji's sweet and unassuming manner, but will he find the answer to the one relationship question he has never been able to solve: how to know when he's met Mr. Right?

ISBN 978-1-941530-25-2

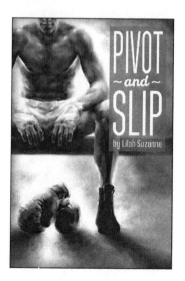

Pivot and Slip by Lilah Suzanne

Former Olympic hopeful Jack Douglas traded competitive swimming for professional yoga and never looked back. When handsome pro boxer Felix Montero mistakenly registers for his Yoga for Seniors class, Jack takes an active interest both in Felix's struggles to manage stress and in his heart, and discovers along the way that he may have healing of his own to do. Faced with the ghosts of his athletic aspirations, can Jack return to his old dream or carve out a new path, and will their budding romance survive the test of Felix's next bout in the ring?

ISBN 978-1-941530-03-0

"... sweet contemporary debut... (with) a delightful pair of protagonists." —Publishers Weekly

interlude ✦✦ press™
you may also like...

Definitely, Maybe, Yours by Lissa Reed

Baker Craig Oliver leads a happily routine life: baking for and managing Sucre Coeur for its absentee owner and ending his day at the local pub. He has a kind heart, a knack for pastry, and a weakness for damaged people. Playboy Alex Scheff is drowning his sorrows, but instead discovers a weakness for cookie-carrying Englishmen. Can a seemingly incompatible pair find the recipe for love?

ISBN 978-1-941530-40-5

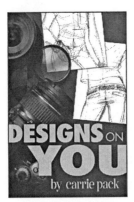

Designs On You by Carrie Pack

If graphic designer Scott Parker has to design one more cupcake company logo, he might lose it. When tasked with retouching photos for a big fashion client, a stunning, lanky model mesmerizes Scott and occupies his fantasies long after the assignment is finished. When the model is assigned to one of Scott's projects, Scott discovers that the object of his desire is nothing like what he imagined. Despite Jamie Donovan's aloof and dismissive behavior, Scott struggles to forge a friendship with him, all the while trying to keep his attraction at bay. Will Jamie follow through on signals that he may be interested, or will he forever be the beautiful man in the photograph, an untouchable fantasy?

ISBN 978-1-941530-04-7

Love Starved by Kate Fierro

At 27, Micah Geller has more money than he needs, a job he loves, a debut book coming out, and a brilliant career ahead of him. What he doesn't have is a partner to share it with—a fact that's never bothered him much.

When a moment of weakness finds him with a contact to a high-class escort specializing in fulfilling fantasies, Micah asks for only one thing. "Show me what it's like to feel loved."

ISBN 978-1-941530-32-0

interlude press™

One **story**

can change

everything.

interlude**press**.com

Twitter: @interludepress | **Facebook:** Interlude Press
Google+: interludepress | **Pinterest:** interludepress
Instagram: InterludePress